Loved By Darkness

By

Autumn Jordon

Loved By Darkness

This is a work of fiction. Names, characters, places and incidents are either the product of the author's imagination or are used fictitiously, and any resemblance to actual persons living or dead, business establishments, events or locales, is entirely coincidental.

COPYRIGHT © 2018 by Dianne Gerber
Contact Information: autumn@autumnjordon.com

Cover design by Vivi Designs
Editor: Pat Thomas
Published in the United States of America
www.autumnjordon.com

ISBN: 978-1-7320801-1-9

Other Titles By Autumn Jordon

Romantic Suspense/mystery
(all written as stand-alone stories)
Seized By Darkness
Obsessed By Darkness
His Witness To Evil
In The Presence Of Evil

Contemporary Romance
Obsessed By Wildfire

The Perfect Love Series
(all written as stand-alone stories)
Perfect
Perfect Moments
Perfect Hearts
Perfect Fall

Dedications and Acknowledgements

This book is in honor of my husband, Jim, who remains my hero. And to my children. Without your support, I could not do what I love to do.

A heartfelt thanks to Nancy Coni, Hope Ramsey, Rita Henuber, Anne Marie Becker, the ladies of Pocono-Lehigh writers and the ladies of the Ruby Slippered-Sisterhood WWF plotting gang who helped bring this story to life. And a huge thank you to my awesome editor Pat Thomas and her team of beta readers. You made this story great! I love you all.

Also, I want to thank James Walp for his help in matters of aviation. Any mistakes concerning plane operations is my mistake. And a huge thank you to the men and women who serve as U.S. Marshals. You are an elite group and inspire me.

PROLOGUE

My heart rattles my ribs. How it has room to flutter wildly is a mystery since my chest is so tight I can barely draw a breath.

I look down the beach once again, making sure there are no witnesses, and then I wade into the cool water, carrying the dark-haired little girl whose bright, round eyes will haunt me forever. But I have no choice. I must believe time will erase this memory from my mind.

The waves slap my thighs. I bite my lip against the stinging pain, realizing the feeling of rage which had freed my soul is gone. Now what remains are boulders in my gut: desperation, disgust, and fear.

I have no choice, I remind myself and turn my back to a wave as I scan the beach again. I need to be rid of her.

No one will believe that I didn't kidnap her. Martha took the child, but Martha will never be found.

If I'm discovered with the child, I'll be the one to pay the price. I can't take that chance.

The child is beautiful. She loves the water— thank goodness—and is anxious to climb into the raft I found in the garage. She thinks I'm playing with her. I'm not.

I wish her safe passage as I release her into God's care.

AUTUMN JORDON

CHAPTER ONE

Letting go and relaxing was something U.S. Marshal Jolene Martinez didn't do well. Behind oversized sunglasses, she studied the seven other people on board the forty-four-foot sailboat as they laughed and sipped wine imported from the Finger Lakes.

She zeroed in on the quiet man who leaned back on the seat with his long tan legs extended out in front of him, his ankles crossed. Though his sunglasses hid his eyes, she'd lay odds he had a piercing stare. He had dark wavy hair which lifted with the ocean's breeze and the lower half of his face wore a day's worth of bristle. His T-shirt didn't conceal his toned muscles underneath. His name was Norris Stiles and he was the new Chief of Police for Cape James, Virginia.

He was also a temptation she couldn't allow herself. Jolene held her sigh and scanned the horizon.

The others only saw her smile, heard her quick wit, and assumed she didn't have a care in the world because she enjoyed the warmth of the mid-June sun on her bare shoulders. Her tranquil facade was a front, however. Too many undercover gigs in service to her country qualified her as a professional actress worthy of an Oscar. She sensed Stiles would comprehend the uneasiness which was her constant companion.

Her fingers found the duck charm on her bracelet and brushed over the form that symbolized "be in the moment." Then her gaze danced over the group of friends again.

She wished she could leave the underbelly of the world behind and enjoy the simple pleasures life offered…but scum floated on the surface of all her thoughts.

Jaded by her past and uninterested in the conversation's direction into politics, Jolene moved toward the sloop's bow. Using her sarong as a pillow, she lounged against the hatch of the cabin. She stared off to her right toward the Chesapeake shoreline where splashy umbrellas and multicolored bodies dotted the silver beaches that quivered with heat. From time to time, Boogie Boards spiraled into the air, resembling leaping dolphins. The sounds of the crashing waves and the jubilant prattle of the beach dwellers were lost to the flapping of the sail above her. She'd no doubt crimes were being committed in the picture-perfect scene, but there was nothing she could do to stop them. Not today. Not from here.

A trickle of perspiration made its way between Jolene's breasts as she repositioned her bracelet on her wrist. Being with her childhood friend, Rose Delgado, again brought back many good memories that made her laugh. Recounting their teen years also released

4

memories of less pleasant events Jolene had kept locked away: The on-going arguments between her and her parents hung on the fringe of every conversation, waiting to be addressed.

She pressed a palm against her flat stomach and filled her lungs with salt air, willing serenity to quiet her thoughts. She exhaled slowly.

Rose came forward on the main deck and disrupted her peaceful view. In her free hand, she clutched a large plastic cup and carried a plush beach towel tucked under her arm. "You're finally chillin'."

The boat dipped and its bow cracked against a swell.

"Oh, my!" Rose grabbed the rail with her free hand, and with her legs spread, she balanced herself against another sudden dip. She caught her breath and said, "I saw you check out Norris."

"Who's Norris?" Jolene turned her face toward the warmth of the afternoon sun, ignoring her friend's grin.

"Wow, Chica. Who are you trying to kid? I saw the look he gave you and how you smiled back at him."

Standing toe to toe with Norris when they'd been introduced, Jolene's breath had actually hitched. He had the whole bad boy look going on with his slight unkempt beard and moustache, dark sunglasses, and a single line tattoo on the inside of his right forearm. God knew she loved bad boys—and so knew enough to put up her guard. "I was being polite."

"The smile was more than a polite glad-to-meet-you smile," Rose said. "You totally checked him out, right down to his boat shoes."

"I check everyone out." Jolene allowed a coy

smile to lift her glossed lips. "Part of the training." Rose knew Jolene worked for the U.S. Marshals, but thought she worked as a desk jockey, pushing files.

"Okay. Have it your way. Here." Rose handed off her white wine and dropped onto her knees beside Jolene.

With the wind cascading over the bow, her friend struggled to position her oversized towel. She did the best she could and quickly trapped the towel with her body. Then she pulled a tube from between her breasts and squirted lotion on her legs.

"So how long are you on vacation?"

"I lied. I'm working a case."

The tube almost fell from Rose's hand and she fumbled to grab it before it hit the deck.

"Really?"

"No." Jolene laughed. Her friend had always been easily duped. "I'm really visiting Martina and her family for a few days." She kept a broad smile on her lips but recalled Will, her boss, had forced this vacation on her after her last assignment—a thrill-seeker's wet dream.

Rose leaned toward her. "Tell me about one of the cases you've worked recently?"

"I can't. I would get jail time for treason."

Rose frowned. "You can trust me."

"I know." Jolene turned her face to the sun. Reality was, if Rose knew the truth about her job and the details of the cases she worked, Jolene doubted Rose would ever sleep peacefully again. It was bad enough Jolene suspected her sister, Martina, knew the truth about her position with the U.S. Marshals. Martina probably wore down sets of rosary beads worrying

6

about her.

Jolene arched her back. "What's Norris' connection to the Hackmans?"

"I knew you were interested in him."

"I'm curious how a chief of police is connected to a millionaire."

"He's a friend to Tony's brother, Joseph, and his wife Grace—a social worker. I think they worked together when he lived in Norfolk. Norris was a detective. I guess he and Grace came together on few cases dealing with families."

Going from a detective in a large city to a small-town chief was a big career change, Jolene thought. "What's his story? Why did he leave the city?"

Rose shrugged. "Not sure. Why don't you ask him?"

"It doesn't matter." She zigzagged her fingers through her cropped hair, skimming her scalp with her nails, and then tugged at a few tufts to spike them. "Why is he here today?"

"Same reason you are. To spend time with friends and relax."

Feeling there was another motive he was aboard, Jolene lifted her glasses and shot Rose a calculating eye.

"Okay. When I asked Jackie if she and Tony would mind if you came along, Jackie got it in her head to play matchmaker," Rose confessed. "She invited him because she thought you two would hit it off since you're both in law enforcement."

Jackie Hackman, a corporate stay-at-home wife, didn't possess a clue about what encompassed being a cop's life, or what a Marshal's life was like, for that matter. It took a very special person to endure the stress the job created within a law enforcement relationship. Sure, she knew a few Marshals who'd found trusting partners—Will and Nicole for example—but she also knew some who nearly lost their minds because of bad relationships. She was a prime example because she'd fallen in love with a man on the wrong side of the law…and then watched him die.

"Did she think we'd bond while chatting about our guns?" she asked.

Rose frowned.

"Sorry." Jolene dropped her sunglasses to the bridge of her nose. "That was uncalled for. It was very nice of her to extend the invite."

"I'll tell her you said thank you, but no thank you."

"No. I'll do it." Jolene settled back on the black and red sarong which matched her new two-piece suit. "In a few minutes."

The yellow sail above them flapped madly.

"Wow. The wind is picking up," Rose said.

"It feels good."

The breeze kept the sun's heat at bay while they lounged in silence for the next ten minutes.

Jolene glanced toward the shore and saw several umbrellas now bowled upward. They resembled wavering martini glasses while their owners fought to right them against the gusts.

Feeling parched, Jolene sat forward. "I'm going to get a drink. Do you want more wine?"

"No, thank you."

Jolene grabbed for her sarong before it took flight into the ocean. She wrapped the thin material around her chest, secured it with a knot, and tucked the ends into her bathing suit's bra before she pointed to the cup between Rose's legs. "Do you want me to get rid of your wine and bring you a soft drink?"

"Please."

Jolene grabbed the railing and concentrated on her footing while she shuffled aft to the stern of the boat. *Was it her imagination or did the sea seem a little rougher?* Maybe the boat was moving faster. It was hard for her to tell since she wasn't a sailing expert. Sunning on the sand and romping in the waves were her preferred water activities.

She noted Norris Stiles no longer sat in the boat's cockpit with his group of friends, which meant he was below in the galley, right where she was headed. And since Eric and the other two couples were staring at her, there was no turning back. She felt compelled to enter the ship's belly and be alone with the man.

"Rose wants a fresh drink." She smiled back at the group and held up the cup. "I'm going to help myself, if it's okay."

"Go right ahead," Tony shouted over the wind whipping the sail as the boat faced more into the wind.

"If you need anything, Norris can help you," Jackie said, brushing back the strands of long blond hair escaping her French twist. "He's been on this boat a few times. He knows where everything is located."

"Okay." Jolene didn't need eyes in the back of her head to know everyone watched her descend the stairs. She heard Jackie's comment that she and Norris would make a handsome couple.

The cabin was made for two very friendly people. Norris stood at the tiniest sink she'd ever seen.

He held a knife poised to slice a lemon. Stepping onto the lower deck would put her in his space.

"Hi," she said, remaining hunched over on the bottom step.

"Hi." He glanced her way for a second before turning his attention back to the yellow fruit he held between his fingers.

Earlier, on deck, his Battle wrap sunglasses concealed his eyes. Now the glasses sat high on his forehead. The black frames were nearly lost in his hair which spiked up around them. Before, she'd thought his athletic build was his best feature, but just a glimpse of Norris' forest-green eyes confirmed his eyes were his finest trait. Staring into them was like looking up at the bright summer sun through lush maple foliage where mature greenery danced with endless golden shards from heaven.

She thought to ask if he wore contacts, but before she could, he cut the juicy lemon and it squirted in his face. He dropped the knife and rubbed his eye with the back of his hand.

The color was definitely genuine.

"Be careful with those lemons," she said.

His slight chuckle matched hers. "Right." The man didn't talk much.

Out of nowhere, Jolene felt like an anxious school girl on a blind date, not knowing what to say or how to stand. After thirty seconds of uncomfortable silence, she said, "I came down for something other than wine to drink."

"Not a wine person?"

"Not today."

"Me neither," he said.

"Not today, or never?"

"Sociably."

"Ah."

"I'm having lemon water. Do you want some?" Now that he'd actually said something more than a few grunted words, she realized he'd been born with a rich, deep voice meant to make the fairer sex want to mate.

"Sounds refreshing. Do you mind if I also grab one for Rose?"

"Help yourself." He nodded to his right. "Bottled water and ice are in the cooler. Plastic cups are behind you on the shelf."

She held up the cup in her hand. "Rose didn't finish her wine."

"The trash is also behind you in the little cabinet."

"I'll just…" Jolene stepped off the last step and reached around him intending to pour the wine into the sink. Immediately his masculine scent combined with sun screen and salt water filled her nostrils. All the blood rushed from her brain to body parts south.

The boat shifted. She lost her balance and stumbled against the hard plane of his back. The ripple of muscle under her palm stalled her pulse. Her survivor's sensor went off and she jerked back. "I'm sorry."

"No problem. Part of being at sea." He glanced over his shoulder with an impassive eye and then turned back to his task.

Jolene ditched the used cup and then grabbed two clean ones before she skimmed past him, careful not to touch him again. She retrieved a water bottle and ice from the cooler.

11

She'd been under the impression Norris was an active participant in Jackie's matchmaking scheme, but his actions pointed to one of four things: Either the man was in on the plan and after seeing her decided he wasn't interested...or he hadn't known about Jackie's plan...or Jackie didn't know he was gay—which was such a waste of manhood for the women of the world—or maybe Norris had known about Jackie's plot and felt the same way she did. Not interested in a relationship.

She was intrigued as she wondered which scenario was the truth. "I understand you're Cape James' Police Chief."

"For the last ten months." Norris dropped two wedges into each of the ice-filled cups she held and then, without the slightest amount of eye contact, turned his back to her.

"And before that?" She heard his sharp intake of air. She moved to his side and watched his strong hands squeeze every drop of juice from a couple lemon wedges into a bottle of water in the sink.

He jammed the rinds through the bottle opening and screwed the cap back on.

"You've been asked the question before...?"

"I was with the Norfolk Police Department." His jaw flexed under his beard while he opened a top cabinet and pulled out a box of sandwich bags. He dropped the rest of the lemon slices into the bag and pinched it closed with a solid zip.

"Did you always want to be a lawman?"

"Yeah, ever since I saw *Tombstone*." He plucked a towel off the hook screwed into the cabinet front and wiped his hands clean. "Are you an Agent Gerard fan? Is that why you chose to work for the U.S.

Marshals?"

She remembered the character Tommy Lee Jones made famous in *The Fugitive* and pride rushed through her. She snorted under her breath and angled her head back to stare directly at him. "I am a Marshal."

"They let you carry?"

In response to the map of lines crinkling the corners of his twinkling eyes, her fingers compressed the cold cups she held. She presumed Rose had told him she was a secretary for the agency, thus the tease. She wasn't an egotistical person, but for some reason, in that moment, she wanted Norris to know she was a full-fledged agent. Her pride needed him to know. "Always."

His gaze drifted down to her breasts. The responsive bow of his lips was enough to confirm Norris was definitely not gay.

"FYI. I'm dangerous even without my M&P 9," she stated flatly.

His eyes lifted slowly.

"So am I." He took the bottle of water she'd retrieved from the cooler and filled the cups, chilling her hands. "Smith & Wesson, huh? I prefer a Glock 22. Why the M&P?"

"I do a lot of night work."

He stopped pouring the water. "Then, you don't work a desk?"

"There are reports." She winked.

He smiled and then dropped his attention to her arm. "What's with the bracelet?"

If her hands were free she would've touched the piece of jewelry which held too many memories. Each charm represented a moment in time, especially the

13

dragonfly. She slanted her head and dipped her chin toward his left arm where she noticed a one-line tattoo reaching from the inside of Norris' wrist to his elbow. "What's with the tiger?"

"It's a Lynx," he said.

"Why a Lynx?"

"I think they're cute. They have spiky hair on their ears." His gaze flickered to the top of her head. "And, like I suspect your jewelry does to you, it means something to me."

"And what is that?" she asked.

"That is something I don't share."

"I understand." Transfixed by the man, Jolene's heart rate increased. She acknowledged the draw between them, but reined it in. Getting involved with someone, especially an officer of the law, wasn't on her agenda this week. "We better get up top before rumors fly."

"Right behind you."

Norris didn't follow her up the stairs immediately. In fact, she'd just approached Rose at the front of the boat when she finally caught him emerging from the cabin.

"You were gone for a while." Rose wore a huge grin. "Did you and Norris hit it off?"

"We bonded over our weapons of choice, so you don't have to lie to Jackie." She handed her friend both cups of water before removing her sarong. Her skin felt flushed despite the breeze. She glanced to the rear of the boat. Norris was perched on the leeward side watching her.

"Oh, look." Rose pointed to the sky. "Someone lost their kite."

14

Holding onto her wrap and the lifeline, Jolene turned and shielded her eyes against the sun's rays. Sponge Bob hovered in the clear sky. Most likely, his string snapped against the ocean gusts and now he free-sailed on the air currents. "I'll bet you twenty dollars some kid is having a fit."

"Not taking the bet," Rose lazily responded, settling back against the cabin.

Jolene stared out over the endless body of water and dismissed all thoughts of Sponge Bob.

Her peaceful state lasted only a few moments before the sea air trapped in her lungs.

"Sweet Mother Mary." She unclipped her bracelet. "Catch." The jewelry clanked against the boat at Rose's hip, and then her sunglasses did the same.

The boat dipped.

She vaulted up and grabbed the shrouds and clung to the thick lines to ensure she didn't lose her footing on the glossy, wet planking. She scanned the ocean again then climbed over the lifeline. The boat's bow rose and cut into a swell, cascading water across the bow.

Behind her, Rose cried, "What the hell are you doing?"

Jolene curled her toes into the deck while zeroing on where she'd seen something on the ocean.

"Drop the sails," she yelled to Norris who'd already jumped to his feet. Without waiting for his response, she dove into the ocean, hoping to save a little part of the world—and steeling herself for the worse.

15

CHAPTER TWO

Should he go for it, or not?

Maybe hostess Jackie had finally found a woman who could fulfill at least one of his needs.

Jolene's bottom was right there in front of his face while he waited for her to climb the steep stairs to the upper deck. The nearly sheer sarong did little to conceal her tight ass. His groin had tightened as he watched the movement of her cheeks.

Earlier, when Jackie told Norris she and Tony had invited a woman friend, a friend of a friend, to join them on the outing he immediately thought his day off had fallen into the crapper. While waiting to meet the woman, his fingers had twitched against his cell and he'd fought the urge to sneak a call to his deputy and order Warren Pickett to call him back with a false emergency. With the excuse of needing to handle police business he wouldn't hurt anyone's feelings and could get the hell out of meeting Jackie's "perfect match" for him.

Jackie was a good person, but she didn't understand he wasn't interested in finding the right woman. The perfect woman for him didn't exist, and that fact had been proven. It was the reason he'd applied for and accepted the position of police chief for the coastal town of Cape James and moved the hell away from Norfolk—away from his biggest mistake.

After his brief conversation with the pixie U.S. Marshal and especially after noting the way her breasts pressed harder against the fabric of her swimsuit when his gaze lingered on them, Norris felt Jolene might be open for a night of hot, sweaty sex while she was home on vacation. He hadn't slept with a woman in well over a year, ever since the break-up of the century which had almost landed him in jail. Maybe it was time to get on with his life.

Hell, a few of his men suggested numerous times over the past month he should hire a hooker and get some release, if only for the sake of their blood pressures and sanity.

He was the chief of police. Hookers weren't an option for him, unlike they'd been for a few public servants he'd known over the years.

He climbed the stairs and saw Jolene headed forward. *Should he follow her?*

Norris felt the weight of interest directed toward him and turned to the group, ignoring the grins. They didn't know what had gone on between him and Jolene below, or what he thought now. He didn't like people knowing his business. Jolene wasn't going anywhere.

"Anyone else need something to drink while I'm playing bartender?"

Everyone shook their heads to the negative, so he crossed the deck and settled near Grace.

"So, did you and Jolene talk?" Grace smirked.

"We did."

"And did you hit it off?"

"Not really. We disagreed on the type of weapon to carry."

"That's all you two talked about? Guns?"

He shrugged. "What can I tell you? No spark." Over the top of his cup, he surveyed the ocean, starting

17

with the view over Grace's head and circling around. Until he saw Jolene climb up on the side of the boat, outboard of the life line.

He lowered his cup. "What the hell is she doing?"

Adrenaline dumped into Norris' bloodstream as he jumped to his feet. He heard Jolene call out: "Drop the sails." Then he watched as Jolene's slim body did a perfect arched dive and sliced into the ocean. With a reflex response he used the boat's lifeline and climbed up on the deck. *Where was she?*

When she surfaced he scanned the waters beyond her, in the direction she swam and every muscle in his body tensed. "Lower the main sail, now! Eric, bring the boat around to the port side. Don't cut it too hard," he shouted over his shoulder.

"Oh my, God." Grace's nails dug into his arm. "Is that a—?"

Everyone, except for Eric who remained at the helm, moved to the boat's side to get a glimpse of what he saw. Their gasps filled his ear.

Norris grabbed Joseph by the shoulder. "Help Tony with the sails. Quick, man." He dug his cell phone from his pocket. It displayed three bars. Good. He punched in 9-1-1. While he waited for the connection to complete, he ordered Jackie and Grace to get the life preservers and blankets. Then he shouted over the cry of the luffing sails, "Rose, watch the boat's bow so Eric doesn't cut too close to Jolene when he comes about." He whipped his glasses from his head and tossed them on the seat. Then he ripped off his shirt.

"9-1-1. What's your emergency?"

"This is Chief Stiles. I'm on a sailboat off the

shore about two miles south of Morgan's Pier. We've found a floater in the boat lane. Get the Coast Guard out here a.s.a.p. The captain of the *For The Good Times* will send them our exact coordinates immediately," he shouted so Tony also heard him. Tony acknowledged with a nod. Norris continued: "Notify the medical team and the examiner. Also, contact life guard stations for any missing persons information. And put all available officers on standby until I know where we'll put in." He toed off his shoes.

"Confirmed Chief Stiles. Coast Guard has been dispatched to your location. Officers on standby. Life guards, medical team and examiner have been notified."

As Norris watched, Jolene reached the victim who floated on the sea swells in something that resembled a child's raft. Bile tickled the back of his throat.

"Forget the examiner. Floater appears to be alive. Stay on the line." He handed the phone off to Grace and slung a ring buoy over his shoulder. *So much for taking a day off*, he thought as he dove overboard.

CHAPTER THREE

The moment she tenderly touched the little girl's soft hair, Jolene knew her life changed forever. She wasn't sure how, but something primal reared its head. She'd felt the instinct to protect someone, something, hundreds of times but this new need was unique and all consuming.

Treading water alongside the little rubber raft, Jolene noted the small child's cherub face and that her shoulders and her arms were fiery red from the sun's relentless rays.

"Hey, talk to me," she said.

The child's sunken eyes sent Jolene back in time, to the last second of Stefan's life. Her heart hitched when the tiny hand slowly lifted from its resting place on the rubber raft and her small stubby fingers brushed her burnt cheek, her lips.

Without warning, the child scrambled to get out of the raft and in her panic, she clung to Jolene.

Jolene fought to control the girl, to keep her in the raft, and in the process she dipped below the surface. Salt water laced her throat and nostrils. When she sputtered to the surface again, she spit out a mouthful of salt water and drew in air. Fighting to keep her own anxiety in check was a challenge. She had to remain calm. She wouldn't drown, but she feared for the child if she gave up the tube entirely.

"You're okay, sweetie. I've got you." Jolene struggled to get the girl to remain inside the tube without tipping it over…"*Shhhhh*." She treaded water with one hand, moving her feet slowly. She didn't know how long she could keep herself and a hysterical child afloat in the ocean current and rising swells. "You must sit," she said with all the calmness she could muster. "You're safe. I'm not going to let go of you."

Long seconds ticked off before the child settled down. The little girl tried to moisten her cracked lips, to speak.

The ocean waves worked to pull them apart and Jolene held the girl's hand to ease her fear and to link them as one.

Something brushed her thigh and Jolene jumped, scanning the water beneath them while the theme from the movie *Jaws* tr…rumped, tr…rumped in her mind. *How could she protect the child, exposed as they were like this?* She quickly realized it was the child's foot that brushed her leg.

She told herself to remain calm and treaded water lightly. It little to quiet the inner dialogue running around in her head. She had to get the child to safety. They were sitting ducks in the ocean for any number of predators and with the rising seas... She saw the crew on board the sloop working to lower the mainsail and turn the boat around. The boat was now at considerable distance, appearing to be the size of one of those remote-control boats she'd once seen in Central Park, and it seemed to move slower as it turned.

"Mama," the child whispered and her eyes drifted shut again though her lips continued to move.

It was ironic they floated in an enormous body of water, and yet there wasn't a drop of drinkable water to fend off the child's thirst.

"I'm here." Jolene lightly brushed her fingers over the girl's scorched soft skin. "I'll get you something to drink the moment we're on the boat."

"Boat," the child repeated. Jolene could barely hear the word.

The child's hollow mumble raised Jolene's concern. She scanned the immediate area again. From her vantage point, she could barely see the shoreline. She couldn't imagine the terror this little girl's parents must be suffering. She didn't have a child, but she knew with complete certainty, if anything happened to one of her nieces or nephews she'd be fanatically searching for them.

Her stomach rolled thinking how the loss of a child would crush Martina and Simon. Then her thoughts returned to this child's parents.

She heard a splash behind her and momentarily let go of the inner tube, swinging around with a clenched fist to punch whatever came at them. "Norris." She expelled the air from her lungs in relief when she saw him swimming toward them.

He must have dived into the water before the boat sailed past her.

"Here." He shoved a buoy at her and floated to the child's side. "She's alive?"

Her arm relaxed somewhat though she continued to cling to the lifebuoy. "Barely. She's showing signs of acute dehydration."

"My people have the Coast Guard on the way. And medical attention is standing by." His eyes turned from examining the girl to her. "Why the hell didn't you tell me what you saw instead of just jumping overboard?"

"I don't know. I saw her. I had to jump."

"It could have been a stupid move."

Jolene's jaw clenched. Her impulsive actions were the reason she'd been encouraged to take this vacation and she was tired of this argument.

"Maybe. Maybe not." She turned her attention back to the child.

"Look where you are," he said, floating beside her. "You didn't know she was alive. You could've hurt yourself going after a floater."

She checked to make sure the girl was calm, before she swished around to glare at him. "Can we talk about this later?"

Someone shouted from the boat and they both turned.

Jolene looked back to Norris. "What did he say?"

"I think that help will be here in two minutes."

The child mumbled.

"She's a lucky little girl. Her parents must be going crazy," Jolene said.

"We're checking"—Norris lowered his legs and submerged under a swell. Resurfacing, he spat out seawater—"life guard stations. Soon they'll know she's been found."

"How do you think she got away from them?"

"Don't know." Norris' biceps flexed with the motion to stay afloat.

The sloop glided over the water, drawing closer. Jolene saw that Rose's fists clutched the lifeline as she leaned over the bow, her expression taut with worry. The others remained at the stern, not taking their eyes off Jolene, Norris and the little girl.

A flare shot upward and then burst into glimmering red shards against the blue sky.

Less than a minute later, in the not-so-far distance they heard the blast of a ship's horn.

"The Coast Guard." Jolene pointed over Norris' shoulder. "Over there."

Within minutes they were flanked on one side by the boat and on the other by the Coast Guard vessel. A small life boat was lowered and two "guards" made their way to the trio. When one reached for the child, she screamed and threw herself backwards at Jolene, tipping over her raft.

Jolene, taken by surprise, let go of the lifebuoy and retrieved the little girl before she went under.

In desperation, the girl wound her arms tightly around Jolene's neck, stealing her breath, and they both plummeted away from their help and sank under the roiling waves.

Jolene sealed her lips tight and kicked furiously, struggling to gain the surface while she held the child tightly against her. If she let go, the girl would surely drown. The little one was too weak to hold her breath for long if she did go under.

Jolene felt the sea's power and knew she was fast losing the battle. The undertow constantly pulled her downward. The girl grew heavier. Her legs moved more slowly.

Her lungs burned. *Would all this be for nothing?*

No. From deep within her a force surged and she lashed out at the sea, demanding to be released.

A second later, strong fingers dug into the tender underside of her arm as they reached to secure her. Immediately her descent ended and she and the girl

24

were yanked back up into the sunlight.

Before she could draw breath or think about keeping her tight hold on the child, she felt the little girl pulled from her arms. The girl howled.

"She's fine and I've got you." Norris' deep-toned whisper filled Jolene's ear.

Clinging to his wide shoulders, Jolene gulped in more air. She blinked the stinging seawater from her eyes and then saw the worry in his.

"Better?" Norris asked. He had one arm wrapped around the lifebuoy and the other held her close.

She nodded, still unable to speak because a fire burned in her chest.

She heard the child's continuing cry and turned toward the lifeboat. "She's alive. Easy honey. You're safe now."

The guardsman confirmed her words with a nod.

"She's going to be okay." She smiled at Norris.

"Because of you." He returned her smile.

"Because I jumped."

"We're going to talk about that later, remember?" He kicked them closer to the lifeboat. "Let's get you on board."

"Give me your hand," the guardsman said, extending his arm over the side and helping her aboard.

She rested against the warm, hard vinyl and let her heart rate normalize. Her head dropped back and once again she enjoyed the warmth of the sun on her face.

A second later she startled when the little girl scrambled out of the Guardsman's embrace and crawled onto her lap.

Jolene took the blanket the man offered her and wrapped it and her arms around the small shivering body. She rested her chin on the girl's head and smoothed her long, wet ringlets back over her thin shoulders. The child's contentment actually made Jolene's racing heart relax.

When Norris was helped from the water he slid headfirst into the lifeboat's belly. He quickly told the Guardsman he was the Chief of the Cape James Police Force. Then he crawled on his knees to the raft's end and sunk down next to Jolene. He was offered a blanket but waved it off. He wiped the water from his face and looked at her.

"So you're on vacation?"

She felt relieved, fortunate and happy all at once and couldn't help but chuckle. "Yeah. And you're off duty today?"

"I am."

"Are you having fun yet?"

"Not yet, but I think the day can only get better from here."

"Copy that." She smiled.

CHAPTER FOUR

They arrived with sirens blaring at the hospital. Wearing a thin white blanket draped over his shoulders and with his semi-dry shorts clinging to his balls, Norris stalked up to the nursing station. "May I use your phone?"

He reached for the receiver and a hefty hand cut him off.

"I'm sorry, but I can't let you use this phone," the nurse sitting behind the desk replied. "Hospital rules."

He frowned as his patience was tested more with each second ticking off the bold-faced clock on the wall behind her. "It's official police business."

"Right. I don't think so." She scowled. "And before you also tell me you have pastoral duties"—she flicked a wary eye over his bare chest— "I'll let you know right now, I won't buy it." Then she resumed studying her computer screen, picked up her cup of coffee and took a calm sip.

Norris pulled the blanket over his chest. There was nothing about his attire that screamed law enforcement. He likely appeared more like a surfer dude without his shirt or shoes.

"Look. I was off duty today. I need to make a call." He'd have flashed his badge but it was still on Tony's boat along with his wallet and phone.

Within the moment, snappy footsteps slapped the vinyl floor, cutting through the emergency room's din. Norris turned. Warren Pickett was headed his way, wearing his official bicycling officer's uniform, a neon Cape James Police Department shirt and shorts. And his unofficial Designer L sneakers. He was returning from a shift riding the boardwalk when Norris' call reached him.

Pickett was Norris' first hire as chief. He'd been right out of the academy, his badge and attitude untarnished. Despite Pickett's lazy gaze, he showed acute sharpness and insight during the interview, and in the ten months they'd worked together, Pickett had proven his value to Norris.

He met his officer in three long strides, tossing the blanket into a laundry bin nearby.

"Where have you been?"

"Retrieving your stuff. I brought you a force-issued shirt like you asked."

"What took you so long?" He pulled on the navy Cape James Police T-shirt over his head.

"They docked twenty minutes ago. I got here as quickly as I could, Chief."

"Didn't you learn how to walk on water yet?" Norris accepted his wallet and stuffed it into his back pocket.

"You haven't taught me that lesson yet, sir."

At Pickett's quick retort, Norris chuckled and accepted the badge. He turned and held it up for the nurse to see. "Told you I'm a cop."

The woman was taking a call and only nodded.

He felt bad resorting to flashing his badge, but he was under pressure and in his current state of mind every mishap and miscommunication perturbed him. He took his own phone when it was offered and headed

28

down the hallway to room number eight. "Thanks," he said over his shoulder to his deputy.

Pickett fell in step beside him. "I assigned Jacobs to take the statements from the passengers before they disembark the boat."

"Good. Did you hear back from—?"

"Yes, sir."

Norris stopped by room three which was empty and stared at the younger man. "How do you know what I was going to ask you?"

"Hunch."

Norris arched his brow. "What was I going to ask you?"

Pickett eased back on his heels. "You were going to ask if I heard back from the Beach Operations Sergeant."

"And did you?"

"Yes. All missing children reported today have been found and returned to their guardians."

Norris shook his head in frustration and waited until a medical team wheeled an elderly man past them on a gurney. They maneuvered it into room four before Norris and Pickett started the trek down the hall again. "All stations were contacted?"

"He assured me they were," Pickett replied.

"Did you check with central dispatch?"

"Yes. No one has reported any child missing. I even checked with Heaven's Port."

Heaven's Port was the closest beach community north of Cape James. *Was it possible for the child to float on the currents seven miles between communities?* It had been a relatively calm day until just before the rescue…

29

He stopped outside the room where Jolene was keeping the little girl company.

"Then where are this child's parents?"

"Could they...*um*...be missing too?" Pickett fiddled with his belt loop. "Just a thought."

"Not a bad one." Norris contemplated that notion for a moment. Then he stepped through the doorway, held up his phone and snapped a picture of the little girl who slept peacefully beneath white sheets as if she were tucked into a fine vellum envelope.

The watchful eye of Jolene Martinez turned his way.

He snapped a second picture, this one of the U.S. Marshal who now wore hospital socks with the non-skid bottoms and blue scrubs over her bikini. She sat at the child's bedside, index finger stroking the girl's pinky.

Norris gave her a thumbs-up and a reassuring smile before stepping back into the hall.

Outside, he stared down at the picture of Jolene's exhausted face. In the photo, the woman still held the child who had refused to let go of her during the entire ride to the hospital—until the sedatives the doctor gave the girl took hold. Only then were they able to place her in a bed, remove her swimming suit, examine her, and after several attempts—because she was so dehydrated—insert an IV into the tiny vein in her forearm. All procedures had been recorded and done under Jolene's and his charge.

Despite everything Jolene had dealt with in the last several hours she still appeared pretty.

He went back to the girl's photo. Hydration had brought some fullness and color back to the little girl's cheeks and her eyes didn't appear sunken any longer. Thank God Jolene spotted her, otherwise… Who knew what would have happened to her. Likely she wouldn't be alive.

He tapped his phone's screen. "I'm sending you the child's picture, Pickett. Check with the local marinas and see if anyone recognizes her. On second thought, we'd better include all marinas within twenty miles up and down the coast."

Pickett pulled out his phone and started tapping notes into his notepad app. "That's going to take time."

"Get help. I'll handle the mayor if he questions paid overtime. I'm sure he isn't going to squawk. Bad news isn't good for the tourist trade and our busiest weeks are ahead. I want this wrapped up before the July Fourth holiday week starts." Norris swiped his nails under his left armpit and ignored the looks he received from the pair of female techs who passed by. "Hand off the info and her picture to the other local departments. Also, ask them to report any boats that don't return to port tonight. And, check with the Coast Guard to see if they received any distress calls last night."

"Are you thinking she was on a boat that went down?"

"We found her sitting in a child's blow-up raft and not even wearing a life jacket, so I'm still leaning toward a beach incident, but let's cover all bases. I've seen people do stupider things than sit their kids on an inflatable and think they'll be safe." He scratched an itch at the nape of his neck. "Have our boys comb the shore for any signs of wreckage too."

"How far?"

"All the way to Haven's Port." He grazed his

fingers over his stomach. "Is this a new shirt?"

Pickett shook his head and then glanced up from his phone with his brows knitted together. "Yes. I didn't have time to launder it."

"Damn." Norris pocketed his phone, feeling the cool dampness of his shorts graze his abdomen while his skin above his waist felt on fire. He was having an allergic reaction to something on the shirt. He grabbed the back of the shirt and pulled it over his head. "Why the hell not?"

"You didn't specify you needed a laundered shirt."

Norris tossed the shirt to Pickett. "You read my mind about everything else."

"Concerning the job. Not about your personal preference on attire and hygiene." Pickett rolled the shirt up and tucked it under his arm. "But, I'll make a note." He tapped his phone.

Norris grimaced and between tight lips said, "Damn it. Don't make a note."

"*Shhh.*" Jolene rushed out of the room. "What is going on out here?"

"Police business," Norris grumbled, reaching behind to his back where he swore an army of ants crawled up his spine. He bit down on his lip.

Jolene glared at him. "Do you normally strip on the job?"

"I brought him a new shirt, right out of the package. He doesn't like it." Pickett stepped forward, smiling, and extended his hand. "Officer Pickett, at your service. You can call me Warren."

Warren held Jolene's hand a little longer than necessary. "Let's keep it professional," Norris said pointedly.

Jolene's attention shifted to him. "That coming from the near-naked guy standing in a public hallway scratching himself." Looking at his chest, her lips parted. "Ah…What's going on? You're covered in red blotches."

When she reached out to touch him he stepped back.

"I have an allergy to the packing stuff or the sizing the manufacturers use to ship the new clothing."

"I didn't know," Pickett declared, putting up his hands.

"I'll find a doctor and get you a Benadryl, and a scrub shirt," Jolene offered.

He grabbed her by the wrist to stop her and was surprised by the softness of her skin. A wave of possessiveness surged through him and he was reluctant to let her go. Probably an aftereffect of their close call. He didn't want her exerting herself.

"I'll find someone in a moment, when I'm done with Pickett," he told her.

"I need to find the restroom anyway." She smiled demurely and the gesture softened her face. She pointed down the hall. "You'll stay here in case she wakes up?"

"No problem." He had no idea how he'd handle the child if she did wake up, but knew he could always call a nurse.

"Nice to meet you, Warren," Jolene said, before walking quickly down the hall.

Pickett watched her. "So… She's the U.S. Marshal?"

Norris frowned. "That's what I've been told."

"U.S. Grade A. Is she married?"

"She's out of your league." Norris' words surprised himself and he hesitated to think why he'd blurted that out. He sounded like he was staking territory. Claiming his woman.

Ridiculous. Maybe Pickett would let it go. But that was not in Norris' cards for today…

Pickett chuckled. "But not yours. I got it." He slapped Norris' shoulder and quickly backed away. He held up his phone. "I'll get on to my to-do list a.s.a.p. while you"—*cough, cough. Wink, wink*— "work the case from here."

Knowing Pickett had read his mind concerning Jolene, his jaw tightened. "You're an ass, Pickett."

"I'm learning from the best." Pickett laughed again and back-peddled a few yards before he turned and headed toward the exit.

Norris looked to where he'd last seen Jolene, but she had disappeared.

Jolene stopped and peered inside room number eight. True to his word Norris sat next to the bed and watched over the little girl who still slept. Did he feel that protective energy rush after a rescue, like she felt? He likely sat there watching over the little girl out of kindness or because she'd asked him to. And if her instincts weren't out of whack too, he wouldn't leave until he had a chance to question the child.

Where were her parents?

She tapped on the window to gain his attention and his electrifying gaze snapped her way, causing her heart to skip a beat. She motioned him to her before turning and sucking in a deep breath. Trying to rein-in her totally inappropriate attraction to him, she pushed a fist under her rib cage. The attraction was likely heightened because he risked his life to save her and the child. She noted the blue scrubs he'd been given were pulling across his broad chest and that coarse curls filled the V-neckline.

"I see they brought you another shirt," she said when he came out of the room.

"Yeah. It'll do until Pickett gets back here with one of my shirts from the office."

"How is she doing?"

"Sleeping like a baby." He smiled and with those words and that smile, his appeal rose even more.

He pinched the thin material above his waist between his fingers and tugged but it didn't have much give.

She forced herself to look up and met his enchanting eyes. "Ah... About something for your reaction to the shirt sizing... Even though you're their chief of police, the nurse told me they couldn't issue you anything, including Benadryl, unless you're admitted. But it's just over the counter. I can run out to a pharmacy and pick some up if you like..."

"I already managed to get some."

"How?"

"I have my ways." He smiled down at her with a sly lop-sided grin. "One of the doctors here is a poker buddy of mine."

Her radar went up. Was Norris one of those lawmen who bent the rules for himself and his friends. A doctor giving away drugs and..."Isn't gambling illegal in Virginia?"

"I didn't say where we played."

35

"Right." She looked at him questioningly.

"Thanks for trying though."

"You're welcome." She knew she was about to step on the chief's toes, and this time he wouldn't take it lightly, but she had to ask. Not asking was irresponsible. Impulsive she was; negligent she wasn't. "Your doctor friend, does he usually distribute the hospital's drugs at will?"

Norris' smile faded. It was the reaction she'd expected. With her chin notched higher too, she waited for his response.

Norris' sharp gaze never wavered from hers. He shook his head.

"Always on duty. I get it," she said.

"No, that's not it. Tim is allergic to cats so he carries it with him, in case he treats a patient who has cat dander on them."

Jolene nodded, accepting his explanation. She'd find out soon enough what type of Johnny Law he was because she was determined to remain involved with this case. Until the little girl's parents were located and took her home, Jolene would be close by.

She pointed toward the window. "Did you locate her parents yet?"

"No. And as of this moment, there are no open missing children cases."

"How can that be? She has been gone at least four hours." She felt the hairs on the nape of her neck bristle and rubbed a hand over them. "It's a miracle she didn't tip that raft over before we found her."

"Even if she hadn't it's likely she would've drifted further out and might never have been found at all. You did good. You saved the little girl's life and her parents, when we locate them, will be overjoyed."

Jolene just thanked God she'd been up to the task.

"We're checking with other municipalities up and down the coast. She was pretty well sunburnt, so she could've been floating for hours.

"No wonder she was so terrified. I know I would be." Jolene rubbed her wrist, missing the familiar weight of her bracelet.

"We're also checking for any missing boats. It might take a day or two to hear back from all the harbor masters."

Her breath hitched. She hadn't thought of that scenario. She shivered, recalling how her lungs had burned while filling with cold salt water. Those few seconds of feeling life being pushed from her lungs and the sensation her muscles were weakening and her limbs going limp were enough to keep her on dry land for a while. Her eyes felt scratchy and tired from the salt water. Every muscle in her still felt weak. She closed her eyes and felt the solid floor beneath her stocking feet. Then she looked up at Norris with renewed appreciation. He *had* saved her life.

She refrained from thanking him again. Instead she drew in a deep breath and said, "Right. It's a possibility." With her mind refocused she offered up another scenario. "Or whoever brought her to the beach wasn't a parent and they're keeping her disappearance a secret for the moment. Or maybe it was someone hoping to find her before they had to tell the parents. You know, like a big sister who got caught up with her boyfriend and the little girl wandered away. Or her grandparents who are a little feebleminded. Although I

37

don't see her climbing into the tube by herself and walking into the ocean without anyone seeing her."

"The beaches are crazy this time of year," Norris said. "Someone could've seen her and assumed someone else watched her. We can't rule out any possibility. If any of those scenarios happened, we'll know soon enough. In the meantime, the ER doctor is going to admit her overnight for observation. Hopefully we'll hear from her parents soon."

"If not, what are your protocols?"

"Once the doctor releases her, she'll be turned over to social services."

So, if her parents weren't located, the girl would be placed in the care of strangers. Jolene recalled the terror that distorted the little girl's sweet face when the doctors and nurses first tried to examine her, and she winced. She wanted to do something, *but what?* She had no rights or jurisdiction in the matter. For now, Norris held all the power over the little girl's safety.

"Do you need a ride somewhere?" Norris interrupted her thoughts. "I can have one of my officers give you a lift to your hotel."

When he grazed his nails over the linen fabric at his collarbone she remembered his rash. She'd contacted poison ivy once and hated the irritation the rash caused, so she sympathized with him. "I'm not staying at a hotel."

"Oh."

Norris' long lashes made his eyes look wider. "I ah... I assumed since you're Rose's friend that you were staying at her father's hotel."

"No. I'm staying with my sister and her family. They live on Mariners Drive." She rubbed her neck, a response to a long day.

He dipped his head to the side. "You okay?"

"I'm fine. Thanks."

"Your sister lives in a nice area. I can have my guy drop you there."

Noticing he watched her closely, she folded her arms across her chest and glanced toward the child. "Thanks, but no thanks. I'm not going anywhere."

"You don't need to stay with her."

She looked up into his concerned face. "Yes. I do. She'll be frightened when she wakes up and since she seemed comfortable with me, I'll stay. However, if I can borrow your cell, I'd like to call my sister and see if she can hook up with Rose and get my phone and bag and bring me a change of clothes. Also, I need to check in with my office."

His brow crinkled. "I thought you were on vacation."

"I am, but I'm on call twenty-four-seven in case of an emergency situation."

Norris' eyes flashed with interest, but he didn't press her to explain what she meant by a situation. Instead, he slipped his phone out of the front pocket of his jeans and handed it to her. "I should've thought... Should have had Pickett grab your things from the boat too. Sorry."

"You had more important things on your mind than getting my personal stuff to me." She ignored the warmth of the phone in her hand and shrugged.

He nodded with understanding as she put some distance between them.

Jolene's nerves tingled, knowing Norris watched her while she walked to the end of the hall to get a bit of privacy. She quickly made a call to her sister, Martina, and then one to Rose, who wanted to hear more details than Jolene would offer. Rose was a witness to what occurred so Rose's statement had to be accurate and not tainted by Jolene's experience or opinions. Rose, or perhaps one of the others on board the boat might have seen something no one else had.

After she hung up from speaking to her friend, Jolene decided to wait until she had her own phone to check in with Will, her boss at the U.S. Marshals' office in Scranton. She joined Norris again outside room eight and handed him his phone. "Thanks. My sister will be here within the hour with my things."

"Good," was all he said then he turned back to the window. "So how old do you think she is?"

"Maybe two. I have a niece who is two and half." Jolene turned to him. "Did you notice how her swimsuit fit her?"

He looked at her quizzically. "Not really. Why?"

She massaged the tightness in her shoulder. Keeping both herself and the girl afloat, had been a strenuous workout for her deltoid muscles. "It might not mean anything, but the suit seemed really small on her. The straps cut into her shoulders."

"So."

He was such a guy. "If it were May and the beginning of the swim season, I wouldn't think it odd, but it's nearly July. I know my sister buys new suits for her kids around Easter."

Norris splayed his broad hand across his chest—the chest she'd been trying hard to avoid looking at.

"I'm not a kid expert by any means, but maybe

her family was visiting someone and they forgot her suit and used an old one, or borrowed one for the day."

"Maybe. Let me check the size?" Jolene quietly padded across the floor into the room. Norris had no forensics team. He needed to rely on the state police forensics lab and until he was able to drop it off at their offices, they weren't leaving the article of clothing or the raft Lia had been found in, out of their sights. She grabbed the evidence bag off the nightstand next to the bed and rejoined Norris outside the room. The bag crinkled as she pulled the suit out. Jolene tucked the bag under her arm and checked the embossed markings inside the suit's back. "It's a size eighteen months. I guess she could've worn it last year. It looks brand new, though." She turned the multi-hued purple suit over in her hands. "The material is not worn on the backside at all."

"The backside?" Norris' brows pulled together. "What do you mean?"

She spread her hand inside the suit and held up the area which would have covered the little girl's bottom. "This is the most tatty area on my nieces' and nephews' suits. Children tend to scoot on their rumps across the sand, the sidewalks, the floors. My nieces and nephews constantly wear their suits out. Martina buys them two or three suits a year."

"Interesting."

"Is it?" She chuckled.

His full bottom lip pursed. "I know nothing about kids. I don't have kids and I'm an only child."

"You're also a man. Most men don't notice such things so you're excused on all counts?"

"So, do you have kids?" he asked.

"Never married." She scowled at his disgruntled expression—and he was right to be put out: She hadn't answered the question. "No. I don't but I have six nieces and nephews and a large extended family of cousins who have bunches of kids. We get together every year which is why I know about things like the tatty backsides of kids' swimsuits."

"It must be nice belonging to a big family."

His smile was the kind of smile that drew a girl to kiss a man she hardly knew. *Whoa... Where did that come from?*

"Being part of a large family has its advantages, but it also has drawbacks. One being, everyone eventually knows your business."

"Is that why you moved away?"

He asked a question she didn't answer honestly for anyone. "Maybe."

Feeling an invisible force drawing her toward Norris, she dropped her gaze to the little nylon suit. Her mind should be on the little girl in the room, not on this police chief, but she enjoyed his wit and candor. And the physical attraction between them was undeniable.

Inside the room, the little girl began to wake and thrashed her legs around. Pain filled her moans.

"Hit the call button," Norris ordered Jolene as he followed her into the room.

Once she called for a nurse, Jolene encased the little girl's hand with her own. "*Shhh*," and she bent over the little girl and whispered into the child's ear. "You're okay, honey. *Shhhh*."

"Ask her what her name is."

"And you accused me of being the impatient one," Jolene said, turning her head to find herself nose to nose with Norris. His expression was an intriguing mixture of concern and excitement. "I think it's something like Lia…"

"Can you check again?"

Her gaze dropped to his parted lips.

As if drawn to her too, he leaned toward her slightly before he jerked away.

She quickly turned away from the attractive police chief and focused her attention on the child. "Give me a minute. I'll confirm the first name once she calms down."

Once this child was reconnected with her parents and the case was closed, Jolene might consider exploring their attraction if there was time before she left for home. She welcomed this attraction as a good sign she was finally ready to move on, away from the past. What could be the harm in having a light relationship for a week or so?

CHAPTER FIVE

The early evening sun cut through the large-paned window at the end of the hall. Someone had placed a chair and a hospital table between the window and the child's room for the officers who watched over her. The recliner-type chair looked inviting, but he was too anxious to actually sit. Norris needed to pace and standing was a better option for him.

In about an hour, the sun would disappear into the ocean and the moon and stars would take over the sky. Then the beach night life would rev up and his small force would need to handle other situations, situations that could erupt into three-alarm blazes if not extinguished immediately.

As each hour passed with no one coming forward to claim the little girl, Norris' blood pressure rose a few points. From the start, he knew in his gut the child hadn't simply been lost on the beach. A much bigger case than that had landed on his shoulders.

Down the hall, a janitor mopped the floor and the pungent antiseptic cleaning solvents tickled Norris' nostrils.

Moving away from the sun's rays, Norris swiped a finger under his nose and read the text updates he'd received from Pickett. There had been no distress calls to the Coast Guard last night, but that didn't mean a boat hadn't perished. No debris had washed up on shore yet, but depending on the currents and manner by which the boat had gone down, it could be days until anything significant was beached.

Also, no one had reported missing children to any of the beach operations along the coast. And no Amber Alerts had been issued in Virginia or in surrounding states.

So where had the girl come from?

A pump alarm sounded from one of the rooms. He watched a nurse from the duty team set down one of the cappuccinos he'd brought them. She leapt from her perch and rushed from the nurses' station to evaluate the situation. He was relieved she didn't head for Lia's room.

The girl's name was definitely Lia. They now knew that much, thanks to Jolene. She had deciphered and confirmed the information from the few words the girl had muttered.

Lia now called Jolene "Mama." The poor child was in shock and had attached herself to Jolene with a vengeance.

Yes, there were signs of trauma bonding between Lia and Jolene, on both sides. Lia clung to her as if Jolene were her mother and Jolene let her. The attachment bond had begun to cement itself even before he had reached them in the water.

Jolene came into the hallway, leaving the door ajar a few inches. "What's going on? You're still here?"

"There's an emergency somewhere... Yeah. One of my officers will be here in about ten minutes. I need to get back to the station and check on things."

She looked more comfortable in her fresh tight short-legged jeans, T-shirt, and sneakers. She still smelled of suntan lotion and the sea.

"Never a day off," she said to him.

45

She understood his life all too well.

"They are rare." On the boat, before she dived into the ocean, he'd been distracted by her trim body and full breasts, so he hadn't really noticed Jolene's spiky raven hair ends tinted a deep purple. He now noticed them when she moved into the rays of the setting sun to stare out over the parking lot below.

She turned, placed her hands on her hips and arched her back to limber up. "It feels good to stand and stretch."

She wearily raised her arms over her head, first grabbing her right elbow and pulling her arm as far back behind her head as possible. Her sun-kissed breasts swelled against the tank top's neckline and he had to look away before his interest was noticed. Then she did the same and stretched the muscles of her left arm.

"I guess there's no news?" she asked.

"Ah… No." He cleared his throat of the desire her stretching caused. Any male would do the same… "She's exhausted and with the sedative Doctor Evans gave Lia earlier she'll probably sleep until morning. We're not going to learn more from her tonight. If she wakes, they'll call me. I can take you home," he offered.

"Thank you. But, I'm going to stay. In case she does wake up." Jolene bent over at the waist and touched her toes.

"She won't," he responded, not daring to watch her moves anymore.

She stood and placed her hands on her hips.

He scoffed at her tenacity. "I figured you wouldn't leave so I grabbed something from the cafeteria for you when I picked up coffee for the nurses." He pointed to the bag sitting nearby on the hospital table.

"Nice. Thank you." She walked over and opened the plastic sack.

"I didn't know what you might like…"

When she looked up at him she wore a huge smile. "A chef's salad and a soft pretzel. And you grabbed mustard too. Awesome." She ripped off a piece of the pretzel and popped it into her mouth.

"The pretzel was for me, but you can have it."

"Sorry." She stopped in mid-chew and trapped a chuckle with the back of her hand and then swallowed. "Thank you. You want some?" She held out the pretzel.

He chuckled. "No. I'll grab something later."

"It's good. Not too much salt."

"I had enough salt today," he responded. "Go ahead and eat it."

"Okay." She quickly ripped the pretzel in half and dropped one part back into the bag. Then she laid the Philly-style pretzel on a napkin, opened the mustard and smeared it over his snack.

"I didn't take you for a carb girl." Good God, he enjoyed watching her nibble the pretzel. He had to order his dick to behave and promise his grumbling stomach a double-packed garlic cheese steak in twenty minutes if it would be quiet for now.

"I'm a total carb girl. Pasta is my Achilles heel."

"I'll remember for next time." His fingers rasped over the bristles on his jaw. Maybe he should've taken ten minutes to shave before heading out that morning.

Her tongue swiped a bit of mustard from the

47

corner of her mouth.

He shifted his eyes and focused on the orangey-pink clouds drifting across the sky behind her. He couldn't get distracted by this woman. This case was the biggest thing to happen in Cape James since he'd taken on the job ten months ago. It was probably the biggest case in a decade and he was on probation for one year, until the end of August. His job might even hinge on him handling this correctly. If he didn't do his job to the satisfaction of his hiring committee, all his hard work to turn this little force into a top-notch team might be for nothing. He'd be looking for another job somewhere.

He enjoyed living here. He seemed to have finally earned the respect and cooperation of Ted Beltz, his second in command who thought the chief of police position should've been his simply because of tenure. He'd come to like his officers: Ted, Frank, Larry, Warren and his one woman officer, Sandy.

He got along with most of the town's administration. However, some of them wanted a chief of police with larger iron fists. They were the teetotalers whose families had walked this shore for generations and who didn't easily tolerate the riff raff who intruded on their quiet seaside life six months of the year.

"You sure you don't want some?"

"No," Norris responded, pulled away from his brooding thoughts. "So, did Lia say anything more? Maybe her last name?"

He'd asked the little girl a few questions when she'd first woken, but she clammed up and sunk into the mattress at the sight of him. Later, when he observed her from the threshold, he noticed she tensed

48

whenever a man came into the room which made him wonder what her father was like.

"She asked me for Boo-boo," Jolene said. "From her description, I think Boo-boo is a stuffed rabbit, a purple stuffed rabbit." She popped the last piece of pretzel into her mouth, tied the bag top and placed it aside.

"Odd name for a toy. Don't you think?"

"My niece named her first doll Hi-bye."

He drew his brows together, confused by the little people language. "Hi-bye?"

"Hi and bye. They were words she could say clearly."

"Huh." Okay. He got the reasoning. He'd taken a class on child psychology which had focused mostly on the troubling adolescent years. The language of toddlers hadn't been included.

He looked past Jolene's shoulder, refusing to watch her lips draw on the straw of her soft drink. He refocused on the case. "So the word boo-boo, which I assume refers to injuries, is a word used often in her home."

"Maybe. Are you thinking abuse? She doesn't show any signs. Except for the dehydration. Doctor Evans said she looks well nourished and as if she's been taken care of. And her swimming suit is an LE, a top-of-the-line brand. Whoever bought it for her, didn't buy it at Walmart."

"So, we might be dealing with a family with an above-average income. The suit could've been a gift." As he considered that, his surroundings disappeared in significance. *Could the girl have been kidnapped, held for ransom until things went south for the kidnappers?*

49

Again, there had been no Amber Alerts in over a month, and the last one had been for a boy age twelve who had been found alive. He'd skipped out on his parents after midnight to pull an all-nighter playing video games with a friend. The father had found him missing from his bed at two a.m. Norris tapped into the notepad app on his cell. "You said LE?"

"Yes."

"I'll have my guys check with the local high-end stores and see if they can help us. Maybe someone will recognize her."

Overhead, Brahms' Lullaby wafted from speakers, announcing the birth of a baby.

"What's the size of your force?" Jolene leaned against the wall.

"There are six of us. Five men and one woman." His cheeks warmed under his whiskers, knowing he'd just made what could be considered a sexist statement. He didn't want Jolene to think he was sexist, because he wasn't. "I know gender isn't important. I just thought you might want to know there was a woman on the force."

"Is she special to you?"

He snapped his head up. "Hell no! I don't—"

Jolene played with the straw poking through the plastic lid.

"Relax. I didn't take you for the type of man who dipped his pen in the company ink." She laughed. "You're too easy, Stiles." She took a long draw on the straw.

Norris clenched his jaw. She'd set him up, teasing him. The woman was maddening—on so many levels. He wouldn't let her get to him again. "Anyway,

May through September we're all full-time."

"You're going to spread your team thin checking leads." She was all business once again.

"We've been spread thin before." He finished his text and pocketed his phone.

The nurse exited the room where the alarm had sounded. She barely glanced their way before returning to her perch behind the desk where she immediately began to type on her keyboard.

Jolene rattled the ice in her cup. "Can I help you work this case?"

"I can't let you help." He glanced down the hall, searching for his relief man.

"Why not? I'm a U.S. Marshal. We're federal and we do help local and state agencies when they request it. While I'm sitting here with Lia I can check on the stores where Lia's bathing suit might've been purchased. And I'm sure I can handle a few other things too. I do have experience running investigations."

He folded his arms across his chest. "I thought you rode a desk?"

Her shoulders lifted and fell quickly in response to his question. "So do a few other people in town. Perception... I want to keep it that way, so they don't worry."

"I had a feeling." He studied her.

"You did, huh?" She pushed off the wall and stepped toward him. "I'm pretty good at hiding my wily ways. What gave me away?"

He looked down at her and noted a small scar in her right brow and a bit of mustard on her lip. He hadn't noticed her scar before because her bangs had covered it. He'd be a liar if he said he wasn't intrigued by and undeniably attracted to the Marshal. If they weren't standing under bright fluorescent lights in the middle of a hospital hallway, outside a young child's room, he might even have touched her. Tasted the mustard on her lips.

"Diving into the ocean to save a possible floater... I don't think a desk jockey would've done that," he answered.

"*Hmmm.* I'll need to remember not to jump next time."

It was so hot the way she stood toe to toe with him. She reminded him of a tigress with her whiskey eyes, her graceful stride and her fearlessness.

"Plus you're very perceptive, among other things." He noted the sudden huskiness of his voice and cleared his throat.

"Like?" she prompted.

He wanted to ignore the smile that curled her lips, but he couldn't seem to look away. She had him under a spell. "You're determined, fearless, quick and as you said yourself, you're cunning. Oh, and annoying?"

Her lips rolled together, holding her smile in check. "How well you know me. Hard to believe we only met a few hours ago."

Her playful smile faded as a code blue announcement cut the hallway. The event occurred on the floor above them.

Once the broadcast ended, she stared at him through thick dark lashes. "So are you going to let me help, at least unofficially?"

An acute sense of the rational tightened Norris' neck muscles. "Unofficially? No." He crossed his arms.

"I don't want any evidence found by you to be dismissed on a technicality. If there is a proper protocol for getting you involved, I want to follow it."

"I bet you dot your i's. Huh?" She chuckled softly.

"I do." Again, he ignored her taunt.

She backed away and leaned against the wall again, looking relaxed and sexy in her tight T-shirt and jeans.

"So, you're thinking Lia…"—a sudden yawn made her raise a hand to her full mouth—"is a victim… Of what? Which way are you leaning?"

"That I don't know yet."

The elevators at the opposite end of the hall opened and Officer Frank Diterich stepped out. "My man is here. You should get some rest. Let me take you home."

Her purple spikes shimmered under the bright lights. "I'm staying."

"You won't get much rest here."

"I've slept in worse places. See you when I see you." Carrying her soft drink with her, Jolene grabbed the rest of the food he'd bought and marched into Lia's room.

As the door closed quietly, Norris wondered what Jolene's position was with the U.S. Marshals. He intended to make some calls and see what he could learn about her. She seemed sharp, but he wouldn't jeopardize his career by letting a wannabe field agent fuck things up for him. Or distract him…

***

53

From her position inside Lia's room, Jolene watched through the cracked door while Norris gave instructions to his officer. It was absurd, but she felt a twang of loneliness when he disappeared from view and as the sound of his footsteps diminished while the distance between them grew. She had to forget how her pulse quickened when she inhaled his scent or how easy and fun she found teasing him.

She liked him too much.

Norris was smart. He'd already thought of more reasons for Lia to be on the water than most investigating officers would've come up with on their own during a week. And he'd already given orders and delegated tasks and received information from his small staff quicker than most large-city detectives she'd ever worked with. He ran a well-oiled machine and she respected him for that.

She glanced at the wall clock. It was after nine. She saw the town lights click on as if falling dominos triggered their switches.

She yawned and dropped onto the chair next to Lia's bed. Waiting for something to crack in the case was the hardest part of the job. The exciting part of the job happened once the perp was known and the hunt for them began in earnest...

She was getting ahead of herself. Lia's story could end happily in a matter of hours.

She yawned again. The day had drained her. She would need her wits about her tomorrow if...

Another possibility popped into her mind as she sat there watching the sleeping girl. Maybe the child had been abducted by her estranged father after killing Lia's mother. The woman's body might not have been discovered yet, thus the reason they'd had no Amber Alert. *But if so, why had she been adrift on the ocean?* Perhaps once Lia's father realized what he'd done, he panicked and thought to make Lia disappear so it looked like a child abduction gone wrong.

But why didn't he just kill her and dump her body? Why would he put her into an inner tube on the ocean to die a horrid death? Was he punishing her for something?

Jolene slid her phone from her jeans pocket, wanting to call Norris, but as she searched for the Cape James Police non-emergency number she decided to wait and talk to him tomorrow. She could share the theory tomorrow—if Lia's parents weren't found.

Norris had enough on his mind right now.

She inhaled and immediately longed for the fresh mountain air of Pennsylvania. The hospital room was cool but the air stale. Even the heavily salted air she breathed in while on the boat today would be better. Feeling restless, she rose and walked around the bed to where Lia's swim suit lay on the table. She glanced at the officer sitting outside in the hall and saw his head drift toward his chest. She wished she could shut down as easily. Chase and Will and her other Marshal's C.U.F.F. teammates were the same way. Maybe it was her X chromosomes which kept her mind whirling constantly. Well, she'd take two Xs over two sweaty balls any day.

There were too many setups for Norris and his men to check out in a timely manner. The first forty-eight hours of any crime were crucial to gather evidence in order to solve it quickly. They needed help.

Of course, she was willing, but U.S. Marshals

didn't get involved with kidnappings of the general public, unless asked. Tomorrow Norris would need to contact the state police, if he hadn't already. And if any evidence was found or there was reason to believe Lia was brought to Virginia across state lines then the Feds would get involved. She knew Norris didn't want to give up this case to anyone.

She dialed Will's number, knowing she'd rest easier if she had her boss' permission to help Norris.

CHAPTER SIX

"Chief, wake up."

Norris swatted at the hand that gripped his shoulder and shook him from a deep sleep.

"Officer Pickett, you better have a damn good reason to wake me." A beam of light from the hallway outside his office cut across his chest and his watch. "I slept maybe forty minutes," he grumbled, holding up his arm and peering at the face of the watch he received from his father the day he graduated from the police academy. His mother hadn't come to the event, but then she hadn't come to his welcome home party after his stint in the Army. He hadn't cared then and he still didn't care.

"Then you had your forty winks." Pickett flipped the light switch and Norris growled his frustration at the fluorescent glare blinding his vision.

"Ted found something in the cold case files online," Pickett stated, ignoring Norris' foul mood. *Or maybe he was used to it by now.* "He remembered a baby with similar features who went missing nine months ago from the Richmond area. By features, I mean hair and eye color and a birthmark on the inside of the left leg."

Norris picked up on the trepidation in the deputy's voice. He shot up to a sitting position and dropped his stocking feet to the cool vinyl floor. He wiped the grit from his tired eyes and then stared up at Pickett. "He knows where the girl's parents are?"

The young officer hesitated. "He thinks so."

"You disagree with him?"

"I have reservations."

When his deputy's gaze shot toward the door, uneasiness pricked Norris' gut. There was something Pickett wasn't telling him along with the something he was. "Where is he?"

"He's in the den."

"Okay. Get me some fresh coffee." Norris reached for his shoes. "I'll be right there."

Pickett did a quick check of the hallway before stepping outside the office.

Norris sighed. He would lay odds his deputy hadn't told Ted he'd be contacting Norris.

He stood and stretched his back before reaching for the shirt hanging on the back of a nearby chair. If Ted were right about the missing child, maybe she would be picked up and the case closed. If so, he would ask Jolene Martinez to join him for a late dinner. They could celebrate jobs well done. And afterwards…

The memory of the swell of Jolene's ripe breasts above her sarong as she stood next to him in the cabin's tight quarters stole his breath. At the time, he'd wanted to peel her shawl away from her body and feel the weight of her breasts in his hands.

The squeal of the dispatcher's mike caused Norris to blink the image from his mind. He yanked on his shirt and focused on the case.

He hoped his senior officer was right. It didn't matter to him that the man who thought he should've been crowned chief of police by the town's counsel had unearthed the girl's identity. Ted would likely crow from the rooftop that he was the hero in this story, even though Jolene was the one who'd rescued the child. What mattered was the little girl would be reunited with her parents.

There still was plenty of case to unravel, such as how the girl ended up in the water and who put her there? To Ted, learning these answers would be grunt work. Work below his status of second in charge. That was a huge difference between them: Grunt work was what Norris lived for.

Leaving his shirt unbuttoned for the moment, Norris stalked into the open office his deputies shared. As he approached Ted Beltz, Ted hung up the phone.

"I heard you solved the case," Norris said.

"I did."

Ted's shitty grin could only be labeled smug. He handed off the file in his hand.

"I recalled reading an Amber Alert a few months back."

"Nine months." Norris read the date on the paper Ted had inserted into their file jacket.

"Yeah. September fifth of last year. It was Labor Day weekend. You were here then."

Norris slid his gaze off the page and toward Ted. Yeah. At that point he had been here for a whole three weeks. His chair hadn't had his ass imprint by then since he was so freaking busy settling into the job and a new house. Ted expected him to recall a case that hadn't been in their jurisdiction? "Your point?"

Ted's expression remained self-righteous. He lifted one shoulder in a negligent shrug.

"Nothing, Chief."

He'd rather the man liked him, but he could live with the fact he didn't as long as he did his job and showed him respect in front of his fellow officers.

Ted pointed to the file. "The Burgess baby, Abigail, went missing from her family's Richmond suburban home while a holiday picnic took place in their backyard. Someone walked in the unlocked front door and snatched her out of her crib, sight unseen."

"Okay." Norris remained silent for a minute while he read down over the notes provided by the local and state police officers who had worked the case before it was handed off to the FBI. The child belonged to Darren and Bonnie Burgess, a happily married working couple of average income. Baby snatching for ransom had been scratched off the scenario list by the investigation team, as was vengeance by a jilted lover. The couple, married for five years, had one other child, a son, Lonnie, age four. *Until that day, the Burgesses had the American dream going on*, Norris thought sorrowfully.

"Good." Norris read the next page. "The parents had her finger and feet stamped and a DNA sample was included with the collected evidence. See how much of the evidence kit is available digitally, specifically the fingerprints and footprints. Let's get them and compare them to our girl. If we have enough matching markers, we'll request DNA testing."

"All that might not be necessary," Ted responded.

Norris' jaw tightened. He knew what was coming before he asked and pressure thumped against his temples. "Don't tell me you called the parents of this missing child?"

"Yeah. I just hung-up with the father. They should be here in about an hour to do a positive ID."

"Fuck it, Ted." Norris slapped the file closed.

Coffee sloshed over the lip of Pickett's cup and he cringed. "*Owww.*" He set the cup down on the edge of a desk and flung his hand in the air, sending droplets spiraling toward the floor.

Larry turned to watch them and his chair's moan fill the dead silence cloaking the room.

"What?" Ted looked up at Norris resentfully. "You're pissed because I solved the case."

Norris' jaw locked, trapping additional choice words. *How could Beltz, an experienced officer of fifteen years, be so stupid?* He stepped forward, crowding Ted, and peered down at him.

"This isn't about me or the problem you have accepting I'm in charge here. Get that straight." He pushed his index finger against the manila folder. "What happens if our girl isn't their daughter? You'll tear the hearts out of the family again. Every step they've conquered toward healing will be lost."

"She has to be theirs."

Norris narrowed his eyes. "Why? Because you said so?"

"She has a birth mark on the inside of her left leg, same as the missing baby."

"Get your head out of your ass, Ted. A lot of kids have birthmarks. There are reasons we have protocols in place to identify and notify next of kin." As a policeman, Norris had learned the importance of self-control. He put the desk between them before he punched the man's self-righteous smile right off his burly face. *Didn't Ted realize the damage he could have done?*

Several phone lines rang at once. Larry grabbed

one.

Norris opened the file jacket and zeroed in on the name he needed. "Pickett, get me special agent, Kyle Carter on the phone. He's with the Richmond office." He turned to hand the file to the deputy and saw that Pickett held out a phone receiver toward him. Apparently Pickett had answered the second line.

"Special Agent Carter is holding for you on line two, Chief."

Norris scowled at Ted. "Would you like to square things away with the federal officer in charge of the Burgess case?"

The arrogant expression drained from Beltz's face.

"I didn't think so." Norris turned toward his junior officer. "I'll take it in my office. Meanwhile, get the fingerprint comparison started. I want to know whether we have a potential match in no more than thirty minutes."

"Boss," Larry spoke, "I've got a reporter from Channel 49 on the line asking us to verify one of our officers found the missing Burgess child."

Ted lurched out of his chair, sending it spinning back against the next desk. His jowls bloomed to a beet red. "How'd they find out?"

"Twitter," Larry answered him and then looked to Norris. "Should I tell him no comment?"

"No. He'll take a 'no comment' as a confirmation the child's been found. We'll be swamped with every reporter in the state before dawn." Norris thought for a quick second. "Tell him I'm in the john and put him on hold. Buy me two minutes with the SA Carter and then ring my line." He looked pointedly at

Ted. "I hope you realize you started a goddamn flash fire. When this case is over, you and I are going to have a heart to heart in my office, one on one."

Norris stormed down the short hall to his office. He inhaled quickly, knowing he was about to be dressed down by a FED. He grabbed the phone. "Chief Norris, here."

"This is Special Agent Kyle Carter of the FBI. Can you tell me what the hell is going on in your office? I received a call from Darren Burgess telling me your people found his daughter."

"That hasn't been confirmed. We found a girl. We're working on the markers for the fingerprints on file right now. I should know something within the hour."

"If you don't have confirmation, why the hell did you contact the Burgesses? And why did you overstep me, the officer in charge?"

"I didn't. One of my officers was over zealous. My apologies."

"Is he fresh out of the academy or some local part time idiot you've hired for the beach season?"

Norris sealed his lips, imagining a red-faced suit, gripping the phone on the other end. There was a lot he could tell the SA, but airing Ted's dirty laundry wasn't his way. "He was only hoping to bring the family's misery to an end."

"What made him think they were the same person?"

"Our girl is about the right age and has same hair and eye color and a birthmark on the left leg."

"That's all?"

"What can I say?"

63

"Well, I hope for Darren and Bonnie's sake your guy is right, because if he's not I'm going to make sure he's gone."

"That's my call, not yours," Norris stated flatly, letting SA Carter know Norris had drawn a line and it would be better for all involved if Carter didn't cross it, federal agent or not. This was still his force. "I've made him aware of the damage he might have caused because he didn't follow proper procedures. And I will make sure he is by my side if I need to tell the Burgesses that the child we found isn't their daughter."

"Understood. Did you get the sons of bitches who snatched her?"

"No. We're still working on scenarios."

"How about forensic evidence? My people can help with that. I can have a team out there in a couple hours. I hope you secured the location."

"There was no evidence to be found."

"What do you mean there was none? There's always something. We know how to do our jobs, Chief. We'll find some."

Carter could search the Atlantic if he wanted. "Not this time."

"The only way we don't is if she was dropped into the middle of the Atlantic. Where did you find her?"

"Floating in the shipping lane off the shoreline."

"*Say what?*" The shock was evident in the SA's voice.

"You heard me."

"Christ. Is she okay?"

"Badly dehydrated and sunburned, but otherwise she seems fine. She's at Cape James Mercy Hospital for observation."

"I can't wait to hear the whole story," Carter said. "I'm in route and have a helicopter waiting for me. I should be there in about forty minutes. The Burgess family is driving there, so they probably won't arrive for at least an hour and a half."

"You can have the pilot set down at Cape James Mercy. I'll meet you there." Norris really didn't want to cough up more bad news but what choice did he have? "FYI, you should know the press have already picked up the story through Twitter. I have a local reporter holding on the other line, waiting for a comment. He reported the story of us finding the girl today. How do you want me to handle it?" Norris asked, hoping the FBI agent's mood might mellow at being asked for advice.

He heard the man exhale. "Just state the facts. The two cases have not been connected, yet."

"They know the Burgess family is on their way here."

There was silence on the line. "Did you speak to the family yourself?"

"No."

"Then tell them you can't confirm if the family is in route—since you haven't spoken to them yourself. Let them know you've made contact with me and you're cooperating with the FBI to learn the truth. That should hold them off until we know more."

"You think so?"

"Not really, but I can dream."

He heard a car door open and then the roar of a larger engine coming to life.

"One more thing before you go." Carter stopped

Norris from hanging up. "Please tell me you have an officer stationed at the girl's door."

"Yes, sir. And I have a U.S. Marshal sitting at her bedside." Norris smiled at that addition and placed the receiver in its cradle. He buttoned his shirt and tucked it into his pants. Time to get to work.

Taking a deep breath, Norris hit line one and told the reporter exactly what Carter had suggested. Then he dialed the mayor's home number and prepared to drop a shit bomb on him.

***

Norris gripped his steering wheel tighter. He hated that the Feds had become involved with his case so fast, but there was nothing he could do about it now. If the girl turned out to be the Burgess child, she was theirs anyway, but if she wasn't, she was his and he had no intention of stepping aside. Instead of thinking about what had happened, he focused on his next steps.

At four a.m. the only vehicles on the road were delivery vans making their way to every little convenience and grocery store in town so Norris' drive to the hospital was made in record time without the use of his flashing lights or sirens. He eagerly exited the hospital's elevator on the third floor. Jolene waited in a room not more than fifty yards away, and with that thought, his heart skipped.

He'd run a check on her and of course the information he received from the U.S. Marshals office was what he'd anticipated. They confirmed she did indeed work for the service, as a desk agent. His gut told him the official information was a cover, as Jolene had suggested on the boat. He'd made a call to an Air Force buddy he'd served alongside in Italy and who now worked for the Marshals in Texas. Rubens returned his call right before Norris stalked out of the station and he confirmed Jolene was a Marshal. However, Rubens stated her jacket was classified. That bit of information told Norris all he needed to know.

Feeling like he had a five-pound weight on his chest and with his pulse racing, he pushed through the ward's double doors. He couldn't remember the last time he'd felt so anxious to see a woman. Yes, she was beautiful, but there was much more about Jolene that raised his interest. She was smart and street savvy. He wondered about her real job within the Marshals and how she had honed her street skills.

Her comments—stated in only a few words at times—held double meanings, which told him she was used to relaying and receiving dual messages. And with only a look she challenged him. Norris was impressed by the woman, and he wasn't easily impressed by women since…

The door to Lia's room was closed and his officer sat on a nearby chair sleeping. His men weren't used to twenty-four-hour shifts. During the busy season, they normally worked twelve- or fourteen-hour days, maybe sixteen on occasion, but every fifth day they were scheduled for forty-eight hours off. Now they would be working longer hours without a break until this case broke, or got ripped from their hands by the state guys, or the Feds. He so wanted to solve this case. It was the kind of case a cop lived for. Though the child was alive the case was still shrouded in mystery and there were a dozen unanswered questions.

Norris shook Frank awake and told him to head back to the station. Then he crossed over to the nurses' station to check on the little girl's condition. He was told Lia Doe—the name assigned her—had slept through the night. The nurse also reported that the woman still sat by the girl's side.

Norris requested the nurse contact the hospital's doctor and have the doctor call him immediately to fill him in on Lia's condition. Whether the girl turned out to be the missing Burgess baby or not, he wondered if it might not be best to move her to another location and he needed to know if he could. Cape James Mercy Hospital was small with maybe two security officers on duty at any given time. They wouldn't be able to handle the surge of reporters and ensure the family's or the girl's privacy when the story broke. His force was already stretched to the limit with the girl's case and the summer crowd to be of much help to the security staff.

He gently pushed the door open and poked his head inside. The room was dark except for the thin band of light from the bathroom slicing through it. In the dimness, he saw Jolene rested on a nearby chair. He hated to wake her, but she needed to know about the federal agent and the family on their way to the hospital to see the girl.

The moment he stepped inside, Jolene's head lifted. She blinked the sleep from her pretty eyes.

"We have a situation," he whispered, feeling embarrassed he had to reveal the incompetency and flagrant disregard for his title by one of his officers. She was someone he wanted to impress.

With his index finger, he motioned for Jolene to follow him into the hall.

She rose from the chair and followed him outside the room.

He walked to the window and looked down on the nearly empty parking lot. Soon a swarm of news vans would clog the area and make it hard for patients and visitors to enter the hospital parking lot. And for them to leave without being spotted.

Jolene joined him. "What's up?"

"Nice badge." He nodded to her belt that encircled her hip-hugging jeans.

Jolene swiped her long fingers over the base of her throat as if she could stop the blush from rising to her sun-kissed cheeks. It was then he got a closer look at the bracelet circling her wrist. Attached to it were a stable of animal charms. He wondered what meaning they held for her.

"I thought it would give me clout and I'd get a free midnight snack in the cafeteria," she said about her badge.

He chuckled. "Did it work?"

She shook her head. "Nah. However, the nurse who came on at eleven did give me a ginger ale and a pudding."

Feeling the unprofessional urge to touch her, he stuffed his hands into his pockets. He nodded toward room 3B08. "How's she doing?"

"She woke up twice, crying. Poor kid. She escaped hell." Jolene glanced toward the door she'd left ajar. "I held her and talked to her and she fell right back to sleep."

He lived along the seaside while growing up. He'd seen evidence washed up on the shore of what the creatures of the sea did to each other. There was no doubt the girl had escaped a horrible death. "Did she say anything more? Her parents' names?"

"No. I doubt she'd call her parents by their names. She's too young." She stretched her back and then checked the time on her cell. "It's been nearly seventeen hours since we found her. No one's reported her missing, have they?"

At the same moment she asked the question, Norris' cell buzzed on his hip and he held up a finger, indicating she should give him a minute.

"Stiles here," he said, answering the call. Hearing Pickett's voice Norris asked, "Did you get it?"

"I ran both sets of prints through two different software applications and the girls had only three similar markers, not enough for a match," Pickett responded.

Norris frowned. Ted was going to be in a whole lot of trouble.

"Did you hear me, boss?" Pickett asked into the lengthening silence.

"Yeah. I heard you." Norris felt sorry for the parents who were on their way to the hospital. It was likely Lia wasn't their daughter and their old wound would take a big hit. He glanced at Jolene and noticed she watched him closely. If he had wanted privacy, he should've walked away from her. "We've already pissed off the Feds, so let's play nice. Send what you have to SA Carter's email address. Have them double check your findings and get back to me a.s.a.p." He hung up and met Jolene's steely stare.

"Feds? What's going down, Chief?"

Norris quickly explained the situation.

"What was your man thinking?" He heard the

frustration in Jolene's tone. Her lips thinned, giving her expression darker angles.

"He wasn't. Thus, the problem." He wouldn't state the obvious. Ted wanted the opportunity to be the hero in this little girl's story and because of his phone call to the Burgesses, had handed the hero status over to the officer in charge.

"You know, this Carter guy is going to want to take the lead," Jolene said.

"Yeah, but that's not my worry right now." Self-consciously Norris rubbed away the tension in his neck. "I fear we're going to be bombarded by reporters soon."

"No doubt. It doesn't take them long to pick up a juicy story's scent." She slid her hands into her jeans pockets. "Do you think we should move her out of here?"

He nodded, glancing down the hall, hoping to see a white coat push through the double doors in answer to his call. However, the doors remained still, and he clenched his teeth together. Their window of opportunity was ticking away. "If the hospital and attending doctors give the okay, I think it would be in the girl's best interest. If I move her without the hospital doctor's okay, I could open the town and myself for a lawsuit."

She nodded. "Where would you take her? Back to the station?"

"It's not the best atmosphere for a child, but we could protect her from the media better there." He searched for the nurse he'd spoken to earlier but apparently she'd taken another patient's call.

Jolene chewed on her lip for a moment. "I have an idea, but first I need to tell you something."

"Okay..."

"This is your case, and I'm not trying to take it from you, but if you need help, I have permission to step up."

He arched his brow. Two things he demanded from his people were discretion in handling cases and loyalty to him. But Jolene wasn't *his* people. She was a federal officer of the law. Now he wondered who else knew about his case? "You have permission, huh? From whom?"

She hesitated for a moment, apparently aware of his irritation. "I called my division's boss after you left us last night."

Norris noticed the slight blush in her cheeks.

"Not to step on your toes," she continued, looking directly at him, "but to obtain permission to help you for as long as it takes to learn who Lia belongs to and how she ended up floating alone on the Atlantic. Assisting in investigations at every level of law enforcement is one of the duties of the U.S. Marshals. We make your arm stronger and longer. So, if you'd want me to partner up with you in this case, I'm yours."

Norris studied her face. Yesterday afternoon, he would've thought of Jolene in another way if she'd said those two little words to him. This morning, he saw her as more than a good time. He trusted her. And he wasn't stupid. With her involvement, the state police wouldn't try to take over the case and the FBI would take second seat.

"I come with resources," she said, pulling him from his thoughts. "And, I have an idea, if you want my opinion."

He folded his arms across his chest, giving her

the impression she still hadn't convinced him to partner up with her. "What is it?"

"Make the girl disappear again."

"Protective custody at an undisclosed location. Where?"

"I have the perfect place."

Overhead he heard the whir of a helicopter and knew Special Agent Carter was about to arrive. He nodded toward the ceiling. "That's the federal officer in charge of the Burgess case. He'll want to know the location."

She shrugged. "I can play nice."

CHAPTER SEVEN

Jolene hated hospital odors. The antiseptic scent only masked the presence of sickness and death and brought back moments in her life she wanted to forget.

She had walked the floors of the twelve-by-twelve hospital room for most of the night, listening to the beeps and dings while she watched over Lia.

No one knew better than Jolene that the world was filled with terrible monsters.

Each time monsters entered Lia's dreams and she'd became agitated, Jolene had brushed back her soft hair and calmed her by softly reciting the fable her older sister, Martina, had read to her many times when they needed to forget their world wasn't perfect.

Now she stood at Lia's bedside with her hands stuffed in the pockets of her light hoodie and studied FBI Special Agent Carter while Norris filled him in on the details of girl's rescue.

Carter fit the physical profile of every other male Fed Jolene had ever met; six-foot-six in height with shoulders that needed to be measured with a yard stick. He wore his hair cut to half an inch and his square jaw was clean-shaven. His suit was darn pretty and probably cost about what she made in a month. His highly polished wingtip shoes would've made her self-conscious if she wore a skirt.

He was as pretty as his suit.

She looked at the chief. With a good two days' worth of whiskers now covering his jawline, he

definitely had the earthy rough look going on. Norris'
whiskers and confident look made her blood run hot—
more so than the immaculate professional style Carter
portrayed.

When Norris told Carter about her impulsive
move to dive overboard, Jolene grimaced. However, the
understanding in Carter's gaze dissipated her
mortification and assured Jolene he had the same heart
ninety-nine percent of law enforcement officers had. He
cared. Too much at times, which the puffy bags under
his eyes revealed.

Carter turned and studied Lia.

"She could be Abigail Burgess. She's about the
right age and the birthmark on her leg isn't quite the
same, but it could've changed shape as she grew."
Carter whispered so he didn't wake the sleeping child.
"However, the fingerprint markers make the case that
she isn't Abigail."

Carter turned away from the bedside and
crossed to the window, gesturing for them to follow
him.

"Not to insinuate your staff is incompetent,
Stiles, because I'm sure they're very competent at
taking fingerprints, however..."

Jolene saw Norris' jaw lock in anticipation of a
pissing match. Pissing matches often occurred when
two males from different agencies came together. The
act was a law of natural order, or physics, or something
to do with the male psyche, Jolene thought. It was best
to stay out of the way and let the bout play out so all
parties knew where each of them stood. When the dust
settled they could get on with handling the case.

"I'd want to have my man take them and run

them again to be sure. You know, put the FBI certification on the docs so there is no inquiry later."

Jolene's stomach tightened. She knew from experience relationships between law enforcement agencies could get nasty. Norris probably had no experience working with federal agents and Carter, who likely knew Norris was new to his command, was trying to take advantage of the fact.

Standing between the pair, Jolene felt like she wore the shoes of the biblical David who faced off against Goliath. She had to arch her head back to look directly into Carter's eyes.

Her heart pounded against her ribs but she kept her expression passive. She'd be damned if she'd let either man see her desperation to keep the situation under control.

She slid her hands into her back pockets, giving the appearance she was relaxed. This was just another day. Another case. Another set of partners.

"I was present when the prints were taken by Norris' officer. And I can assure you, Special Agent Carter, officer Pickett followed protocols to the letter for every procedure and dotting every I." Jolene notched her chin higher. "If need be, I'll put my name to the file as a witness."

She waited for Carter to pull his shiny badge out and compare it to the one she wore on her belt.

Norris' gaze shifted to her.

She didn't look at him. Engaged with Carter, she wasn't about to back down. Yes. Carter cared, but damnit, they all did.

"We all want the same thing. To learn who Lia belongs to—Lia, is the name she calls herself, by the way—and return her safely to her family," Jolene said firmly. "Then we need to catch the bastard who kidnapped her and set her adrift on the ocean to die. So, let's work together."

Carter inhaled.

She'd squashed the match and continued: "As I see it, Chief Stiles is the one who gets to call the shots concerning this child's welfare until she's identified as your missing girl."

"And your role?" Carter looked down his nose at her.

"I've offered any assistance he might need."

Carter pursed his lips, before turning them up into an amiable smile. "You know, I wouldn't be here if his officer hadn't called the Burgess family."

"I know the jurisdiction laws in kidnapping cases," Norris stated flatly. "We're not sure Lia is an Amber victim. And FYI, my officer has been reprimanded for not following protocol."

Carter stuffed his arms across his chest. "What are your plans, Chief Stiles?"

"I'm moving Lia, now." Norris checked his cell phone. "Grief clouds reason. The Burgesses will insist she's their child. They'll want to take her home immediately. If we allowed that and then they found out later she isn't their daughter it will tear them apart again."

"And if she is their daughter, and you make them wait, Chief?"

"I'll take the heat."

"What about her condition?"

"The hospital doctors say she's fine. We have their permission to move her."

Jolene glanced at the wall clock. Fifteen minutes had passed since the federal agent walked through the ward's doors. Time was ticking. They didn't need Carter's permission to move Lia, but she and Norris wanted Carter on their side.

"That would be hard on her too," Jolene added, pointing to Lia. "We don't want to placed her in a home with strangers only to be removed again in a few days."

Carter dropped his gaze to his shiny shoes and sighed. "Okay. I agree. It would be heartbreaking for all of them. It would be better for all to wait a few days and we can rush the DNA testing."

"Good," Norris said. "I'm moving her to a more secure location. The hospital doctors approved her release. The hospital security staff is small, as is my force. We can't protect her from reporters or someone else taking pictures of her with their cell phone here."

The lines in Carter's forehead deepened. "Where are you going to take her?"

"My sister volunteers for the county as a temporary foster parent," Jolene said, drawing the agent's attention. "I'm staying with her and her family while I'm here on vacation—which just got canceled with this case. Lia can stay there. It's a secure, gated community which will add some defense against reporters if her location becomes known. She'll be with other children. My niece, Clara, is two and half, so Lia will have someone close to her age to play with. And I'll be there to check on her and watch over her too."

"Okay," Carter responded. "I'll want the address of course. I'd like to check on her there so I can reassure the Burgess family she's in good hands."

"Not a problem." Feeling relieved Carter was in

agreement with their plan, Jolene glanced at Lia. "I hope she is Abigail for everyone's sake, but until we know without a doubt she is, Chief Norris and I are going to work the case under the assumption she isn't."

"Let's get her out of here before the parents or the press show up." Norris was growing impatient. "I'll bring my car around back to the loading dock. You stay with Lia since she feels comfortable with you. Hospital transportation personnel will show you the way there."

Jolene had a thought. "You have your cruiser, right?"

"Yes. Why?"

"I think it would be better if I take her in my SUV. Reporters are likely watching your car already."

Norris' brow arched. "Your vehicle?"

"My brother-in-law dropped it off last night. He put my niece's car seat in it."

"You knew I'd move Lia out of here?" Norris asked.

He was a smart lawman. She was a smart agent. They thought alike. "I thought you might want to."

Norris held out his hand. "Give me your keys. I'll drive it to the back."

Jolene crossed the room and grabbed her purse from the back of the chair she'd slept on. She fished the keys out and tossed them to Norris. He caught them against his chest, like a pro football player catches a pass. "It's a black SUV."

"Of course it is." He turned the key fob over in his hand. "Does it have any knobs I shouldn't touch?"

She ignored both his jab at her being a federal agent and his smirk. "It's parked in section H3. Don't scratch it. I'm still making payments."

79

Jolene hit the call button for the nurse. They had to get moving. Outside the sun was already perched on the roof of the four-story building across the street. In another hour, the streets would be filled with early risers heading to work or to walk the sandy beaches.

Apparently aware of the game going on between her and the chief, Carter cleared his throat to draw their attention back to him. "I'm going down to the lobby to wait for Mr. and Mrs. Burgess."

"I don't envy you, Carter. It's going to be damn hard holding them off," Jolene said.

"No doubt." Carter headed for the door.

Norris stepped up and stopped Carter from opening the door by placing his hand on the handle. "I'm going to stay with you," he told the agent.

"That might be a good idea since you were one of the people who found her. You can decide how much to tell them, without hampering your investigation."

Norris' chin notched up. "I'll also let them know it was my man who prematurely contacted them."

Carter gave a nod, acknowledging the chief's integrity. Jolene had to admit she was impressed with the chief.

"I'll meet up with Agent Martinez later, some place other than the station. I'll review what my team has learned and discuss where we go." Norris said.

Carter looked at the chief quizzically. "Why not meet at the station?"

"I want to keep Agent Martinez's involvement in this case under wraps. I don't want a reporter following her back to Lia. You're welcome to join us, as a consult."

Again, her respect grew for Stiles. He had made

it clear whose case this was.

Jolene saw the lines around Carter's mouth deepen as he pinched his lips. Feds were used to giving the orders.

She was actually surprised when Carter replied, "Thanks. I think I will. You have my cell number. Text me where and when and I'll be there."

The nurse pushed on the door and both men stepped back to allow her a clear path into the room.

"I'll be staying in town for a few days," Carter said. "Do you have any recommendations where I might get a decent room?"

"I'll call my friend Rose. Her father owns the Seaside Hotel. I'll make sure she has a room for you," Jolene answered. "And for the Burgesses, if they'd like one. Rose was on the boat with us when we found Lia. I'll instruct her not to mention it to them."

"That would be for the best."

While Norris and Carter headed down the hall, Jolene watched the nurse disconnect the IV needle used to give Lia hydration and meds when necessary.

Lia moaned and Jolene's heart winced. She inhaled and silently swore she would find the person who did this to the little child and she'd make sure they paid.

***

By noon, Lia was wide awake, fed, and playing in the backyard with Jolene's niece Clara.

Under a bright sun in a crystal-clear sky, Jolene sat on the patio and watched the two little girls playing in Clara's playhouse, feeding and rocking dolls as if they were their mothers.

The two little girls were about the same in height and weight, so Clara's little sundress and pull-ups fit Lia perfectly. The turquoise dress was ideal for Lia's bronzed coloring just like it was for Clara. In fact, if it weren't for a few distinctive facial differences which revealed their different ethnic heritages, the pair could be mistaken for sisters. Lia, of course was slathered with sunscreen.

Martina came out of the house carrying a tray with a pitcher of lemonade, two ice-filled plastic tumblers and a dozen juice boxes for the children playing in the backyard or swimming in the fenced-off inground pool.

"What are you working on?" Jolene pointed to the file folders Martina had placed on the table.

"A church project. We're starting a program to help families from poverty-stricken countries relocate to the United States."

"Cool." Martina was such a giving person: fostering children, volunteering at their family's church and other organizations. *Where did she find the time and energy?*

Jolene nodded in the direction of the spirited children. "Clara and Lia hit it off."

"You'd swear they were best friends." Martina poured a glass of lemonade and handed it to Jolene.

"I can't believe she is running around as if yesterday never happened," Jolene replied, before she took a sip. The cold liquid soothed the dryness in her throat.

"Kids are resilient."

Jolene swallowed quickly. "And they forgive

too easily."

"We can learn from them," Martina responded.

Jolene dropped her tumbler against the table's glass top with a thud. She knew that tone. Martina was approaching a subject she'd promised Jolene she wouldn't bring up when Jolene agreed to come home for a visit.

"We're not going to go there," Jolene reminded her.

Martina sat down across from her in the shade provided by the table umbrella. "At some point, you will need to forgive them. If you don't, and it becomes too late, you'll carry the burden of it for the rest of your life."

Jolene flexed her arms over her chest, stretching her taut back muscles and rubbing her bare shoulders. "There is a lot of weight on these shoulders already. What's a few more pounds of flesh?"

Martina wiped a condensation ring from the tabletop with a napkin and then set her glass on the napkin. "You've become very cynical."

"It's a side effect of the job."

The chair in which Martina sat screeched against the concrete when she jumped up from the table. She crossed to the pool fence and proceeded to scold her oldest child for ducking his brother.

Jolene leaned back on her chair, pushed her sunglasses back on top of her head and turned her face toward the sun. She shoved away the guilt Martina tried to hand her. It was a perfect day for the beach but Jolene had other plans. Ones that included Chief Stiles. There was no way she would want to be in his shoes or those of SA Carter's this morning when they'd faced

Mr. and Mrs. Burgess with the update. The couple probably went bat-shit crazy on them both.

Coming back to the table, Martina interrupted her thoughts. "I'm changing the subject, sis."

"Okay." Jolene slid her glasses down.

"Be honest with me." Her sister's face was tight with worry.

"I always am. You know that." She casually picked up her drink and sipped.

"No. I know no such thing. You're not a secretary for the U.S. Marshals, are you?"

Jolene knew sooner or later she would need to come clean with her sister about her job. She thought maybe the time would come when she'd been wounded in action. Or maybe the discussion would never happen—for instance if she were killed in the line of duty. Knowing how betrayed her sister would feel under those circumstances made her confess. "I know you've suspected... I'm a field agent."

Martina's hefty chest pushed against her tank top. "I thought so. Why didn't you tell me?"

"When we were kids, you were always protecting me. We're not kids anymore. You can't protect me and I didn't want to worry you."

Martina's hand covered hers. "I'll always worry about you. That will never change."

Tears blurred Jolene's vision. She had missed her sister and wondered why she'd taken so long to return home to spend time with her. She rolled her lips tight and nodded, noting moisture also glazed Martina's walnut eyes.

Martina squeezed her hand and then let it go. She notched her chin toward Lia. "What time do you need to meet Chief Stiles?"

"At three. We're going to meet at the coffee shop on Lexington. What time is it?"

Martina glanced at her cell phone that lay in the shade of the umbrella. "It's a nearly two-thirty."

"I'd better go change out of these shorts." Jolene pushed back from the table. "I should be back in a couple of hours, in time to help you with dinner. Are you sure you'll be able to handle Lia?"

Martina laughed and waved her hand toward the scene in front of them. "*Really?* I have four kids of my own and two foster children who come with a whole bunch of friends. One more only adds to the fun."

"With our background, how did you become such a great mom?" Jolene asked in a serious tone.

"I didn't want my kids growing up feeling the way we did. One day you'll be a great mom too."

Jolene shook her head. "Not me. I don't ever want children."

At that second, Lia ran up to Jolene and tossed the doll she'd been playing with onto Jolene's lap. The little girl babbled something and it took Jolene only a second to realize Lia had removed the doll's clothing and wanted her help putting another outfit on her. When she'd done so, Lia gave her a smile that had the power to melt her heart and—if she weren't careful—to start her biological clock ticking.

***

Jolene's black SUV pulled into the parking spot next to his Jeep at the same moment Norris pushed open the driver's door. She was right on time. Good to know she was someone he could count on to be on time. He climbed out and met her at the rear of her vehicle.

Seeing him, she pulled up short. Then she nodded toward his "baby" whose shine had been lost nearly a decade ago. "Ditched your cruiser, I see."

On a slight breeze, her soft floral scent surrounded him.

Again, he ignored the urge to touch her tanned skin though his fingertips itched. Yesterday, in the Coast Guard's raft, when his upper arm had rested against hers he'd enjoyed the softness covering her hard muscles. "It wouldn't make sense for me to drive my cruiser to our meeting, would it? And if a reporter followed me when I left the station, he'll think I'm a dimwit, local flatfoot who still works his nine-to-five shift even when a big case drops in his lap."

"But it's only three," she replied, cocking her head.

He shrugged and smiled. "So I took time off to meet my girlfriend. I worked extra hours last night."

"Girlfriend huh?" A smile lifted her lips and Norris felt something give in his chest.

Jolene wore sunglasses so he couldn't see her eyes, but from the timbre of her voice he knew desire was there. She liked being with him. And he sure liked the idea of being with her.

Dressed in a red tank top and black capris and high-heeled sandals that took her out of the pixie realm, she was hot!

A car horn blared behind them at the intersection, drawing their attention. Witnessing a near mishap extinguished the flirtatious mood between them and it was back to business.

"That guy ran a red light," Jolene remarked, shifting to his side.

"It wasn't a female driver?"

"No. Definitely male. He had a beard. And he was a blonde."

"Lucky bastard. He could've hit someone. The vehicle was a 2010 Saturn. Popular model around here." Norris looked down at her. Even with her wedge heels, her chin barely reached his shoulder. "I couldn't see his plate number. Did you?" He'd call the infraction in if she had the number.

"I couldn't. The shrubbery blocked my view."

Norris frowned, pissed he hadn't caught any of the plate numbers himself. He couldn't have his officer who worked traffic today chase down every person driving a blue Saturn, looking for a blond dude with a beard.

He let the incident go, hoping the guy used better judgment in the future and then Norris refocused on Jolene. "Did you sleep?"

"Yeah. About four hours." Jolene cupped her hand over her sunglasses and looked up at him. "How about you?"

"I caught a few hours." He was glad he'd gone home and showered and changed into clean jeans and shirt before coming to the hospital.

The heat from the tarmac wafting up at them suddenly seemed to be getting hotter and he pointed to the coffee shop. "We don't need to wait for Carter out here. We can go inside and wait in the air conditioning."

"That does sound better," she said and grabbed his hand.

Surprised he opened his mouth to ask what she was doing, but she cut him off.

"In case we're being watched." She grinned and tugged him forward playfully.

"Ah. Right." He liked the smoothness of her skin and shifted so Jolene's hand was wrapped in his. He also enjoyed having her walk by his side into the shop he patronized at least four times a week. The owner took a double take when he looked up from placing warm blueberry muffins in the display case. He had never brought anyone into the café with him and doing so now had the staff glancing their way and whispering to each other.

"I thought this would be a good place to meet." He suddenly felt self-conscious. "It's small and blocks away from the ocean, so its customers are mainly locals who want to get away from the summer tourists." He babbled on and couldn't seem to shut up. "And at this time of day, it's very quiet. And it's not too far from your sister's."

"I know." Jolene laughed.

"What?"

"You're very cute when you're nervous, Chief."

"I'm not nervous. Why would I be nervous?" But he was.

Her eyes narrowed in the sexiest way. "I don't know. I seem to make you nervous?"

Unconsciously he inhaled, expanding his chest. Then he took her small, soft hand in his again, wanting to prove he was not nervous around her. "You don't."

The longer her sparkling almond-shaped eyes remained on him, the stronger the urge grew to kiss her.

He felt himself leaning toward her and jerked

away just in time, changing the direction of his gaze to look toward the menu on the wall behind the cashier. "I-I'm going to grab a breakfast sandwich," he stammered and pushed his sunglasses back on his head. As he stood to walk to the counter he asked, "Do you want one? They make great sandwiches. My treat."

"Thanks, no. I had lunch. But I'll take a French Vanilla Cappuccino." She slipped her hand from his, allowing him to pull his wallet from his back pocket.

After they ordered and received their drinks and his sandwich they took a seat at the rear of the shop away from the other patrons. She studied the half dozen people who sat at various tables reading books or using their electronic devices. He watched as she snagged her glasses from her head and hung them from the scooped neckline of her tank top. Then she carefully removed the plastic lid from the cardboard cup and set it aside. She blew across her drink and rich, aromatic steam rose from the liquid toward her full rose-colored lips.

Norris didn't want to look away but he had to because his erection would prevent him from standing otherwise.

Goddamn it, he needed to get laid. No, he needed to think about the case...

Instead of thinking about how much he desired to taste the sweetness of her lips, he made small talk. "I would never have taken you for a French Vanilla Cappuccino girl." It was a weak attempt at making conversation, because his mind was busy going down a different path.

Jolene stopped blowing across her drink and smiled mischievously. "Really. What did you expect me to order?"

"Swiss Mocha. Women love chocolate." He unwrapped his sandwich and bit off a bite.

"Not all women."

"You don't?"

"I do." She chuckled. "Honestly, I teetered between this and mocha."

As he watched her sip her drink and lick her lips Norris' cock twitched. Immediately he glanced away, reminding himself they were working together and he had to keep this on a professional level no matter how much he'd longed to taste every inch of her compact, tanned body.

The front door's bell system dinged, telling them someone entered the establishment. Both of them looked to the door, expecting to see Carter but instead saw a pair of teenagers walk in.

"He's late." Norris' tone made it clear he was annoyed with the agent.

"It's tactical." Jolene leaned back on her chair. A knowing smile curled her lips.

After a bite of his sandwich, Norris wiped the napkin across his lips. "What do you mean?"

"He's testing you. He wants to see if you'll wait for him to make decisions concerning the case. And when he gets here he'll make suggestions, expecting you to go along."

Again, the woman impressed him with her working knowledge of the Feds. "He'll be disappointed then. This is my case. I'll bring you both up to speed if he ever decides to join us. In the meantime, how's Lia doing at your sister's?"

"Amazing. She and my niece were best friends forever before I even woke up. She ate really well and right now she's playing house with Clara."

"That's good."

Her smile faded and her expression turned serious. "How did the Mr. and Mrs. Burgess take the news?"

"Not good. Carter calmed them down when he stated he had doubts that Lia was their child. They seem to trust him."

"Did they stay here or go back home?" She mixed her cappuccino with a wooden stirrer.

"Oh, they're here. At least for a few days. They're hoping DNA results will come in quicker than what we told them. They've seen the news reports saying rapid DNA results are now available to law enforcement agencies."

"They haven't heard about the long waiting list however."

"No." Norris frowned. "They ignored that part when we spoke to them. I'm going to continue to approach this case as if Lia isn't their child. It might be counter-productive if she turns out to be theirs, but in the meantime I don't want to miss or lose any other leads." He took a swallow of his own coffee and welcomed the swift rush of caffeine.

"I agree." She tapped the stick on the cup, laid it aside and then propped up her head with a fist pressed to her temple and stared at him. "What has your team learned?"

He swallowed a bite of his egg and sausage sandwich and wiped a napkin across his mouth. "So far my team learned that all boats launched within a fifty-mile radius and during the seventy-two hours prior to finding Lia have now returned to port. So the possibility of a small craft sinking is unlikely."

"But not impossible?"

"No, if they sank after putting to sea outside the fifty-mile radius or from a private dock. I'll have one of my staff check further. Maybe the Coast Guard can help us out but I don't see a small boat carrying a child—"

"Or children," Jolene added.

She was right. There could have been other children aboard. Lia might have been the lucky one to survive. "Or children, making that kind of a trip. Again, not impossible." Norris pulled his cell phone out and tapped a note into it. "The Coast Guard and beach services are still watching for wreckage."

"No one has come forward looking for a lost child?" Jolene asked.

"No. So I'm crossing off the possibility of her wandering away on the beach."

Jolene's charm bracelet jangled against the tabletop. "What if whoever was caring for her—her mother or babysitter—can't report her missing? This case could be as clear-cut as an estranged father killing Lia's mother and taking off with her."

Norris arched a brow. "If he wanted the child for himself, why dump her?"

"Self-preservation. He didn't mean to kill, but now that he did, he had to get rid of her and any witnesses who might've seen him take her. He'll need to disappear and try to set up an alibi because he knows he'll be the first name on the police's suspect list. Sadly, it's happened before."

"Shitheads."

"You're being kind." Jolene picked up her cup.

"I'll have my people request information on any

homicide cases occurring within the last forty-eight hours and going forward, just in case a body hasn't been discovered yet." Norris brought his phone to life again. Only this time he sent Pickett a text then popped the last piece of his sandwich into his mouth. He wiped his mouth and hands off on the paper napkin, rolled it into a ball and tossed it into the plastic basket sitting in front of him. "You sound like you've seen a similar case or two."

"No. My cases are a little off the wall. How about you? Did you handle any homicides when you worked in Norfolk?"

"Two. And quite a few domestic violence cases. None of them led to a homicide however."

"When children get involved it's a different game."

"Definitely."

"And seeing what we do is hard on relationships, makes it hard to get close to anyone, doesn't it?" Jolene said, and quickly looked away.

Norris stared at her, wondering if she wanted to share something personal. Before he had a chance to ask, Jolene pointed out the window. He followed her gaze. She waved as Carter crossed the parking lot.

The federal agent had easily caught Jolene's eye and for a second Norris felt jealous.

"He finally made it," he said, snuffing out the sting he knew too well and that threatened to unleash memories he'd purposely buried. He took a swig of his rich coffee and waited.

Jolene's eyes finally slanted his way and she must have recognized his reaction because she said, "Remember, we agreed to play nice."

He licked the coffee from his lips, telling himself he didn't care if Jolene was interested in the man. He wasn't looking for a relationship. "Haven't I been nice to you?"

"I found the girl first." Jolene grinned.

Damn he liked her smile. "Whatever."

SA Carter seemed to ignore them when he entered and headed straight for the front counter. Only after he'd place an order did he turn and nod to them.

He approached them a minute later, carrying a large iced coffee.

"We thought you got lost," Norris said after Carter pulled up a chair to join them at their round table.

What did it say about their trust issues that none of them sat with their backs to the storefront? Norris looked from Carter to Jolene as she peered at Carter over her cup.

"Nah. I don't get lost. I only take detours." Carter chuckled before sipping his drink. "It's damn hot out there today."

"You could take off your jacket," Jolene said.

"I don't think so." Carter leaned against the chair spindles and they moaned in protest. "So, what have I missed?"

"Chief Norris' team hasn't received any new reports of missing children."

Norris knew it shouldn't, but Jolene's statement made him feel incompetent. He and his entire small force were working as hard as they could to gather any information which might help them learn something, anything.

"Which leaves us with an earlier kidnapping or

abandoned-child scenario. Don't you agree?" Carter asked.

The man placed his hand on the table near Jolene's.

Norris shifted on his seat. "We're still checking on missing boats," he stated flatly. "That might take another day, since some ships go to sea for a few days." He hooked his thumb toward Jolene. "Agent Martinez suggested we consider the girl's guardians. She said we need to consider that her mother, father…grandparents could be dead."

"And they haven't been found yet," Jolene interjected.

"Custody battle." Carter nodded. "Good thought."

"If that's the case, I think we'll hear something within the next twenty-four hours, if a missing person report is filed," Norris added.

"What's your game plan in the meantime, Chief?" Carter asked him.

Norris drank his coffee before he answered. "We need to find out if any locals saw Lia in the last few days and who was with her."

Carter shifted on his chair and rested his elbows on the table. "Then you've decided to release her picture to the media?"

"No. I think—"

"Why not?" Carter interrupted him. "That would be the fastest way to get leads."

"This is a tourist area. People come, and go. They don't get to know the people around them. They're on vacation and they see what they want to see. If we put her picture out to the media, we're going to get hundreds of sighting calls. Yes, it could be possible that one would be a genuine lead, but by the time we weed through all the calls it could be too late. We need to go old school first." Norris sat forward on his chair. "I think we can assume Lia is not from here or close by. We would've heard something by now which means she has to be from somewhere else. There aren't many places to stay in Cape James. We have ten hotels and eight bed and breakfasts, and a campground ten miles north. Plus, the surrounding towns also have a few places to stay. I want to get my people out to those places and see if any staff recognize her."

"You're assuming too much," Carter said. "You have miles of beach fronts with private homes. What's to say someone involved isn't renting one of them?"

Norris sighed and set his cup down. "I'm sure you know I've only been chief here for nine months."

Carter nodded.

Norris knew the man had run a check on him. He would've done the same thing if their positions were reversed. "With the exception of me, every man and woman on my staff have lived here all their lives. They have connections to almost every family in town. They've told me that there are only two houses on the beachfront for rent. We've already contacted the listing agencies to get information on the people renting them now. We'll also do checks on them."

Carter leaned toward Norris' space. "And if whoever had Lia merely drove by to drop her off in the ocean, how will you find them?"

In his peripheral vision, Norris saw Jolene shift on her chair. She didn't lean forward. Instead she reclined back, informing him she was enjoying the game he and Carter played.

"If that was the case, we might never know who dropped her off. However, we'll also check with the local gas stations and restaurants. Our service stations are very busy. People fill up here before they head home instead of waiting until they get nearer the turnpike or Interstate."

"I still think you should release her picture, Chief," Carter pressed.

Norris gripped his cup in his hand. "And I disagree. I want solid tips right now. I don't want my people running around searching for leads that don't exist." He could see Carter was chomping at the bit. Regardless of what Carter said about not stepping on Norris' toes with this case, it was obvious the man wanted to take the lead. And Norris wasn't going to let it happen.

"I agree with Chief Stiles," Jolene said.

Norris shot her a look of thanks.

Carter rested back on his chair. "Of course, you would."

"What's that supposed to mean?" she asked, continuing to play with the little tab on the lid of her cup.

She was used to the games the FBI agents played.

"It means you want this case as much as I do," Carter said.

"What I want, SA Carter, is to learn who put the child adrift on the ocean to die. I don't care who heads the case. I want to help." She sat forward and with her arms on the table top leaned toward the federal agent. "We're on the chief's turf. He hasn't asked for our help yet. He asked us here to review what he's learned and tell us the steps he plans to take, as a courtesy."

"From my view, you're already involved with the case. You're guarding the girl."

"I was the one who found her."

Even though he was enjoying the sparring match between the federal agents, Norris' flat palm hit the top table with enough force to cause them to look at him. Unfortunately, he also gathered some curious looks from other customers. He smiled, relaxing his features, and looked directly at Carter. "There is no argument here. As long as I hold jurisdiction over this case, I'm going to work it my way. You both can offer advice and I'll consider it, but my decision is final."

"Until we learn the girl is the Burgess child."

The man needed to have the last word it seemed. "Agreed."

Norris held Carter's glare until the Fed pushed his chair back and stood.

Carter looked down at Jolene. "Thanks for setting me up with a room."

"No problem."

"I'll call you when we get the DNA results. Call me if you learn anything." He turned and walked out.

Jolene and Norris sat in silence, watching the FBI agent exit to the street and climb into his car.

Jolene turned to Norris. "When *will* your people start showing Lia's picture around?"

"About an hour ago." He winked.

She laughed. "You are sly, Stiles."

Her enjoyment chipped away at the ice with which his ex had encased his heart. "You want to ride with me?"

"Where to?"

"I'm going to check out the rented beachfront properties."

She held up a painted nail. "Let me call Martina and make sure Lia is okay. I told her I'd only be an hour. I'll meet you outside. I want to use the facilities first."

"I'll wait here. It's cooler."

"Right." She smiled and rose.

Jolene walked toward the ladies' room and Norris took the opportunity to admire her backside. The view was grade A, as Pickett had mentioned yesterday. He had to admit he was glad she offered to stay and work the case. This case, and her presence, somehow had brought back to life parts of him that had been stomped to hell a year ago.

He wanted to solve Lia's case.

CHAPTER EIGHT

Jolene relaxed against the cushioned seat and appreciated the warm breeze flowing in through the open window. She couldn't see the ocean. The view was blocked by homes and shrub-covered dunes, but she could smell its unique scent in the air. She did her best to ignore it though. The salty, fish-infused odor brought back memories from yesterday. She had to work past them if she was ever to enjoy the beach again.

She drew in a deep breath, expanding her chest and then slowly exhaled. Norris was one interesting guy. She respected that he didn't back down when Carter pressed to gain control of the case. Most backwoods lawmen she'd dealt with were more than happy to hand off a case to the Feds and go home to their dinners. Norris wasn't them though. He intended to see this case through.

Recalling the tension on the two men's faces made her smile.

"What are you thinking about?"

She raised her eyes from his hands that gripped the steering wheel, to his smile. He had nice lips. "Not much."

"It made you laugh."

"Did I laugh?" With the wind whipping around them and the Jeep's canvas flapping overhead, she hadn't realized he could hear her chuckle.

100

"You did. Tell me. I need a good laugh."

She pulled her sunglasses from on top of her head and placed them on her nose. She lied, not wanting to tell him the truth: "It was nothing. Something my sister told me about Lia."

"What was it?"

Great. What the hell was she going to tell him? Her mind tripped over things Martina had said earlier in the day. "Nothing really. Lia and my niece were playing house and insisted they serve the afternoon snacks. She had to eat a cracker layered with peanut butter and a dill pickle slice."

Norris chuckled. "What a combo. Where did they come up with that?"

She shrugged. "Who knows."

"You like her, don't you? Lia I mean."

Jolene shrugged. "Sure. She's sweet. I'm glad she is staying with us. She had such dreadful nightmares last night in the hospital. Today she acted as if nothing had happened to her, except the sunburn. It bothers her sometimes. She's too busy playing with Clara to notice it most of the time."

"That's good. Maybe this nightmare will be over for her soon."

Jolene studied his profile. "Are you hoping she is the Burgess girl?"

He braked for a car turning into a driveway. "Sure."

With the road in front of him clear, he glanced her way again. "It would make for a happy ending and she would be back with her parents."

He pushed down on the accelerator.

She spoke louder over the whipping canvas. "But you don't think she is their child?"

"No." His lips turned down and he frowned. "I don't. But I could be wrong."

She understood his feelings. Hope that the world would right itself had been her constant companion since childhood. It's what had driven her to become a U.S. Marshal.

Jolene turned and gazed through the passenger side window. Norris was a nice guy. She wondered why some woman hadn't snagged him from bachelorhood and married him.

You couldn't have what couldn't be gotten. Wasn't that the old wives' tale? So maybe it was something about him. Being a law enforcement officer was hard on marriages and families. It took two special people to make it through the years together, even without the stress of an angry world knocking on your door every single day.

They rode in silence for the next few minutes. Then Jolene felt the Jeep slow down.

He veered off the main road and made a right turn into a driveway. As he did, the muscles in Norris' forearms flexed and the tattooed lynx came to life on his arm.

He braked suddenly and she put her hands up in front of her so as not to hit the dashboard.

Eight cars filled the half-moon driveway. The shrubbery alongside the driveway had kept them hidden until they turned in.

"Looks as if there's a party going on."

Norris inched his Jeep forward, careful not to tap the bumper of the Dodge Caravan parked in front of them. He maneuvered around it and drove alongside the line of cars. He stopped next to a cherry-red van sitting near the front door then shifted the Jeep into park.

The moment the engine cut, cries for help became clear in the distance. Jolene grabbed her purse from the floorboard and pulled her gun and badge from inside. She glanced back as her sandaled foot touched the pebbled drive. Norris' door was already closing behind him and he rounded the front of the vehicle.

Only the sounds of crashing waves filled the air now.

They stood side by side, muscles tense, listening.

A blood-curdling scream cut the air.

"What the hell?" Norris sprinted forward.

She followed, backing him up. The snap of his holster sounded and she checked whether he'd drawn his gun. He hadn't. She understood why he hadn't. They were in a beach community which catered to families. Until Norris knew what they were facing he kept his weapon sheathed. Jolene followed suit and shoved hers into the waistband of her capris and looped her badge around her neck.

Immediately her heart thumped against her ribs. It always did the moment she entered an unknown situation that had the potential to turn deadly within seconds. She scanned the windows of the house while they kept moving around to the side in the direction of the cries for help. She saw no movement.

The house appeared deserted except there were eight vehicles in the driveway and someone was calling for help from the back of the two-story brick home. *A picture-perfect cover for a meth lab,* she thought. She wondered what was running through Norris' mind.

"That sounds like a child," Jolene whispered, falling into step behind Norris. Cautiously they followed the narrow brick-lined path to the rear of the house. She especially hated the drug producers who used their kids as fronts. She'd witnessed scenes where labs had blown up and children had been badly burnt or found dead later. Her stomach knotted, praying this scenario wasn't going to play out the same way.

At the rear corner of the house an eight-foot planked fence had been constructed to keep out those seeking beach access. Heavy undergrowth lined the fencing to the south, making access more difficult. However, a small handle insert and a slightly wider space between the boards indicated there was a gate. Norris lifted the latch and the gate gave way.

The sun was at their backs, so whoever was on other side would need to face into the sun.

With his hand on the handle, Norris looked back over his shoulder at her, his look asking if she was prepared for what was on the other side.

The child's scream pierced her eardrum and caused her nerves to twist tighter in anticipation of a confrontation. Then through the wailing she heard a man order, "Do not move."

Jolene nodded to Norris that she was a go. With one hand resting on his back in case she needed to yank him back from an assault of bullets, she slid her other one over the butt of her gun and drew in a breath.

Slowly, he cracked open the gate and peered inside.

She felt his back muscles relax before he stood taller. With a nod, he indicated she should look.

Jolene released her grip on her gun and peered around him.

On the other side of an inground pool, a man stood next to a built-in grill with a click lighter in his hand.

He was clean cut, shaven and wearing expensive beachwear with a Phillies baseball cap. A few feet away a little boy, about four years old, sat on a lounge chair with a towel wrapped around him. Tears glistened against his sunburned cheeks. He pulled his legs up under a plush beach towel and huddled further into it.

"Your mother told you not to go down to the beach without us…" The man continued his lecture while he lit the gas grill. "You have no idea how powerful the ocean is. I don't even know the extent of it and I'm ten times your age." He waved his hand toward the ocean, the child and then himself. "And I don't want to find out. You could've been seriously hurt. You need to listen to us. We love you and don't want you to get hurt. Do you understand, Trevor?"

The boy sniffled and nodded.

"Good. Then go inside and get changed."

The boy didn't need to be told twice. He scrambled off the chair and dashed toward the slider door. That's when he saw Norris out of the corner of his eye—and slid to a halt. "Daddy. There is a man." He pointed toward them and Jolene backed up.

The man turned and jerked his free hand up to shield his eyes from the sun. Immediately his relaxed demeanor turned defensive. "Can I help you?"

Norris tugged his badge off his belt while he opened the gate wide, exposing both of them. He raised his hands, displaying the insignia in his palm. "I'm Chief Stiles," Norris said, identifying himself. "I'm sorry to interrupt your afternoon, but we stopped to gather some information and heard the boy scream. Is everything okay?"

"Yeah. Just the usual stunts," the man responded,

putting the clicker down.

The boy seemed frozen in place. His head, up to his nose, disappeared into the towel much like a turtle retracts its head. His curious blue eyes remained wide above the white roll. He studied Norris, looked to his dad and then back to Norris.

"May we come inside?" Norris took a small step forward, indicting he was going to anyway.

"One second." The man quickly crossed to his son, opened the sliding door and while ushering him inside, told Trevor to go get his uncles. Once the door closed again, he motioned for them to enter. "Information about what?" he asked.

The sun's rays were no longer directly in the man's face and Jolene saw him blink a few times.

Norris stepped inside the area far enough to leave her room to stand in the gateway. It was his way of letting the man know they were no threat, and to keep her safe if trouble showed up. Also, she could watch his back.

He pointed to her before clipping his badge back on his belt. "This is U.S. Marshal Jolene Martinez."

The man's gaze had been drifting down over her but at Norris' introduction it snapped up to her face. "U.S. Marshal?"

Jolene was used to people's surprised expressions when they learned she was a Marshal. She lifted her badge from her chest and smiled. "Yes, sir."

"We have a few questions to ask, if you don't mind?" Norris asked, stealing the man's attention from her.

"Sure."

The door slid open and four more men stepped

outside onto the cement patio. They varied in height and weight, but one could tell by looking at them that they were related. They had the same deep-set dark concerned eyes and hairlines that cut back sharply on each side of their foreheads.

The man quickly told his relatives the little he knew and they looked to Norris and Jolene.

"What do you need to know?"

It was quite amusing how each man then folded his arms across his chest. So much so, Jolene had to grind her teeth together to keep a smile from forming on her lips.

"Are you Gary Webster?" Norris asked.

The man blinked his surprise that Norris knew his name. His brothers passed a look between them and then at their brother. The expressions on their faces clearly asked the question, "What the fuck did you do, man?"

"I am." Gary's tongue swiped his bottom lip. "How did you know my name? What's this about?"

"I got your name from the property owners."

Gary's shoulders relaxed with that information.

Norris pulled out his phone and began to tap away on it which seemed to make the man all the more nervous. "You're renting this house, right?"

Norris was putting Gary at ease asking him no-brainer questions.

Gary looked between her and Norris. "Yes, for a week."

Even though her attire was less than professional Jolene kept her stance and expression all business. She knew the men facing the sun couldn't see her eyes behind her sunglasses so she took in every detail of their appearance and the surroundings. One brother had come outside with a towel wrapping his waist. The other three wore nylon shorts and T-shirts that hosted various sports teams—unlike their brother Gary who clearly dressed on the higher end of style. If she had to guess, she'd say Gary was footing the bill for the house rental.

Jolene relaxed a little, sensing this truly was a family vacation. On the outside however, she remained on guard.

"How long have you been here?" Norris continued his questioning and tapping. She studied the man while the beep of Norris' phone filled the brief periods of silence between them.

"We arrived three days ago. Tuesday afternoon about two," Gary stated. "The owners let me in early. My brothers and their families arrived later, around five."

Webster dropped his arms to his sides and took a step forward. "What's this all about?"

Norris looked up at him, ignoring his question. "How many children are here?"

Jolene saw Webster swallow. The others dropped their arms to their sides and seemed to become fidgety. They darted looks at one another again.

"Ten," Gary Webster responded, stepping back to his brother's side. "If this is about the house only holding eighteen, we didn't think we needed to include Luke's twins," his voice took on a friendlier tone. "They're only three months old. Luke and his wife, Alice, only decided to join us at the last minute."

The door opened again and five women exited the house. Each took a stance next to their mates. Questions filled their eyes.

The brothers had very different tastes in women, Jolene noted. Gary's wife, Alice, was tall and slim while the others carried more weight and were shorter than their spouses. Most of them were blond, except Alice. She had dark hair similar to her son Trevor's.

"Are all the children accounted for?" Jolene asked, studying Alice.

Gary's face tightened. "They are now. Trevor, my son. The one you heard me screaming at decided he wanted more play time on the beach and slipped out while my wife and I were showering."

Alice's face brightened. "He is a handful."

"Again, Chief Stiles. What is this about?" Gary stuffed his hands on his hips.

"We've found a missing child." Norris swiped his finger across his phone's screen.

He produced a smiling picture of Lia which Jolene had taken after lunch and forwarded to him. It was a much better picture for him and his officers to show people than the one he had taken of Lia in the hospital.

Norris crossed over and held the phone up for all to see. "Have any of you seen her before? Maybe on the beach?"

They all shook their heads.

"Was she kidnapped?" one of the women asked.

"That we don't know, Mrs.—"

"Webster. We're all Mrs. Webster." The full-figured redhead giggled. "I'm Brandy."

Jolene's spine stiffened at the woman's attempt to get Norris' attention. Behind her sunglasses, Jolene narrowed her eyes. She had figured Brandy was a flirt even before she batted her eyelashes at Norris.

He totally ignored her. For some reason that made Jolene feel better.

Brandy's Mr. Webster—the one wrapped in a towel—seemed not to care or had no clue his wife was coming on to the chief.

"If you recall seeing her, please call the station," Jolene said, drawing everyone's attention toward her.

Norris' lips curled slightly.

She pasted a big old friendly grin on hers.

"We'll let you get back to your vacation. Enjoy your stay in Cape James." With a jut of his chin, Norris indicated she should lead the way. He stopped at the gate and then turned back to the group. "I'd try to secure this gate. It opened easily. You don't want Trevor or one of his cousins to wander out front. Route 177 is busy this time of year."

"We'll contact the owners right away and get it secured. Thank you."

Norris dipped his head again. "Thanks for your help."

They walked back to the Jeep in silence.

"That was a total bust." Norris climbed inside the vehicle.

She shrugged. "Checking out leads is what we do."

"The other house isn't too far north. We'll check it too before we head back into town."

"Fine by me." Jolene latched her seatbelt.

Five minutes later, they pulled into the driveway of the second home. The house was a large two-story cedar-shingled Cape Cod with a front porch wide enough to host a party. It sat back further from the road, giving the renters more privacy from the traffic that whizzed by. One could tell by the home's exterior and landscaping that this house was built using a very large construction budget. Chain linked fences, partially hidden by large scrub pines and fast-growing exotic grasses stretched out from the rear corners of the houses and along the sand dunes for a few hundred feet.

There were no cars parked in the driveway and with the shades lowered halfway in the over-sized bay windows the house looked empty.

"It doesn't appear anyone is here. I'm going to check anyway." Norris unlatched his seatbelt. "Wait here if you want."

Jolene purposely arched her brow high enough to be seen above her sunglasses. "Now, what kind of sidekick would that make me?"

"Pretty shoddy, I guess."

"Well, I don't do shoddy." She snapped open her seatbelt and put her shoulder to the door.

"I didn't think so, Marshal."

She quickly climbed out of the vehicle. In less than twenty-four hours— trying hours, filled with the stress to quickly solve the mystery of the unclaimed child— the sexy chief was becoming an obsession for her. She couldn't stop looking at him, studying every muscle of his toned body; or drawing in enough of his scent. *Good God! Male musk poured from him.*

Even during the few hours they'd spent apart, he had remained in her thoughts. In the shower this morning, she had thought about his face, his body—and she'd longed for him to be there with her. Her body ached with a deep-seated need to have him possess her mouth and breasts.

Norris sauntered around the front of the vehicle and came to her side.

Jolene quickly refocused on the case and checked the second-story windows for any movement behind the crisscrossed curtains. The quicker this was over, the quicker her fantasy might become a reality.

Her shoulder only reached his muscular forearm as they walked up the slate walkway. The roses planted at the front of the house sent their perfume wafting on the sea breeze. The only sounds they heard as they approached the house were the traffic behind them, the sound of clashing waves in front of them and the crunch of the pebbles under their feet.

"When I was growing up, the homes along here were wooden shacks," she said quietly and climbed the porch steps beside him. "Their paint was faded and in some places blasted totally away by the sand and sea. If only I knew then what I know now about property gains, I'd be sitting pretty. Look at this place. It's gorgeous. What do you think they rent it for?"

"With a hundred yards of private beach, it could be a thousand dollars a night."

She let out a low whistle. "Damn. I should've gone into real estate." She stepped to the side of the front door.

Norris rang the doorbell and the *In The Good Old Summertime* melody played from within.

She leaned down and peeked in the window. From what she could see the living room opened to a dining room. She shifted forward and saw the Atlantic through the French doors in the dining room. "I don't see anyone."

The door chimes ended their melody.

She turned to Norris. "Are you sure this is a rental? The furnishings look high end."

"One forty-two." He pointed to the black house numbers on the porch column. "Route 177 is considered Crane Lane."

"Who would build a place this beautiful and not live it themselves?"

"Someone who has more money than the U.S. Treasury and uses everything they own to make more." Norris rang the doorbell again. "I'm sure their clientele are also rich."

"I would guess so."

Inside the house the chimes played a different tune: *Take Me Out To The Ball Game*.

"Maybe they went to a game or to the store for groceries," Norris said.

She lifted her brow. "Really? If they rent this place they'd just go out to dinner."

"Too early for dinner."

"It's not." Jolene pulled her cell from her pocket. "It's nearly five." Her phone vibrated in her hand signaling she had a text message. "It's my sister. She wants me to call her."

"Lia?"

"Don't know. Give me a second."

"I'll check around back while you make the call."

They walked off the porch together and then split up. Jolene took the path back to the Jeep and stood near the rear where she could see Norris pass by the hydrangea shrubs. She heard a noise and focused on the rear gate he approached. Beyond the gate a huge gull darted into the air, carrying what appeared to be a half-eaten candy bar.

She let out the breath caught in her lungs and hit the speed dial number for Martina.

"Martina, it's me. Is there something wrong? Is Lia okay?"

"She's fine. I only wanted to know if I should expect you for dinner?"

"Of course."

"Are you still at the coffee shop?"

"No. Chief Stiles and I are checking out a couple leads. I should be there soon to help you."

"Oh…"

"Oh what?"

"I thought maybe you might be having dinner with the chief. You know working late. He is one good-looking man. And single."

"Martina, I am very aware that he is single. Stop the matchmaking. I'm not interested. I simply rode along with him to check on a few things."

"What did you learn?"

Why did the general public find the underworld so exciting? If they had to work one of the cases, most of them would triple the locks on their homes, or maybe not ever come out again. She rolled her eyes even though her sister couldn't see her. "You know I can't tell you anything."

Jolene heard Norris' cell and turned to see him answer it.

"Who would know if you did?" Martina responded, sounding disheartened. "I wouldn't say anything to anyone."

"You'd tell Simon and then he would tell someone else because he wasn't sworn to secrecy by me. No. The case is off limits. End of discussion." She could hear kids yelling in the background. Their cries grew louder.

"Okay. Okay," Martina responded to one of the

children pleading for her attention.

"I'll be home as soon as we're through here. It shouldn't be too long." She heard the child whine again and Martina's firm response to hold on a second. "Sounds like you had a busy day. Why don't I pick up pizzas for dinner?"

"Sounds wonderful. I could use a break. And bring Chief Stiles to dinner."

"I'm sure he has better things to do."

"Who has?" Norris' deep voice sounded right behind her.

Jolene jumped and turned to find her face almost touching Norris' chest. She hadn't heard his approach because of the commotion at Martina's.

Norris' earthy scent immediately sent her blood rushing through her veins. She looked up and with her eyes traced the line of his full lips. Lips she'd fantasized about while showering that morning. A daydream which had left her body quivering.

"You. M-my sister asked if y-you..." she stammered.

"I'll chill a couple bottles of wine," Martina said and then disconnected the call.

Jolene stared down at the phone that prevented her fist from closing. She was going to kill Martina.

"Asked what?" Norris prodded when she said nothing.

Jolene unclenched her jaw and smiled. "That was my sister."

"I know. You told me."

"Yeah. Right." She felt heat rising in her cheeks and ducked her head. "Who called you?"

"Pickett. So far no one at the hotels and B&Bs

115

recognized Lia so they're going to start combing the restaurants."

Jolene frowned.

Norris pushed his sunglasses back further on his head. Concern dulled the familiar brightness in his eyes. "Is everything okay at your sister's? You look distracted."

She shook her head. He had enough on his mind without her adding to his stress. "Yes. All is well. Did you find anyone at the back of the house?" She pointed to the path around the house.

"No. The place is locked up tight. I found a bucket and was able to stand on it and see over the fence. The place, beach included, is deserted. I'll check back later and see if anyone is around then. Are you ready?"

"Sure." The afternoon had not provided any answers and that disappointed both of them. Time ticked away and their chances of learning anything new diminished each hour.

Dropping his sunglasses back on his nose, he stepped back and opened the passenger door for her. Once she was settled inside, he rounded the rear of the vehicle and climbed into the driver's seat. He started the Jeep, but before he put it in gear he turned to her. "Are you sure everything is okay at your sister's house. You look worried."

Jolene smiled. "Everything's okay. The kids kept Martina busy all day. I told her I would pick up pizzas for dinner so she doesn't need to cook." He was a detective, for goodness sakes. Norris must have realized he was the one she referred to when he overheard her tell Martina he probably had plans. He would need to be dense not to and, so far, Norris had proven himself quite perceptive.

"Want to join us?" she asked quickly before she changed her mind. "It's short notice. You probably have other plans."

"Other than going in to the station, I don't."

"Then why not join us?" The idea of spending time with him appealed to her. Then she remembered dinner time at the Gomez table was like feeding time at the zoo.

What she was worried about? She wasn't trying to impress him. He wasn't potential boyfriend material.

"Only if you let me pay for the pies."

Norris popped the clutch and the Jeep lurched forward, pushing her back on her seat.

"That is not what joining us means."

"That's my offer."

"We'll split the bill."

He waited for on-coming traffic before he pulled out and crossed over the northbound lane of Route 177 and headed south into town. Then he glanced her way. "I can see now how this relationship would go."

"What relationship?"

"Us."

"Us?" Was it the warm breeze caressing her cheeks or had the warmth come from within? She didn't blush ever, but Norris seemed to make her do that easily.

"Yeah, 'us' as if we'd hooked up yesterday the way Jackie Hackman intended us to."

"Oh, right. I forgot about her." She had forgotten about their matchmaking hostess.

However, hooking up with Norris was definitely rising on her want-to-do-on-this-vacation list. It wasn't like she got the opportunity to hook up with a hot guy every day. The hot guys she worked with on the C.U.F.F. team were off limits.

She picked up her purse and put her gun and badge inside then dropped it back on the floor.

"I try to avoid her." Norris passed by a few cars slowing to make turns for local shops which sold everything from colorful swimwear to guaranteed authentic shark teeth. "I bet Jackie was overjoyed to learn we're working together. I'm sure Rose has told her."

That peaked her interest. *Why would a stranger be happy over her involvement with Norris?* Jolene shifted on her seat so she could easily see Norris' face without getting a Charlie horse in her neck. "Why would us working together make her happy?"

Norris' fingers stretched over the steering wheel and then tightened around it. "She's been trying to set me up with the right woman ever since—"

Hmm. Was Norris about to share something of his past? "That many women, huh?"

"Yeah." He had a nice chuckle. Deep and sexy. It matched him.

"Do you ever want to get married?"

His eyes slanted toward her. "You asking me?"

"No."

He laughed at her alarmed expression.

"I don't know. Maybe." He shrugged. "I guess I haven't found the woman to make me want to. How about you?"

"Once."

He threw a double glance at her. "You thought about it once or you met the right guy once?"

"Both."

"Ah."

She saw disappointment darken his expression and knew he thought the guy she spoke about was waiting for her somewhere. "He died. He was killed in an operation. Saving me."

She didn't know why she told Norris about Stefan's death. She just felt she had to. However, she hadn't disclosed, the how, why and who had killed him.

She had secrets too.

CHAPTER NINE

Norris watched Jolene wipe sauce from Lia's chubby cheeks and hands. For a kickass federal agent she handled the child patiently and with tenderness while Lia tried to play with Jolene's charm bracelet.

The little girl was a mess with sauce from dimple to dimple. She'd eaten as if she hadn't had anything to eat for days, which he knew wasn't the case. Earlier Martina had told Jolene that Lia ate all day long between meals, juices and snacks.

It was just shy of a miracle Lia hadn't managed to get tomato sauce on the little dress Jolene had changed her into before they sat down to dinner.

When she lifted the child off her chair, Norris noticed the toned muscles in Jolene's arms flexed, reminding him of her strength when she'd battled the ocean swells to reach Lia.

Once put down, Lia didn't hesitate a second to join the other children in the play area. Norris chuckled, watching her long chestnut hair swinging back and forth. Her little twig-like legs wheeled into the middle of the action like she'd done so a million times.

Placing her here with Martina and her husband Simon, instead of keeping her at the station or with a social worker, had been the best decision. The little girl was happy and fed, and by the way she acted, he'd swear yesterday had never happened to her.

"Whoa, did you see that flash?" Jolene laughed, staring after Lia.

"You'd think she be exhausted after what she's been through." Martina began clearing paper plates from the table. "She and Clara have been going non-stop since this morning. I made them lie down after you left, Jolene, but they didn't sleep. Not one wink. They talked and talked and talked, and then they started to play in the room. I finally told them to go back outside before they woke Fina."

Fina was a four-year-old foster child who seemed to have some developmental issues. Though he ran after the other children, he tended to hang back and watch them play.

"I wish I could bottle their energy," Simon said, picking up his beer and taking a gulp.

"I wish I had a dollar for every time I heard that expression." Jolene wiped down the chair rails with a dish towel.

Norris rose and grabbed one of the empty pizza boxes from the grill station behind him and held it open for Martina to deposit the used plates. "What would you do with all that money?"

Jolene grinned. "Maybe I'd buy that house on Crane Lane."

The way her whiskey eyes sparkled when she was happy made him forget about the world. She must feel relaxed, like he did. And the ceiling fan above them kept a balmy breeze swirling around them, making the place more than comfortable.

"What house?" Martina looked between them.

Jolene glanced his way before answering her sister. "A beautiful place we passed by today. They've built a lot of big houses out on Crane Lane."

"I worked on a few of them." Simon leaned back

against his chair.

The man's shirt was undone midway down his chest and Norris could see Jolene's brother-in-law kept in shape.

"What do you do, Simon?" Norris put the box back on the counter and sat down.

"I'm an electrician." Simon pointed to his glass. "You sure you don't want a cold beer?"

Norris shook his head. "Nah. Thanks, but lemonade is fine. I need to stay sharp."

"Right." Simon lifted his beer in the air. "You've got a big case going—"

"We can't talk about it, Simon," Jolene interjected and then dropped onto the chair across from him. She gave him an I'm-sorry look before picking up her wine glass and slanting it toward Simon. "So, don't go asking questions."

"That is not what I was going to do, little sister." Simon made a face at Jolene before he picked up the bottle of wine and poured her another half glass. "I know the rules. I guess you don't need to be sharp?"

"I can handle a glass of wine," she clipped.

When Norris first met Jolene, she seemed a lone wolf, much like himself, but she was very comfortable in the family surroundings. From what he'd gathered during the conversations over dinner, she and Martina were the only siblings but they had a dozen first cousins. Simon was one of six children which meant they had huge family gatherings. They spoke freely about so many people but the only time Martina mentioned her and Jolene's parents, Jolene changed the subject quickly, pretending she hadn't heard Martina's comment. He wondered if Jolene and her parents didn't get along, and if so, why?

Everyone had family disputes. He had his own mother issues, so he let his question slide away to enjoy the banter that now included Martina.

Norris' phone vibrated on his hip. He looked at the screen while Jolene and Simon continued a friendly game of mockery. His spine stiffened when he saw SA Carter's text asking for an immediate return call. Could Carter possibly have the DNA results already? Norris hadn't expected to hear anything until tomorrow at the earliest.

Norris looked at his hosts and held out his phone. "I'm sorry but I need to make a call." For a second his gaze connected with Jolene's before he rose from the table. With the slightest nod of her head, she indicated she understood the call had something to do with Lia's case. Her expression remained serious for only a split second before she turned back to Simon, cutting him off at the knees with a seemingly horrid remark about his choice of power tools.

Norris walked to the driveway and stood next to his Jeep and made the call. When it went to Carter's voicemail he ground his molars.

Hearing children's laughter, he smiled and glanced toward the family party in the backyard. Then he dialed the station. Ted answered on the second ring. Normally, the older man was gone by eight, but it was near nine and he was still working. Norris guessed Ted was trying to make up for his mistake by putting in the extra hours. "Hey, it's me. Have Pickett and Frank reported in yet?"

"Yeah. About ten minutes ago. I'd just picked up the phone to call you when SA Carter walked in."

Norris' pulse kicked up. *Had his men found*

something and told Carter before telling him?

"What does he want?"

"To talk to you, I guess."

Ted's tone sounded off, hesitant. *Was he holding something back?* "What's going on, Ted?"

He heard Ted smack his lips. Doing so was an action Ted did when he didn't want to tell you something. It was one of his ways to buy time.

"Fuck, Ted. I don't have all night."

"Okay, okay. You know old man Mackey?"

Mackey wasn't old by today's standards, only sixty-five. He simply looked ancient. Mackey was a veteran and agent orange was used during a few of the operations he'd been involved in. He'd had a rough life. He sympathized, and in January Norris had tossed the older man's ass in jail to keep him from sleeping with the dogs at the animal shelter. Then he'd listened to the guy rant all night, stating he'd rather lay with those dogs than the ones that ran the government. The old guy claimed the dogs had souls and cared. At times, Norris thought he was probably right.

"Yeah. What's he done?"

"He wandered in here a few hours ago to get out of the heat and away from the noise. He was angry because there are so many people in town so I let him use a cell to cool off and take a nap. I went to take a piss and when I got back SA Carter was coming out of your office."

"What the hell was he doing in my office?"

"Apparently he saw someone in there and thought it was you."

Norris closed his eyes. Behind them he felt the inkling of unease and the beginning of a major headache. Ted didn't need to tell him what happened, but he did.

"Mackey was sitting at your desk when SA Carter walked in."

"Fuck. Don't tell me," Norris spat out between clenched teeth and then rubbed a hand over his face. Now the a.s.a.p. followed by an exclamation point in Carter's text made sense. Carter wanted to tell him how incompetent his men were and to remind Norris again that he didn't have control of his team.

And if Norris didn't have control, Carter would take over the case.

The federal agent was probably placing calls to his superiors when Norris tried to call him.

The pizza Norris enjoyed earlier turned sour in his stomach. *Fuck. Fuck. Fuck.*

"Sorry, Chief. Mackey went into your office looking for the stash of peanut butter crackers he knows you keep there," Ted said with remorse.

Norris wondered if Ted was truly sorry the incident had happened or that he was the one who had let it happen. Probably the latter. Ted knew whichever way the incident played out, Norris would ultimately be the one held responsible for it.

"The moment I saw him with Carter," Ted continued, "I shuffled Mackey out of your office and locked him in a cell."

Norris wanted to hit something. Instead he kicked the Jeep's rear tire and then stalked to the end of the driveway. "Where's Carter now?"

"He used your phone to make a couple of calls. Then he asked if we had any leads. I told him, we didn't and he left."

Of course you told him, Ted. Norris gnashed his molars together at the thought. In frustration he swiped a hand over his face again. His men hadn't found anyone who'd even seen Lia.

Ted broke the silence between them. "Carter said he would call you."

Norris inhaled and let it out slow. "Before you tell a federal agent anything, you check with me. Do you understand me, Ted?"

This was the second time he dressed down the man in less than twenty-four hours. Three strikes and he didn't care what the city council thought. Ted would be history.

"Yes, sir."

Norris imagined Ted flipping him off. "Did Carter say why he stopped in?"

"No. I think he was bored and needed someplace to go."

And he picked the best comedy show in town, Norris thought. "Ok, I'll call him."

"Should I kick Mackey out?"

"Why? He didn't do anything wrong."

"He was in your office."

"He's hungry. Call Popmanli's and order him a meat special pizza. He loves those. Have it delivered. Tell Nino to put it on my tab and I'll square it with him tomorrow. And get Mackey a soft drink or coffee or water—whatever he wants. I'll check in with you later."

Norris disconnected the call before Ted had a chance to debate the impropriety of feeding a guy who he felt was using the system. He paced the width of the driveway, stared up at the star-filled sky and filled his lungs with fresh air. He let go of the anger he felt

126

toward Ted, and with that refocus in the direction of his thoughts, he felt his neck cords relax. Only then did he dial Carter's number.

Finally, the federal agent answered. Norris identified himself and asked, "Did you hear back on the DNA already?"

"No," Carter answered flatly. "We're in the top one-hundred the last time I checked. The lab estimates an answer by zero-ten-hundred hours.

That's tomorrow morning."

Norris let the jab about military time slide. He'd assumed Carter checked him out. He already googled SA Carter's name and read the available information on the Burgess kidnapping. He checked his watch. Thirteen hours minus two.

"I stopped by your station," Carter said.

It didn't take long for Carter to bring up the topic. He didn't like that Carter had been in his house without him there. "I heard."

"If I were you, I'd consider retiring that man of yours, Ted Beltz. He's not a team player."

Surprised at Carter's words, Norris blinked. "I'm sure you're familiar with small town politics. Beltz started on the force when most of the city council members were in elementary school. Hell, he probably caught a few of them doing stuff they shouldn't have done during their teen years. But, lately, he's giving me a lot of reasons to dismiss him."

"If you decide to go in that direction and need backup with the council, let me know," Carter said, again dumbfounding Norris into silence. "Did your field guys learn anything?"

Feeling a slight bond with the Fed, Norris nodded

even though the agent couldn't see him. Carter probably had experience working with men who were like Ted so he undoubtedly understood the position Norris was in. "No. Not yet."

The same moment Norris finished relating everything his team had done since their meeting that afternoon and ended the call Jolene walked through the gate separating the backyard from the driveway.

The area was well lit because the light was positioned near the peak of the garage.

He could see by the set jaw that she was concerned.

She'd ditched her heeled sandals earlier in the evening and now wore flip-flops which sucked at the warm pavement. "Everything okay?"

"Carter stopped by the station looking for me." He held up his phone before sliding it into his front jean pocket. He wasn't going to tell her what occurred at the station. Ted had embarrassed them all, which now included her since she'd taken his side with Carter earlier today.

"Did he hear anything?" Stopping a mere two feet away from him, she looked up and immediately read his thoughts. "What happened?"

He'd never had the connection with his ex-fiancé that he seemed to have with Jolene. Ella had been in a world of her own…

Norris shook his head, forgetting about his past and concentrating on the woman in front of him. "Nothing. We'll know something tomorrow morning."

"For Lia's sake, I hope the Burgesses are her parents." Jolene glanced over her shoulder but when she looked at him again he saw sadness written all over her face.

From the way Jolene cared for Lia that evening, he knew the attachment she felt toward the child was growing stronger. The sooner the link was severed the better for both of them. "Yes. It would be the best scenario."

Jolene dropped her gaze to her feet.

He saw her neck muscles constrict and her tongue skim her lips.

"Then the case would automatically be transferred over to SA Carter but I'm sure you would still be involved," she said. "Your office would be credited for finding her."

"This is not about me. However, you were the one to see her out there on the ocean."

"You would have."

"I'm not sure about that. I was busy watching you."

"Me?"

He laughed at her surprised expression. "Don't sound so surprised. You look pretty darn good in a bikini, agent Martinez."

"Thank you." She ran her long nails through her short hair as if she were tucking long locks behind her ear, in an unsuccessful attempt to hide her blush.

Her charm bracelet tinged with the motion and made him smile. He'd rattled her.

His fingers itched to caress the soft skin of her arms again, but he wouldn't just reach out and pull her into an embrace. Instead he dug his hands into his pockets and firmly planted his feet on the sidewalk. He looked down at her, knowing his opportunity to have a non-committal night of hot sex with Jolene was no longer on the table. He knew her too well already. He liked her too much and had to admit he longed to know more about her, a desire he hadn't felt in a long time.

He stepped back from her floral scent.

He'd decided a year ago, he wasn't going to let any woman rip his heart to shreds again. Somehow, he sensed if he let his guard down with Jolene he might never recover. Following in his father's footsteps because his mother had left them. Years later, Dad was still just a shell of a man. Norris would rather walk through life alone with at least his pride intact than become an empty shell of a man like that. It was difficult to reason standing so close to Jolene like this.

"I think I'm going to take off. Would you thank Martina and Simon for inviting me?" He turned toward his Jeep.

Jolene fell in step beside him. "You don't want to tell them yourself?"

Damn. He enjoyed having her by his side. He lengthened his stride. "Please, do it for me. I want to drive out to Crane Lane again, to that home you loved, and see if anyone has returned there. Before it gets too late. It's already past nine."

"Okay. Sure. You'll call me if anything turns up?"

She looked disappointed. Was it because she didn't want him to leave? Or because she wanted to go with him? He climbed inside his vehicle and turned the engine over. "I will."

Jolene stepped back as he put the Jeep in reverse and drifted out of the driveway. "I don't care what time it is," she called after him.

He jammed the stick into first and gassed the engine. In his rearview mirror, he saw Jolene standing in the street looking perplexed.

She'd stay far away from him if she knew how

messed up he was.

***

Jolene walked toward the house with an unsettling feeling in her stomach. Norris was upset about something and since his behavior had changed after he'd spoken to SA Carter, she assumed the reason why had to do with the case. *Was he keeping something from her? And if so why?*

The backyard was kid free when she entered. Thinking about Norris, she hadn't even noticed their whoops and shouts of joy had ended.

Simon still sat at the table. He looked relaxed, leaning back in the cushion chair and had his sandaled feet propped up on another. A fresh beer sat within easy reach on the cleared table.

"Don't ruin it for me. This time of day is my moment of peace." He looked beyond her and sipped his beer.

Simon was a good man. Martina had always dreamt of a large family and after Clara was born and Martina was told she couldn't have another child. It was Simon who had suggested they become foster parents and so far they've helped a half-dozen kids feel loved.

After the living conditions she and Martina had survived while growing up, many people wouldn't understand why her sister would want so many children, but Jolene did. Her sister wanted to make the world a better place. Their goals were the same but their approaches were different. Martina had chosen to make her children's lives and lives of others good while Jolene took on the evil in the world.

"Don't you sleep?" Jolene asked Simon.

From inside the sprawling ranch home, a child screamed, Martina yelled and then another child cried.

Simon smiled. "Sometimes. When they all do."

Jolene laughed. "I'll go see if I can help her get them settled."

"I'm going to stay right here." Simon picked up his beer and took a swig.

The second Jolene opened the slider door and stepped into the eat-in kitchen she almost regretted her decision. The cries for Martina grew louder. She found her sister in the boys' large bedroom refereeing a fight between her two older sons, Diego and Angel and their foster son Jeffrey. Emmanuel, Martina's youngest son sat on his bed playing with his Captain America and Hulk action figures, ignoring the nearby battle entirely.

Jolene stood in the doorway. A good spot, if attacked. She could bolt down the hallway and perhaps make it to the front door before the boys latched on to her. She'd have to lose the flip-flops though. The kids were squirrelly fast. "What is going on?"

Immediately all three boys turned to her and began to cry for her to take their side.

Jolene curled her toes into the rubber soles while her gaze bounced from boy to boy, watching them, waiting for their move.

Martina stood next to a highboy dresser. Growing tired of the argument, she slapped the top with her the flat palm then threw up her hands. "Stop, right now! You all know the rules." Her index finger became her scepter. "Diego, you're the oldest—"

"By two months," Jeffery interrupted her.

With her hands on her hips, Martina swung around

to face her foster son. "Which still makes him the oldest. It's his night to take a shower first." She pointed to a color-coded calendar on a nearby wall. "You're second and then Angel is next. Tomorrow night you're first, Angel is second and Diego is last."

The last one in the shower had the job of making sure the bath towels and rug were hung up and the sink and counter wiped down. The boys had quickly learned to respect their use of the space and not to leave all the work for the last one to take a shower. Payback was a bitch.

"What about Emmanuel?" Angel spoke up, pointing to the one son with his father's fair skin and hair. Features inherited from Simon's English mother.

"He'll take a bath in my tub tonight," Martina said. "Now get your things Diego and get in the shower before I call your father."

Diego rushed into the bathroom and Martina opened a nearby dresser drawer and rummaged through the clothing inside. "While he's in there, Jeffrey and Angel, I want you to pick up the puzzle pieces you dumped out on the playroom floor earlier today."

"What's Diego need to clean up?" Angel asked, lifting his defiant chin and taking a step forward. Of all Martina's children, Angel reminded Jolene of herself. He questioned everyone.

Looking over her shoulder at her middle son, disappointment flashed in Martina's glare. "He and Andrew put their game away before Andrew went home. Now get." The boys passed by her with their chins nearly touching their chests. "And no fighting. I hear the slightest skirmish and I'll count out one-hundred pieces for each of you and you'll pick them up again," she called down the hallway.

She looked to Jolene, snagging a strand of her long hair and trapping it behind her ear. "Sorry. It's usually not this bad. They're played out. I should've called nap time for all of them today."

Jolene could see Martina was tired and guilt threaded its way through her. She'd brought Lia here—of course she had asked Martina before suggesting it to Norris—but now she was torn between her job and taking on watching Lia 24/7 herself.

Martina put a smile on her face and held her hand out. "Come on Emmanuel. Time for your bath."

Carrying his action toys, the boy scampered off his bed and skipped over to take his mother's hand.

Admiration for her sister's stamina warmed Jolene's heart.

"Where are the girls?" Jolene asked, wanting to pitch in.

"Clara and Lia are in the girls' tub right now. I put bubble bath in the water. Can you check on them for me?"

"Sure."

"And check Lia to make sure she didn't have a reaction to the bubble bath," Martina said over her shoulder before she headed down the hallway to her and Simon's bedroom.

Jolene stiffened. She knew nothing about children. "How do I—?"

Martina halted and turned. "When you towel her off, check her skin and see if it is irritated. I laid pajamas out on Clara's bed. Clara wanted to wear the ones with Elsa's character on them and Lia wanted Anna's."

Anxiety threaded its way into Jolene's lungs. She hid her gulp by pretending to scratch a spot on her throat. "How do I know which is which?"

Her sister barked with laughter. "Really?"

She'd never run in the Disney Club. She placed her hand on her hip the way Martina had earlier. "Seriously? Neither of *them* are on the government's most wanted list."

"Don't stand that way. It doesn't work for you." Martina's hearty laugh filled the hallway. "You're too skinny. The girls will tell you which is which. After you empty the tub, tell Sofia and Fina it's their turn. Tonight they can shower together if they want. Tell them to keep the shower curtain inside the tub. I don't want water on the floor again tonight."

How in the hell did Martina keep herself together? "You run a tight ship."

"If I didn't, more things would get lost or need fixing."

"When did you become such a good mom?"

"I guess I started training when I took care of you." Martina winked and then turned and ushered Emmanuel into the master bath.

Later, Jolene stood at the girls' bedroom door and watched Lia sleeping next to Clara. While she marveled how different people were, two questions popped into her mind. After the childhood she and Martina had survived, how was it possible her sister had become such a great loving mom? They'd had no role model. And second: Had Lia been discarded like an old shoe?

How could anyone throw a child away? Any child.

Jolene wouldn't profess to having the same feelings Martina did for her children, but she loved her nieces and nephews and would kill if anyone tried to harm them.

She'd killed a few people. The memories of their lifeless stares tormented her some nights and were the reason she'd never have a family life like Martina. She and Martina were different. They'd taken different paths.

She couldn't change her past.

Looking at Lia, a surprise band of yearning coiled through her and she backed away from the door, unsure what it meant.

A few minutes later, she slipped out into the night.

CHAPTER TEN

Jolene walked along her neighborhood beach with her flip-flops dangling from her left hand. The inky blackness of the sea encroached on the beach with a lapping sound. Above her, the half-moon hung low in the velvet blue sky and provided enough light to see the tracks she left behind. *Why was the sight of a single set of footprints so dispiriting?*

She sighed and moved forward, putting one foot in front of the other.

Her impulsiveness troubled her. Running out of the house, needing space and going for a walk indicated she wasn't good mother material. Mothers didn't leave their children.

She picked up a beach stone and tossed it into the waves.

She had dived into the ocean to save Lia but since bringing her safely ashore a silent battle waged inside her.

She wasn't a mother, she reasoned; Lia wasn't her child. None of the children she helped feed, bath and clothe that night were hers. She was only another person in their lives. A secondary character who might be missed a bit when she left, but not for a lifetime.

A gust rolled over the ocean and carried cool air ashore along with the scent of seaweed.

Jolene rubbed the chill from her arms before she unfolded the scarf which hung around her shoulders and draped it over her arms.

Once she *had* thought about becoming a mother. That seemed a lifetime ago, when in reality it had only been five years. She had loved Stefan enough to want to have his child. However, he'd been a mafia warrior. She'd seen how Gorgon Novokoff, the mafia lord, had trained his son from the age of four to be the heir to Novokoff's empire. She couldn't bring a child into the world knowing her and Stefan's child would be raised a killer.

She doubted it, but maybe she could've convinced Stefan to escape with her. If they had, there was no doubt in her mind they would've spent their lives running and hiding from the Novokoffs. She hadn't wanted that kind of life for any child they might have…or for them.

In November, she would turn thirty. Her time for having children was running out. She kicked at the white foam and then let her feet sink into the sandy earth. With her arms wrapped around her waist she stared up at the stars and then let a hand drift over her stomach.

Where were these thoughts coming from? She swore she'd never have kids. She was a loner.

A cough came from behind her. In one fluid motion she let the scarf fall from her shoulders and spun around, planting her right foot into the sand ready to do battle.

Norris had returned and stood about fifty feet away. His hair lifted in the breeze and he raised his hands as if surrendering to her.

Relief expelled from her lungs and she dropped her arms to her sides. "What the hell are you doing here?"

"I could ask you the same thing?"

Jolene reached down, picked up the scarf and shook the sand from it. "I'm taking a walk. You're lucky my scarf didn't get wet." She flipped the scarf over her head and onto her shoulders.

He strolled toward her, keeping above the lapping waves. "That would have been the least of your problems, if I had been someone else. The beach is a dangerous place at night, especially for a lone female lost in thought."

She wiggled her toes into the cold sand and looked at him shyly. "Are you worried about me, Chief Stiles?"

He flashed her the cocky grin she loved. "I'm more concerned for the guy who might have followed you?"

She leaned to the side to look around him and glanced up the beach and then twisted and scanned the area behind her before she turned back to him. "He must be very good at hiding, because I don't see him." She chuckled, on some level pleased Norris was concerned about her.

"How did you find me?"

He hitched a thumb over his shoulder. "I saw you pulling out of the gas station on my way back into town."

She cocked a brow. "And you followed me?"

"It looks that way."

She stepped closer to him. "Why?"

Norris' tongue moistened his lips before he folded his arms across his broad chest. "I-I wanted to see what you were up to?"

Jolene was thrilled she made him nervous. She chuckled inside at how he tried to cover it up with his caveman puffed-out chest and his you-don't-frighten-me stare. "Did you think I was headed over to Carter's room to do some super cool federal shit?"

"Nah. I think you're tired of the super cool federal shit."

"You do, huh?"

He nodded once.

Maybe he was right. No one enjoyed dealing with the scum of the earth day in and day out. Still, something inside her and others, Norris included, drove them to put on their shields and strap on the guns and dig out the evil son of bitches. Lately, however, she'd been feeling there had to be a better way to protect the world...

She pushed away her thoughts concerning her future and drew a deep breath. "So, do you want to escort me to the pier and back? Or do you need to go and fight crime?"

"I have time."

They walked side by side, creating two trails of footprints in the sand.

Aware of Norris' body's heat, the hair on Jolene's arm stood at attention waiting for the instant his arm would brush hers. Thinking about what she would do if he did touch her had her a little jumpy. She didn't want to do anything hasty that would cause Norris or her any embarrassment so she put a little distance between them. However, a few feet later the distance had narrowed again. *We're two freakin' magnets with nothing between us to stop us from connecting.*

After several long minutes, his coarser hairs grazed hers and sparks of electricity charged up her arm, prompting her heart to skip and stutter. It happened again and her heart raced.

Each time, Norris mumbled half-heartily, "Sorry."

There was no denying the attraction between them. If she were carefree and stupid and he wasn't the authority figure in this town, she'd dance seductively before him. Then while he was mesmerized by her she would link her arms around his neck and lift herself up over his chest and bind her legs around his waist and kiss him in a way he'd never been kissed before.

She noted the number of people still hanging out on the pier in front of them. She wasn't carefree even though she made herself seem so to others. Besides, she wouldn't jeopardize Norris' respectability.

Even so, Jolene felt herself grow wet thinking about Norris' possible reaction to her dance and her kiss and where it might lead.

With her mind on sex, she hadn't watched where she was stepping and pain cut through the pad of her right foot.

"Ouch!" She stumbled against Norris.

He grabbed her arm and steadied her. "Are you okay?" Under a furrowed brow, his eyes displayed concern.

"Sorry. I stepped on a shell." She picked up the broken shell and threw it into the sea.

"Maybe you'd better put your sandals on."

He held her steady while she swiped away the sand with her scarf and examined her foot under the moonlight. "No. I love the feel of the wet sand between my toes. I'll be more careful and watch where I walk."

He stood still, not letting go of her arm and stared down at her. "You should put some antiseptic on the cut. It could get infected."

"I will." Slowly, she withdrew her arm from his embrace. While she loved talking and teasing Norris, she had to draw the line and stay on her side because crossing it could be bad for both of them. She knew what shaky ground she stood on when it came to relationships. And she had a feeling Norris also had something in his past he needed to work through. "I'm okay." She walked ahead and he quickly fell into step beside her.

Music drifted toward them from the pier and after they'd strolled a little further in silence listening to a classic summer time tune, Jolene said, "I take it you didn't find anything at my dream beach house?"

"I met the owner, Mark Branka. We'd actually met before, at several town functions." Norris guided her around a beached jellyfish. "The day I came here for an interview, the mayor gave me a tour of Cape James. He'd mentioned Branka was one of several millionaires who bought up property here years ago. He actually bought up four older homes seven years ago. He had rented them out for several years until he tore them all down and built his home. He's been living there off and on for nearly three years."

"You didn't recognize his name when the realtor gave it to you?"

"Peggy never gave me the owner's name. She said the owner wanted to remain anonymous." He scowled and dipped his head to the side. "It seems Peggy might've given us the wrong address on the rental house. Branka thought maybe she read the house number wrong. It's one-hundred ninety-two Crane Lane that's for rent, not his one-hundred forty-two address."

A rasping noise caused Jolene to look up and see Norris scratching his beard at his jawline.

"So, he doesn't rent out his house?"

Norris shook his head. "No."

"Damn." She kicked out with her uninjured foot and sent sand flying into the air.

"I'm sure he'd sell it to you for the right price."

"I'll check my off-shore accounts in the morning and have the funds available." She smiled, enjoying his company.

Norris nudged her elbow with his and returned her grin. "Or if you tell him you're a U.S. Marshal, maybe he'll let you stay there for a few days. But then again he probably wouldn't since some bad guys might be looking for you."

She laughed and let the scarf slip off her shoulders. "I've learned to cover my tracks pretty well."

"I bet." Norris looked down at her. They both worked in a dangerous world and there was no need to say more. They knew at any given moment their lives could change forever, or end. The thought of everything ending and not having experienced enough of what stood right in front of them made the draw between grow stronger. Their pace slowed and their bodies turned as if they had no control over them. His hands lingered over her arms for a moment before letting his fingers graze her arm.

Jolene longed to kiss him and it seemed he had the same desire because his head dipped, bent toward her lips.

Behind her an explosion occurred. She jumped, feeling the whoosh of warm air across her shoulders. Her ears rang and she swore she heard popping sounds.

Norris grabbed her by the arm and propelled her behind him. His hand tugged at his left ear which probably also buzzed from the bang.

Her right hand automatically reached to her back where she'd normally tucked her gun into her waistband when not wearing a holster, but her palm only felt the soft material of her scarf. Shaking the ringing from her ears, she wound her arm around the material and took an offensive stance behind Norris. If he went down, she'd be an open target. *Who the hell was shooting at them?*

Jolene looked right, then left while she listened for rounds biting into the sand or flesh. The pier's vertical columns would be their best protection from gunfire but she calculated them to be at least twenty yards away. In sand, that would be at least four seconds. Four seconds was plenty of time for a crack shot to fire off a few rounds.

She heard muffled laughter and peeked over Norris' shoulder where sparks drifted downward toward the sea. She scanned the area and exhaled the tension gripping her lungs. Some guy on the pier above them had thrown an M80 firecracker and it exploded midair above the water. Then his buddies followed up with smaller fireworks.

The damn fools had scared the crap out of her. It was a good thing she didn't have her firearm with her. She'd be tempted to pop off a couple of rounds out to sea to scare the shit out of them.

Norris pressed the heel of his hand against his ear for two seconds before he stepped forward and yelled at the guy, identifying himself as the chief of police. The man showed signs of drunkenness and told Norris to "fuck off."

The pole light on the pier lit up the area somewhat and Jolene saw Norris' jaw tense. He took another step

144

closer to the pier and threatened to arrest M80 guy if he and his friends didn't leave the area immediately. There wasn't any more Norris could do other than to shout at the guy because there were no stairs nearby leading up to the pier.

Norris slid his two-way radio from his belt and adjusted the volume up, causing a crackling sound. He pushed a button and an officer responded, "*Go ahead, Chief.*"

"Do I call it in?" Norris shouted.

"*Chief, are you there?*"

"Stand by," Norris spoke into the phone.

Apparently hearing the reply from the home-based officer, M80 guy and his gang grumbled curse words and began to move out. When they reached the pier's exit another smartass found his balls and yelled, "Hey man, the beach is closed. What the hell are you doing on it?"

"I'm special," Norris answered him.

"And her?"

"She's special too and she's with me. Move along before I have one of my deputies escort you to our overnight accommodations. Make sure your designated driver is behind the wheel or call a taxi. I'll have your asses if you drive drunk."

"At least you didn't say, I'm looking for assholes and found a few," Jolene said so only he could hear her.

"I was tempted." Norris kept his eyes trained on the group.

It would be stupid of the guy to toss another M80, this time directly over their heads. M80 guy didn't appear to have a high IQ. But in the end, he surprised her.

Jolene stepped alongside Norris and watched the rowdy six disappear from sight.

When they no longer heard the group's chatter, Norris requested one of his officers check out the vehicles leaving the pier's parking area for a possible DUI before he looked at her. "Where were we? Oh, yeah. I'll check with Peggy in the morning."

Jolene tugged her scarf up over her shoulders. Norris seemed to have forgotten about the kiss which had almost happened. Or had she wished he'd kiss her and only imagined the moment before the blast. Either way they were back to business. "So now we wait, again."

"Not much more we can do." He checked the pier entrance.

She turned away from him, knowing the moment was gone. He was in professional mode.

Silently they strolled leisurely along the beach, letting the sound of the waves wash away the rush of adrenaline that had dumped into their systems.

"You defused the situation nicely." She nodded over her shoulder toward the pier. "I know they're here to have fun, but with *quarter sticks*? Drunken fools."

"I agree. With West Virginia, South Carolina only hours away, it's hard to keep fireworks out. We moderate them the best we can."

It was an endless battle.

"Why am I telling you?" Norris said, looking down at her. "You're from here, right? You know."

"Born and raised, and I do know very well. My older cousins drove to South Carolina one year and bought some fireworks, quarter sticks included. Their nine-year-old sister found them and—"

"Don't say it. She okay?"

"Now she is. One went off in her hand and she lost all her fingers but her thumb."

"Oh man." Norris shook his head. "I'm sorry."

Jolene frowned. "She was lucky."

"It's hard to look at it that way but you're right." They walked in silence for a minute before Norris asked, "So does your family still live around here? I heard Martina mention your parents earlier."

Jolene's back stiffened. She simply nodded.

He put a hand to his ear. "I'm sorry I didn't hear you."

She knew sooner or later her parents would pop up in a conversation. "Yes. They live a few miles south of town. Dad works as a mechanic at Swapfield's Marina."

"And your mom, what does she do?"

Jolene almost choked on the word mom. Her mother was never a mom to her or Martina. She pulled her scarf around her. "She's a lawyer."

"A mechanic and a lawyer. You don't hear that combo very often."

"No, you don't."

"I haven't run into a Martinez at the courthouse yet."

"She handles divorces mostly."

"I get the feeling you don't get along with your parents," Norris said.

"I get along with my dad fine. But my mother, no."

"I don't have much of a relationship with my own mother either."

She slanted her gaze up at him. "Are you telling me that to make me feel better about my relationship with my mother or do you really not get along with yours?"

"I don't." His eyes widened at her questioning brow. "Really. I get along with my dad. He's a great guy, but he wasn't good enough for mom."

"Ah. Then they're not together any longer."

"No. They're not. Mom moved on to greener pastures when I was five. And then when I was nine. And again, after I graduated high school."

A little astounded, a small chortle rumbled in her throat. "Three husbands?"

His chest expanded with his intake of air. "She's on number four now."

"Wow."

"I take it your parents are still together?"

"They are, but I don't think either one of them is happy."

"Why stay together then?" he asked.

"I guess they took their vows seriously."

"Or they really do love each other."

She hadn't been around her parents for years and had no idea what their relationship was like now. Martina said their mother had changed. She wasn't the controlling bitch she had been all their lives. "I don't know. Maybe."

"What made you become a Marshal?"

She shrugged and threw the question back at him. "What made you become a cop?"

"I asked first." Norris smiled.

She pulled her scarf tighter around her shoulders and knotted it. "I don't know. I didn't want to stay here. I wanted to do something that mattered. You know, help people."

Norris flicked a charm on her bracelet. "When I saw this, I thought maybe you were a vet or animal activist.

148

Were the bracelet and charms gifts?"

"The bracelet, yes. The charms… Most of them I bought." Her fingers found the dragonfly. Stefan had bought it for her while they were in Palm Springs.

"Is that one special?"

Norris' lips parted slightly while he waited for answers to questions she wasn't prepared to give.

"Not really," she lied, while she let the charm slip from her fingers. She shook the bracelet to lose sight of it. "I like otters. I think they're fun. They symbolize joy." She didn't tell him the creatures also embodied transition and healing.

She quickened her step and headed up the beach to the path that led to the lot where she'd parked her SUV. "It must be getting late. I've got to go, in case Martina needs my help with Lia."

She knew the odds of Lia waking and not being soothed by Martina were very low. The child was exhausted and Martina had the singing voice of an angel and could lull any child back to sleep with its calming timbre.

Jolene heard the muted sound Norris' soles on the sand behind her.

She turned around to face him and immediately put her hand out and made contact with his solid chest. "You don't need to walk me to my car."

He pointed past her. "I'm parked beside you."

"Oh." Right. He had followed her. Ignoring his smirk, she turned and clutched the ends of her scarf. She'd hadn't seen him following her and that was a rookie mistake. He knew she hadn't spotted him.

What the hell had she been thinking about? She hadn't picked up his tail. Aware of what was happening behind her was one of her best assets. Her C.U.F.F. team members swore she had eyes in the back of her head and that was why she wore her hair so short. For God's sake, she'd ridden in Norris' Jeep only hours before. She should've seen him.

Jolene spun around and bit down hard on her lip. She'd been condemning herself for her lack of mothering skills. Fuck it. She wasn't a mother. She was a badass federal agent. Saving the world was what she did.

At the edge of the lot she stopped and dropped her sandals to the ground. She lost her balance trying to remain upright while wiggling her feet into them instead of bending over and presenting her ass to the hunk behind her.

Norris' hands gripped her hips and steadied her. Immediately, she felt the urge to lean back into his hard body and bring his hands to her breasts, but doing so wouldn't be the right move for so many reasons.

The more time she spent with Norris the more she wanted to get down and sweaty with the sexy chief of police, but she also liked the man he was and didn't want to hurt him. She would be leaving when this case was through, which could be as early as tomorrow morning if Lia turned out to be the missing Burgess girl. She sensed Norris needed something more than a quick lay anyway. He might not say it or believe it himself for some reason but she thought he longed for a lasting relationship. She didn't do those.

"Thanks," she said over her shoulder, shoving her left foot into her strapless sandal. She quickly found her footing, but he held her in place.

"Did I do or say something wrong?" His breath

stroked the back of her neck.

A shiver of excitement tumbled down her spine and she shivered. "No." She stepped out of his hold.

While crossing the lot, she pulled her keys from her pocket and hit the unlock button on her key fob. Her running lights flashed quick and bright like blinking cat's eyes in a dark alley.

At her vehicle's front fender, Norris grabbed her elbow and stopped her from reaching her car door. She spun to face him.

"If nothing is wrong, why are you in such a hurry all of a sudden?" Norris asked.

She shrugged. "I simply think I should get back to Lia."

His cocked eyebrow indicated he didn't believe her. "I put her in Martina's care under your advisement. Are you now saying you don't trust your sister and brother-in-law to watch over her?"

"No."

"And if Lia's DNA doesn't match the Burgess couple, are you planning to babysit while I work the case? Because I thought you'd told SA Carter you were working the case with me." His head tilted in the opposite direction of hers and he stared down at her waiting for a reply.

Jolene's jaw clenched. He was playing her good. She glared up at him. "No."

"No. You're not babysitting or no you're not going to help me find out who put Lia in the flimsy raft on the ocean to die?"

He didn't know who she was because she hadn't proven anything to him yet. "We'll find who did this to her whether she's the Burgess child or not."

"I thought that would be your answer." He stepped closer to her. "So then Lia isn't the problem. So what's your hurry to get away from me?"

"I think you know."

While they tried to read each other the attraction between them grew stronger. The heat from his body rolled toward her, circling her like strong arms and pleaded with her to draw closer.

Jolene ran her tongue over her suddenly dry lips. "This between us … I don't think it's a good idea."

"What thing?"

He was the devil and he was going to make her say the words when he damn well knew what she meant.

She cocked her head to the side and glared. Maybe if she were brutally honest she would make him back off. "If we hadn't found Lia yesterday maybe you and I would've hooked up last night. I think both of us need to get laid, but" —she raised her chin—"we're working a case together now, and I don't get involved with men I work with."

Norris remained silent for only a second, studying her face. "Well fuck, if I'd known that I would've refused your help."

"Well you didn't and we are, so let's step back." She laid her hands on his solid chest and immediately she considered breaking her own rule, just this once. Only this one night.

On his face, in his eyes, she saw her own desire to be held and loved reflected back to her.

He moved closer.

She caved against his charm and slid her hands higher over his beating heart. Immediately his earthy scent, which the ocean breezes had kept at bay, filled her nostrils. She felt her insides quiver.

Norris cupped her jaw, tilting her face higher and ran a finger over her bottom lip. "One kiss."

Jolene admired the breadth of his shoulders while under her palm his heartbeat matched hers. "That would be a bad idea," she said.

Norris' lips curled upward. "Maybe I wouldn't enjoy it."

She latched on to his amused gaze. He was going to kiss her. Unless she jabbed her knee into his groin he was going... To. Kiss. Her. "You really think you won't enjoy it?"

"Only one way to find out." He pulled her closer, winding his strong arms around her, lifting her up against him. Then his head dipped and those lips she'd been admiring for the last day and a half brushed against hers in a soft tantalizing caress. He gently kissed her again, but this time he parted her lips with his tongue and sweetly claimed her mouth.

As the heat between them grew, Jolene's resolve disappeared and she willingly melted against Norris' hard chest. The fire in her belly grew to a roaring inferno and when he tried to pull back, she fisted her hands around his shirt, held him in place and kissed him harder, wanting more.

Behind them a car pulled into the lot and the highlight's bright beams found them.

There was no way the driver missed the way Jolene jumped back from Norris.

"Step away from vehicle, sir," called a static voice over a loud speaker.

Realization hit and Norris expression turned livid. He shook his head and held up a hand, shielding his eyes from the light. "Pickett," he growled. He looked at her and inhaled. "I'm going to kill the bastard. You better not watch."

Jolene had to admit she was also annoyed at Pickett's intrusion but maybe it was a sign that hooking up with Norris wasn't a great idea. She laughed, hoping that would dispel some of the chief's anger toward his deputy.

The lights cut off and they heard a car door open before their vision had time to adjust to the dim lighting.

"Hey, Chief." Pickett remained by the front of his car.

"What the hell do you want?" Norris snapped.

Whatever Pickett needed to talk to him about had better be important, because Jolene sensed Norris was pretty pissed at the interruption. She wouldn't want to be in the deputy's shoes.

"Apparently, he needs to talk to you in private," Jolene said softly. "I'm going to go."

"Don't." Norris touched her arm, stopping her.

She smiled. "I think it's for the best." She opened her door and climbed inside. "I'll see you tomorrow morning bright and early, Chief Stiles."

"Okay." Norris' shoulders drooped in surrender and he pushed her door closed.

Jolene eased her car from the parking spot.

His fingers lingered on the door as long they could.

Leaving was the right move. She knew it. But damn she felt empty as she widened the distance.

She looked in the rearview mirror. Norris watched her for a full three seconds before he swept his hand through his hair and stalked toward his deputy.

Jolene touched her lips. Norris' kiss was probably the best first kiss she'd ever received. Too bad she wouldn't find out if he was good in the sack. She'd bet a year's salary he was great.

CHAPTER ELEVEN

From my position, I watch him via the reflection each time he passes by. He wears me out with his tedious pacing back and forth, working his thumbnail between his teeth.

I know he knows about Lia now. He had to have found her.

I know he'll take care of her—he's a good man, despite the fact he keeps me locked away.

He wouldn't give her back, would he? He can't. I love her.

What will he do with her?

She's my daughter, damn it!

I don't regret taking Lia. She stole my heart the moment I saw her chubby little face. I was alive, enjoying freedom, for the first time in decades—thanks to my sweet mother—when I found her. She brought me such joy and fulfilled a deep-seated need I never had a chance to experience before.

I'm evil for taking her. I know it. And it should break my heart he's so worried, but it doesn't. He's lived a good life while mine has been an empty shell.

I can't stop picking away at this wall. My existence depends on me breaking free again. I want my baby.

Damn him.

CHAPTER TWELVE

Norris yawned. With his elbow propped on his desk, he pinched the corners of his eyes and then blinked several times. He hadn't slept well. He'd spent the night on his office couch, again, listening to the normal radio chatter between Larry, who manned the desk last night, and Pickett and Frank who had patrolled the streets and answered calls. While he'd tossed and turned he thought about the woman whose kiss started a blaze inside him. Even hours later the fire still demanded to be fed.

He swiped a hand down over his face and shook his head. Kissing Jolene had been a totally unprofessional move, and it was one he could not take again. No woman, not even his ex-girlfriend had ever tempted him in the primal way Jolene now did.

Over the last few days he'd seen Jolene in many roles: playful vixen, daring soldier, clever agent, fair-minded mediator, and loving family member. Though tough, he knew she was a compassionate human being. Each facet revealed to him made her more and more interesting too. And made him long to learn everything else about her.

He'd heard it said that things happen in life for a reason. Something at home had caused Jolene to take a walk on the beach. What *it* was, was a mystery to him. If *it* hadn't happened, he wouldn't have seen her pull out of the gas station and then he wouldn't have followed her there. They wouldn't have walked the beach together, getting to know a little more about each other. And they wouldn't have been there to tell the M80 guys to stop their dangerous games. Then he wouldn't have put the call in to one of his officers to watch out for them. The responding officer, Pickett, wouldn't have swung by the parking lot looking for him at the very moment his lips had met Jolene's...

If fate wanted them together, why do so much to put them together, only to have something pull them apart?

He heard a chair scrape the floor and looked up to see Ted rise from his desk chair. Passing Norris' office, he kept his eyes trained forward and headed to the station's restroom.

Norris leaned back on his chair, sighed and stretched. He had so many questions running through his head about so many different things and right now he had to concentrate on his job.

He rose and walked into the main office and stood next to Pickett's desk. He scanned the list of places his officers had already gone to show Lia's picture to business owners and their staff. They had covered all of the hotels, B&Bs, campgrounds, gas stations and most of the businesses along the half-mile boardwalk. So far no one remembered seeing her.

He noted that Pickett had even contacted all the staff who had worked the public restrooms yesterday.

Next on the list were the town businesses and then, working on the premise Lia might be a local child, they would start with the pre-schools and local churches to see if anyone recognized her. They'd done a hell of a lot of work in the forty hours since Lia was plucked from the ocean.

He glanced up at the wall clock above Pickett's

desk. It was nearly zero nine hundred hours. Within the next hour or two they should have the answer to whether or not the little girl was Abigail Burgess.

Having to wait a few hours to get the results had Norris antsy. He needed to know which direction this case would take and if he'd remain in charge. Thankfully, patience was one of his virtues. He began to prioritize other tasks and assign them to whomever he felt could handle them the best. They still had regular duties to perform in the small community now engorged with tourists.

He laid down the spreadsheet his deputy had produced before going home at six to catch a few hours of sleep. Picket had spent the night working calls and planned on being back by noon and ready to work another eighteen-hour shift, if necessary.

Behind him, he heard the slap of Ted's shoes growing louder. Norris noted Ted's chalky skin looked even paler. "Are you alright?"

"Yeah. Okay." Ted tucked his belt into the spot below his paunch. "Mackey is still snoring away."

Norris understood Mackey. He'd come back from serving his country to find his wife had written him off and built a life with another man. From then on, Mackey had never regained his footing and with each passing year grief had hardened his heart.

Do you want me to heave him out of here before the SA gets here?"

"Nah. We don't need the cell. Let him sleep. It's probably the best night he's had since the last time we picked him up."

"It's you're call, boss."

By the sweat beads forming on Ted's forehead and

the fact he'd used the john several times since his arrival to work at eight, Norris knew Ted was nervous over the outcome of the DNA testing. There was a fifty percent chance the man's head would be on the chopping block with the mayor if it wasn't a match.

He was glad he wasn't in the guy's shoes.

The front door to the station opened with its usual grazing of the planked floors that had been polished several hundred times since the small jail was built in 1902.

Norris had expected to see Jolene come through the door before the federal agent but it was SA Carter wearing another expensive suit and red tie who crossed the small lobby.

"Morning, Officer." Carter flashed his badge to Sandy Lehane who manned the front desk.

The smile Sandy flashed at the pretty boy made Norris shudder.

Of course, Carter ignored her and passed by Sandy without a second glance. He entered the police den and scanned the area while clipping his badge to his breast pocket. Finally, he met Norris' gaze. "Good morning, Chief."

Skimming over Carter's pristine pressed suit, Norris was glad he'd taken the time to change into a clean uniform that morning. He would lay down a large bet that Carter even looked official while he slept.

That image made him wonder if Jolene would choose to cuddle up to such a stuffy guy at night. He doubted it. She would prefer a lover who was confident, without pretension.

"Is it good?" The Fed seemed a lot more relaxed than he had yesterday. *Had Carter learned the DNA*

160

results already?

"So far. There's nothing more relaxing than waking up to the sound of the ocean. You're lucky to live here."

"Some days I feel that way, others not so much. Did you get the DNA results yet?"

Carter shook his head while checking his expensive watch's time against the time on the wall clock. "We should hear something soon though."

The front door of the station burst open and shouting covered up the familiar scraping noise. Mr. Burgess, shielding Mrs. Burgess from the onslaught of reporters snapping their pictures, pushed through the door. Exasperated, Mr. Burgess shoved it closed behind them, knocking a camera from one reporter's hand.

Norris and Ted helped keep the media on the other side of the door, while Sandy ushered Darren and Bonnie Burgess to a waiting area in the back corner, usually reserved for law breakers.

Norris ordered the reporters to remain on the public sidewalk and not block entrance to the building. He ignored their questions and returned inside where he ordered Sandy to arrest any of the media who tried to cross the threshold. Then he walked into the den and turned his glare toward Ted who had returned to his desk. Ted with his head bent down, was apparently trying not to be noticed. He didn't want the couple to know he was the one who had called them. He would wait until the DNA results were in and then either quickly disappear or strut over to the Burgess couple and get his ego stroked. Ted's actions had never been about the girl or the young couple and that pissed Norris off. Ted was the kind of officer he didn't want on his force.

The federal agent stood in front of the couple. They were so tired and anxious they didn't notice the bench they sat on had rails damaged over time by handcuffs. Their faces were trained on Carter and nothing would distract them from what he was saying.

Norris nodded to Carter to join him by Pickett's desk. "Why are they here?" He knew it was a stupid question the second he asked it.

"Apparently they saw me leave and followed me. They thought I was going to see the girl."

The couple sat on the edge of the bench and stared at them, desperate for answers to the hundred unanswered questions that had plagued them since their daughter was kidnapped. Their number one question: Had she been found?

The switchboard phone rang and everyone's attention jumped to Sandy. She answered the police line and then proceeded to radio Frank, who was on patrol, to swing by The Sea Crest Restaurant where a couple of kids were using the rear parking lot for skateboarding races.

There was never a lull during the summer season.

Norris exhaled a sigh of relief. There was enough going on that morning without having another real emergency drop in their laps.

From his position, Norris saw the front door open a third time. Jolene walked through it with concern tightening her brow. Today, she was dressed more businesslike instead of the casual vacation attire he'd seen her in since they met on the Hackman's boat. The off-white summer dress, covered with bold red flowers with black stems, accented her curves, and her black flat shoes showed she didn't need extra height to be

162

self-assured. Her poise shone through.

She pulled out her badge from her small purse and clipped it to the black belt at her waist.

Sandy gestured Jolene toward the den out back while she answered another call: "Cape James Police Department. How may I direct your call?"

Jolene stepped up to Carter and smiled as she entered the police den. "Good morning."

She briefly glanced at Norris and nodded but he noticed her smile lacked something. "Chief."

Norris' heart dropped and for an instant he felt second best. And that was a shock. After last night, he hadn't expected her to throw her arms around his neck and kiss him senseless like at the beach, but he hadn't expected her to act cold either. He thought he'd at least be the recipient of a mischievous smile, the one he adored.

"U.S. Marshal Martinez."

Jolene turned a shoulder to him and jerked her head toward the couple perched on the bench. The ones who studied them with undisguised hope. "I see we're all here."

"They followed me." Carter frowned. "I wasn't checking for a tail."

Norris smiled at her arched brow. She ignored him.

"Well, if Lia turns out to be theirs, we'll be front and center to a happy ending." Jolene's smile wavered. "I don't know about the two of you, but I don't get to see happy endings very often in my job. And even if she isn't their child… They'll have the attention of the media and it will give renewed life to their daughter's case. Either way, this will go viral."

"That's true." Carter's phone chimed and he pulled

it out of his breast pocket. He glanced at the screen and then looked up. "Do you mind if I use your office, Chief Stiles? My cell signal is spotty for some reason."

"Not at all." Norris stepped back, clearing the way for Carter.

Jolene stopped Carter by stepping in his path. "Is it the results?"

He shook his head. "It's my boss."

After Carter left them, she looked at Ted. "I take it he's the guy who started this mess."

He glanced Ted's way and saw the man's head was still bowed over a file. "How could you tell?"

"His body language speaks volumes. Whatever he's reading must be important."

Body language always told the truth, and right now Jolene was telling him she wasn't wanting to connect in a personal relationship with him. She kept her distance and the space between them felt iceberg cold. "I think it's his contact with the city."

Finally, a smile pulled at her lips and she chuckled softly.

Norris couldn't help his reaction. Her unexpected light throaty laugh made his heart do a free fall and he smiled back at her. "Can I get you some coffee? It's not Starbucks quality but it keeps us awake."

"Thanks." She followed him to the small cabinet stationed alongside the far wall.

Norris grabbed two fresh mugs from the shelf above a small sink and then filled them with coffee. "How do you take yours?"

"Black is fine."

"We have sugar and cream in the refrigerator." He didn't know any women who took their coffee black and pointed to the mini-unit under the counter.

"I'm used to drinking it black. It makes life easier when we're on stakeouts."

"Right," he responded. Her comment was meant to remind him of what she did for a living and why she was there. Yesterday's attraction for him seemed replaced with a level of detachment.

If the lady wanted to act as if last night hadn't happened, he wasn't going to let his disappointment show. He focused on the couple sitting across the room.

With an easy yard between them, Jolene and he stood silently sipping their coffee for a minute before they both spoke at the same time.

"When we have the results—" Norris said.

"What's the game plan after—" Jolene started.

Her cheeks flushed and he felt the attraction rising between them again.

"Sorry," she said. "What were you going to say?"

If Lia were the missing child, the case would remain open until they learned who had kidnapped her and since she was found in Carter's territory he would be assisting in the case.

He told Jolene about the checks and inquiries his officers had done and continued: "So, in the aftermath, if the results show she's not the Burgesses' daughter, I'm going to head out and check with local pre-schools and churches. I have my man who is on patrol, checking with other businesses when he can between calls."

"In the aftermath... I'm sorry. That sounded a little cold. We're talking about human beings with feelings here," she nodded toward Mr. and Mrs. Burgess.

"I didn't mean to sound cold." He peered down at her. If she'd learned anything about him in the last forty-some hours, she should know he was a compassionate man. He thought his actions—jumping into the ocean to save her; his handling of Ted; putting Lia in Martina's care instead of the system—had proven that already. "I want their nightmare to be over just as much as you do. I didn't mean to sound cold. My focus is on catching the son of bitch who put her in a little inflated raft on the ocean to die. I'm trying to figure out where else to go for a lead, because right now we have nothing."

He felt her watching him and gulped his coffee. Then he rinsed the mug off in the small sink. He cleared his throat and turned to face her. "Pickett will be back in at noon. He'll also do some checks."

"Checking with the pre-schools is a great move," Jolene said.

"I should've probably started there."

"You didn't because you felt no one in your community could do such a thing. You believed our perp had to be an outsider. The way people come and go on a daily bases here, you needed to scratch newcomers and transients from your suspect list first. You did the right thing concentrating your search on local businesses utilized by tourists. If I'd been in charge I would've done the same thing."

Norris saw sincerity in her eyes. The frustration he'd felt in his gut lessened. She was right. They'd learned a lot.

Over Jolene's head Norris saw Carter come around the corner. The agent's tight expression revealed the DNA results weren't what they had hoped for. Once again Carter would need to face Darren and Bonnie Burgess and give them heartbreaking news.

When the federal agent entered the room the couple stood. Their white-knuckled interlocked hands matched their stressed-out expressions. And the hope on their faces faded with each step Carter took toward them.

"I'll be right back," Norris said, knowing his voice sounded tight.

Jolene's soft fingers touched his wrist, stopping him in mid-step and his heart in mid-beat. "Where are you going?"

"I told Carter I was in this to the end. The end is now."

Beside him, Jolene drew in a deep breath.

Norris met Carter and together, shoulder to shoulder they faced the couple.

"Did you get the results?" Mr. Burgess asked before Agent Carter had time to open his mouth.

"Yes," Carter answered, sounding disheartened. "I'm sorry. Lia isn't your daughter"

Bonnie Burgess' heart-wrenching wail caught Norris off guard and he blinked and jerked back. Her face seemed to melt into a multi-layered mask of agony that bore no resemblance of the young, pretty mother. She crumpled as if the floorboards had given away under her and all three men lurched forward, hoping to stop her from hitting the floor.

Her fists wound into the material of Norris' shirt's sleeve and he felt the seams at his shoulder split.

He scooped her up.

Her heaving chest pressed against his thundering heart. Her questions and agonized moans hammered his eardrum, his soul.

A lump wedged in his throat and all Norris could do was look at the woman's husband Darren and reassure the man that he had her.

The man didn't look strong enough to hold her up at the moment so Norris placed Bonnie on the bench. Quickly, Darren took a seat next to her and cradled her protectively. He murmured reassurances that they weren't going to give up searching for their baby and they would find her.

Carter, looking helpless and angry, stepped closer and placed a hand on Darren's shoulder.

Norris glanced over his shoulder at Jolene and saw her put a finger to her eye.

He looked over at Ted. The seasoned officer's head had dropped to his chest and a tear trailed over his weathered cheek, landing on the contract lying on the desk.

At the expense of others, Ted had learned a hard lesson. He would pay dearly.

Norris encased his right fist in his left hand. He vowed this case would stay open until they found out who Lia's parents were and returned her to her family.

CHAPTER THIRTEEN

Why am I lighting a candle for her? I loathed her for what she did to me.

She gave me life, but I wasn't enough. Never enough.

She made me do unspeakable things, caused me so much pain.

When I think about her my nerves rattle and I feel weaker. Bile tickles the back of my throat and I choke it back, quietly, so as not to disturb the others behind me who pray for the sad lots life dealt them.

My hand shakes as I place the lighting stick down. Through my trousers, my fingers scrape the welts on my thighs and a sense of safety blankets my shoulders. My father is with me.

I was enough for him. He saved me. God, I worshipped him.

Going to see her was a mistake.

Because of her, I've sinned.

I ignore the searing of my flesh and quench her flame as if it was her life.

CHAPTER FOURTEEN

Norris pulled up to the curb next to Saint Paul's Church, their third stop.

Church bells rang loudly above their heads.

He shifted his SUV cruiser into park, set the brake. Through the windshield he stared up at the church's towering steeple where a golden cross glistened in the sunlight. Saint Paul's was the largest and oldest of the Cape James churches, sitting on a swell nearly two acres deep and wide and situated almost dead center in town. The foundation and walls, comprised of field stone, had been dug out of mainland Virginia fields and shipped across the Chesapeake. The old church undoubtedly served as a fortress at one time.

The modern fenced-in playground equipment off the basement was definitely a contrast to the historical building.

When he'd moved here last summer, he was surprised to learn the town of Cape James had four daycare centers and during the summer several of the churches ran day camps so the children's parents could take on the abundance of seasonal jobs.

The bells ended the melody on a lingering note and then proceeded to bong twelve times.

Jolene laced her purse strap over her shoulder and turned to Norris, her eyes hidden by her sunglasses. "They say the third time is the charm."

"Let's hope so." He cut the engine and immediately the car warmed. He unlatched his seatbelt, shouldered his door open and was slapped in the face by the humidity and heat. A bead of sweat quickly formed and rolled down his spine under his vest. He rushed around the car, hoping to find relief in the daycare's air conditioning.

His cruiser—with wide tires made to travel the beach, if necessary—sat higher and he intended to give Jolene his hand. But, by the time he rounded the rear quarter panel she was stretching to put toe to ground. Her dress slid up her thigh and he got a great view of her shapely legs. The sight of their full length aroused him yet again. His dick urged him to walk up to her, part them and…

He caught her eye over the rim of her glasses and quickly looked away and buried that image.

"Don't think I don't know you checked out at my legs."

"What do you mean?"

"Right." She glared up at him.

He closed the door behind her and mumbled, "You're the one who wore the dress."

She spun around on the sidewalk and he nearly walked into her.

"I didn't bring a pant suit with me. I'm on vacation remember."

"You brought a dress that shows off your legs," he said, trying to contain his chuckle.

"In case I decided to go out to dinner at a nice place."

He arched a brow. "Alone?"

"Yes. No. Maybe. What does it matter?" Her mouth snapped shut.

There was the answer to his question. He loved the

way her dark eyes lightened with sparks when she was goaded. "It doesn't."

She spun around, sending her purse to swing outward and hit her hip. She clutched it to her side and marched up the walkway to the church.

Norris followed, biting back a smile brought on by their bickering.

She stepped to the side and let him press the intercom button on the daycare's front door.

A voice from inside crackled a greeting: "Good afternoon. Can I help you?"

"It's Chief Stiles. I need some information on a child. Could you open the door and let us in?" He pushed his sunglasses to his head.

"Of course," the voice responded. "One minute."

The radio on his shoulder came to life the second a young woman pushed through the interior glass door and saw him. "Chief."

Norris put his finger up, indicating the girl should wait a second before opening the outside glass door. He stepped back a few steps on the sidewalk, squinting against the sun's rays and answered his deputy's call. "Go ahead, Larry."

He saw Jolene smile at the woman through the glass as he listened intently to what was being said by his officer.

"I stopped by Mercer's Grocery."

"Has Mercer seen the girl?"

"He's not sure. But, he has an employee who hasn't shown up for work. A Greg Hittler. He stocks shelves. Mercer's called the house several times and there's no answer."

Damn it was hot. Rivers of sweat ran down his

back. He stepped into the shade of a nearby tree and felt immediate relief. "Ok, so the guy quit without notice."

"Greg Hittler has a daughter about two years old. Mr. Mercer only saw her once or twice in the backseat of Hittler's car."

Norris looked at Jolene and noted her spine had stiffened.

"Go on," he said.

Jolene walked into the shade next to Norris.

He filled her in: "You told us we needed to consider all possibilities including a possible domestic violence gone bad, so I questioned the employees there. Greg's wife Cheryl works at Suntan Zone on the boardwalk. I hiked over there and guess what?"

He watched Jolene's lips curve up at the ends. "She hasn't shown up for work in a few days."

"You got it," Larry responded.

Inside the glass door, Norris saw the daycare worker anxiously looking back into the building and then at him. She was growing impatient. It was noon and she was probably in the middle of dispensing lunches.

He gave her a smile and held up his finger again which prompted a frown that time. "Get their address and head over there. Text it to me. We'll meet you there in twenty minutes."

"One more thing, Chief. The woman here at Suntan Zone stated Hittler's daughter went to St. Paul's Daycare."

Jolene's smile bloomed.

It felt great when a piece of the puzzle fell into place, but the ramifications, if Jolene's theory played out, could be heartbreaking.

"We're there now," Norris spoke into the mike. "Let

173

me show the girl's picture to the child care workers and then I'll meet you at the Hittler's home. Don't approach the house until I'm there. Understood?"

"Roger."

The mike went silent.

Jolene's shoulders lifted in a shrug. "It's better to know now than have someone report a God-awful smell in a few days."

He frowned, recalling the time during his rookie year when a man from the gas company was checking the meters. He'd noticed a foul smell coming from inside an older home via an open window in the Westover area. He'd called 911. Norris and his partner had found an elderly man dead in his Norfolk home during a scorching five-day heat wave in August. In the heat, flies already inhabited the body and there were signs of rodent nibbles. It was a memory he'd buried deep and he shook it back into place.

The neighbors who normally checked on the old man had gone away on vacation for a week. The medical examiner was removing the body from the home when they'd arrived. It was a heartbreaking scene—so yeah, Jolene was right. It was better to know now, especially since the forecast predicted temperatures in the mid-nineties all week.

Norris heard the lock click. The woman inside opened the door for them. He introduced himself and Jolene and then explained why they were there. Betty Morgan was the manager of the daycare so she knew all forty-five children who attended it.

Jolene had peeled off her sunglasses. With her free hand, she held her cell phone. She pulled up a picture of Lia and held it out for Ms. Morgan to view. "Is this child one of your charges?"

It was a different photo than the one she'd sent to him yesterday. In this one Lia was sitting on top of the slide in Martina's backyard, laughing as if she were on top of the world.

"Is she the daughter of Greg and Cheryl Hittler?" Norris asked.

Ms. Morgan's gaze jumped from the picture to him. "The answer to both of your questions is no. Greg and Cheryl's daughter does attend school here, but that's not her. Their daughter Skye is in our toddler class. She's having lunch right now." Morgan's hand covered her heart. "Is everything okay with Gary and Cheryl? They haven't been in an accident, have they?"

Jolene looked at Norris.

Norris looked back to the woman. "No. I'm sure they're fine. Their employers were worried. Neither of them were at work today or yesterday and they didn't answer any calls." He hated white lies, but Lia's case apparently had nothing to do with the Hittlers and he didn't want Ms. Morgan to draw unfounded conclusions.

"Oh." Ms. Morgan sighed her relief and smiled. "That's because a good friend of Cheryl's passed away. She lives in Maryland. Or lived in Maryland. Skye is staying with Greg's sister for a few days while they're away for the services."

"Do you know Greg and Cheryl personally?" Jolene asked, while she slipped her phone into her purse.

"I do. Ever since we were in elementary school together. They're a nice couple. Great parents." She pointed at Jolene's phone. "Why would you need to speak to them about her? Is she the girl that was found floating on the ocean? I read about it in the papers. Just heart-breaking."

"Thank you for your time," Norris said.

"But is she the one?"

"Sorry. We're not at liberty to say," Norris responded. "Again, thank you."

He held the door open for Jolene. She quickly skirted her way past him. Her soft scent momentarily brought back last night when she'd pulled him to her for another kiss.

"I assure you, Cheryl and Greg are good people," Ms. Morgan was saying behind his back. "I'm sure they have nothing to do with whatever happened to that girl."

"Thank you for your help." Norris dipped his head again and then pushed the door closed.

Once they reached the main sidewalk, Jolene settled her sunglasses back on her nose and turned to him. "Why do people always assume they know someone when they can't possibly? No one ever knows what goes on behind closed doors or in someone's mind?"

Norris didn't say anything, instead he studied Jolene and wondered who'd hurt her.

"What's next?" she asked, seemingly uncomfortable under his scrutiny.

His phone buzzed and he looked at the scene. "The Hittler's address is 87 Seaweed Lane. I'll tell Larry to forget about meeting at their house and then we'll keep searching."

He reached for the mike on his shoulder and Jolene stopped him by stroking her warm fingertips across his wrist.

"Doesn't it strike you funny that neither Greg's nor

Cheryl's boss mentioned a friend's death? Your deputy did say they simply hadn't shown up for work, right?"

"Yeah, he did."

"Maybe there really wasn't a death. Maybe they left town for another reason."

He rubbed the back of his neck, feeling a bit embarrassed. Jolene was sharp. He was so focused on this case he'd closed his eyes to part of the world around him. Something he always warned his staff not to do. His mentor had once advised him that a good cop stayed alive because he remained aware of his surroundings at all times.

"If they left town," he said, moving toward his car. Jolene walked beside him.

Drugs were a problem year round, but during the summer a small-time supplier in this area could acquire a huge bankroll catering to the party crowd. *Could the couple be on a drug run?*

"I'll have Larry poke around a little at the Hittlers' house and ask the neighbors about Cheryl and Greg. I don't think they're involved with Lia but I'll have Larry show Lia's picture around the neighborhood too. In the meantime, we'll finish checking the daycares. If we don't find anything, four o'clock is the deadline for the local evening news broadcast. We'll release Lia's picture to the public then. I have a local station and the local papers meeting us at the station at three-thirty."

"Your station will be swamped with calls for at least twenty-four hours once her picture is released." Jolene reached to open the passenger door of his sedan but he grabbed the latch first and held it open for her.

"I've made arrangements to have a few part-time officers from neighboring districts help out with phone

177

calls for the next forty-eight hours." He watched Jolene lift her legs into the vehicle then blinked to refocus. "Their forces are also strapped with the influx of summer tourists but a few officers were willing to forgo a second day off to help us out. Hopefully they never have a scenario where we'll need to return the favor, but if they do, we'll be there."

"I hear you."

CHAPTER FIFTEEN

I lift my face to the sun and expand my lungs with the sea breeze. I love bike riding. Even more than walking. I think it's the most refreshing form of travel. And in a seaside town I'm invisible among the many.

Chi-ching sounds behind me and I move to the right and allow a family of five to ride by. I laugh at the father who tries to impress his following by riding without holding on to the bike handles. The boardwalk is too uneven for the trick, however. He nearly loses his balance and awkwardly gains control before he tumbles.

I shake my head at his stupidity but I laugh just the same and slow down, watching the children lift their hands from their bike handles for a quick second. They tried to accomplish what their father hadn't been able to do.

What is it about the sea air that brings out the child in everyone? It seems everyone rents bikes when they stay in Cape James. It isn't a cheap pastime but for twenty dollars an hour they relive part of their childhood. They love it and I love that they do. I can cruise any street while riding my vintage 1970 Schwinn five-speed without turning heads. No one notices me and that's so freeing.

I peddle faster and zoom by the family of five.

A minute later, a gust carrying an icy chill and particles of sand pelts my uncovered arms and I slow my pace.

Placing the girl on the water, the way Jochebed,

Moses' mother, had done with him, had been the right thing to do. The child was saved from serving a demon for a lifetime, as I had hoped.

Even if she had died she'd be better off.

Lightening flashes over the gray sea off to my right.

I draw another long, deep breath and inhale the storm heading toward shore.

It's time to head home. There is still work to be done. I need to deal with the one who kidnapped the child in the first place.

Only then will I truly be free.

CHAPTER SIXTEEN

A weather front headed out to sea ran up the eastern seaboard instead, hit a low-pressure area at two p.m. and shifted suddenly, taking an easterly turn. By three-thirty p.m. it was directly over Cape James and swept onto shore with wild gusts and driving rain. The news conference planned for on the courthouse steps was now a washout. Norris had no choice but to move it down the block into the police station. The small lobby of the Cape James Police Station quickly became a zoo gone mad.

Standing in the den with Jolene by his side, Norris watched Ted try to control the situation while local television, radio and newspaper personnel shook off their rain-soaked slickers and battled for floor space. The mayor and city council had suspended their decision on Ted's disciplinary actions until next week because of the shortage of manpower.

Today the mayor and some council members stood behind the railing off to the side watching the scene unfold.

Sandy and Pickett scrambled to roll up every industrial carpet they had in the place and laid them out in the lobby to prevent people from slipping on the slick wood floor. They even borrowed a couple of mats from the pizza shop across the street. Meanwhile a borrowed 911 operator from Newport helped with incoming calls.

The noise level was almost deafening and didn't help ease the tension building in his forehead. Norris turned his back to the scene and drew a deep breath. He hated being in front of the cameras. This part of the job he'd gladly hand off to Ted who seemed to enjoy acting as the delegate for the Cape James force. But Ted wasn't the one in charge of this case and he wasn't the one the news people wanted information from. They wanted him, the chief.

He exhaled slowly.

"You look very"—Jolene leaned against the kitchen counter, holding a warm cup of tea and flashed him a smile—"official."

He'd seen her nervous swallow and wondered if "official" was the word she had intended to say. *Had she meant to say something more personal?* For a second, thinking she admired what she saw took his mind off the sea of vultures pounding the walls of his gut.

"You can say it. I look as if I'm about to face a firing squad."

She laughed. "You'll do fine."

"You must be used to this kind of thing?" He lifted his chin, stretching his neck, trying to get some air past the fastened button and tie circling his neck like a noose. He stared down at her. "I don't have a lot of details to give them."

The reporters who could see them watched Norris and Jolene with speculative glances.

Mark Branka, wearing an expensive looking raincoat over his business suit, slipped in through the front door on the tail of yet another cameraman. He wore a stylish pair of the L sneakers that he sold as part of the cycling enthusiasts' line. Probably afraid to get his Italian loafers wet.

Norris watched the man make a beeline toward the mayor and council members. Everyone wanted to know firsthand what Norris was about to share.

"You're not providing them with answers." Jolene drew his attention again. "You're stating the facts as you know them and are asking the public for help in gathering further leads."

"We haven't had any leads yet." He frowned.

"We've had possibilities and checked them out."

She was right, but... "True enough. Still, that won't stop them from asking questions I don't have answers for."

"Give them the normal lines."

"What are those?" He'd never had to do this before.

Laying a hand on his arm, she smiled. "Tell them, because this is an on-going investigation, you cannot share details of the case. At this time, you're asking for help in pinpointing where the child might've been sighted in the area and with whom."

Ted rushed into the den. "They're ready for you, Chief."

He nodded to Ted and then inhaled again. "The sooner I get this over, the sooner I can get back to work."

"It's part of the job," Ted reminded him.

"You'll do fine." Jolene's eyes shifted to the lobby.

He turned and saw that Carter had entered the lobby—the last person he wanted to witness his on-camera interview debut. "What's he doing here? I thought he left this morning after the results came in."

Jolene shrugged. "I did too."

Carter kept a low profile, skirted the media and swiftly made his way to the den.

"SA Carter." Jolene set her cup down and took the lead. "We thought you headed home this morning."

He pulled a handkerchief from inside his breast pocket and dabbed the rain from his face and then smoothed the cloth back over his hair. "I decided to stay a day or two in case you needed some help."

Norris didn't like the way the Fed's eyes lingered on Jolene as he spoke.

"We'll be fine," Norris stated flatly. "Shouldn't you be working the Burgess case?"

"I can work from anywhere." He slipped out of his coat and hung it over the back of a plastic chair edging the wall. "Man, the skies opened up as if someone unzipped the clouds."

"Would you like some hot coffee?" Jolene offered.

"Yeah, help yourself. To coffee," Norris added.

"Thanks, I will."

Jolene shot Norris a warning glance before she turned.

Norris didn't care for the way the Fed watched Jolene pour his drink.

"Chief," Ted interrupted him, touching his shoulder and bobbing his head toward the media. "We've got to do this now if they're going to meet their deadlines."

"All right."

The questions started the moment Norris walked into the lobby. He ignored the cries for information until he stood behind the podium Pickett had borrowed from the mayor's office. He waited until the group grew quiet before he started with the short speech he'd mentally prepared. He laid out the facts he knew: where, when and by whom Lia had been found. He conveyed her condition and the fact that so far no one had come forward to claim her. He also quickly revealed the DNA test results which eliminated Lia as the missing child of a northern Virginia family whose child had gone missing over a year ago. When he was through, hands shot up and questions flew from many directions. He put up his hands and quieted the small but hungry crowd. "One question at a time. Jones, you're first."

"Where is the girl now?" the journalist from the *Cape James Record* asked.

"In a safe location." He pointed to the next reporter.

"Has the FBI been notified?"

"Special Agent Carter of the FBI was contacted when it was thought the child could be the missing Burgess girl." There was no need not to use Darren and Bonnie Burgesses' names. They had already spoken to reporters this morning before leaving Cape James.

"Is he still working the case?"

"Since we don't know if the child has crossed state lines, I remain in charge of the case, but Federal agencies have offered their help."

"What are they doing?" Another reporter called out.

"They're using their resources to check DNA on all open cases of children abducted in the last two years."

"Two. Is that how old the child is?" another reporter asked.

"We believe so."

"You said agencies," another newsperson shouted. "What agency besides the FBI are involved?"

He glanced at Jolene. She and Carter had followed him as far as the den's archway. Now they stood behind Ted who guarded the den's entry with his feet spread and his arms folded across his burly chest. Norris wasn't sure Jolene wanted to be identified as part of the team working the case. The reporters had seen her there this morning and now she stood only a few feet away. There was no doubt some had questioned her part in all this. His questioning gaze held hers.

She dipped her head slightly, giving him permission to acknowledge her involvement.

"U.S. Marshal Martinez has been immersed with the investigation from the start since she was the one who found and rescued the girl on the ocean."

Heads turned toward Jolene and Carter, and a few cameras clicked. Jolene brushed a hand through her hair and leaned back against the wall, using Carter as a shield from the cameras.

It seemed she didn't want her picture taken and again he wondered what her job function was with the U.S. Marshals.

Norris held up a large picture of Lia and drew everyone's attention back to him with his next statement. "At this time we're not certain if the child is missing or if her guardians are the ones who are missing."

"Do you think that's the reason they haven't come forward?"

"Are you thinking foul play?" another asked.

"How did the girl get to be floating on the ocean?"

The questions came at him like rapid fire. Norris put up his hands, refusing to say anything until the group quieted. "We need to look at all possibilities and that is why we're asking for the public's help."

He held up Lia's picture again and told the group: "We need to know if anyone knows this little girl or has seen her in the area this week. If you have, please call this hotline number: 555-757-0000."

Five minutes later, the bright lights from the cameras clicked off and Norris stepped down from the makeshift stage. Hopefully they would receive good intel from this circus.

The local T.V. news station reporters and their cameramen packed up in record time, hoping to edit their video in time for the five o'clock news. In this digital age, they'd make it.

Norris told Sandy to tell the others to prepare for calls.

After answering a few more questions for the local paper, he walked back into the den to find Carter helping Jolene into her rain coat. Jolene smiled at him. So did Carter, but his smile was smug.

"You did great, Chief. You were firm and showed you cared," Jolene said, slipping her arm into a sleeve.

She called him "Chief," not Norris which was a definite sign their relationship had taken a step backward.

"Where are you going?" He wanted to tell Carter to move away from Jolene but he didn't have that right.

"We thought we'd have an early dinner and share war stories." Carter shrugged into his own overcoat.

What the hell? They were leaving just when there might be a break in the case? Norris' molars gnashed together and then he reminded himself Lia's case wasn't theirs. Certainly not Carter's. It was his. And until that moment, he'd thought Jolene considered herself his partner.

Was this the way she worked? Both sides.

"Do you want to join us? We're going across the street to the pizza shop," Jolene said.

"Nah. I'm going to stay here and get ready to follow up on calls."

She pulled her hood over her head and seemed to disappear inside the material. Her dark pixie eyes stared up at him and Norris couldn't help thinking she was damn cute. Despite his anger, he wanted to tell her not to leave with Carter. Better yet, he wanted her to decide that herself…

"How's Lia?" he asked once again hoping she'd choose to stay with him. After getting to know her, and kissing her, he wanted her for himself… "Have you checked on her?" he said, stalling.

Her eyes narrowed to slits. She tilted her head to the side and studied him for a second before replying. "I spoke to Martina when we came back, remember? Everything is fine. Princess Lia and Princess Clara are probably having their milk, tea and cookies right now."

"Right." Of course, he knew she'd checked on Lia and that Jolene felt responsible for the little girl.

"Is there a back door we could use?" Carter asked, stepping up alongside Jolene.

He stood too close and Norris wanted to act the caveman and push him away from Jolene.

"It's down the hall. Code to disable the alarm is 898," he replied soft enough for their ears only, even though Pickett was the only other one in the den at the moment.

"Shall we go?" Carter clasped Jolene's elbow and nudged her toward the hallway.

Norris' molars ground.

"You sure you won't come?" Jolene walked backwards while Carter continued to lead her.

Wearing a frustrated frown, she pulled away from

Carter's grasp and turned to Norris. Her hand rested on the wall beside her and her index finger tapped the drywall. "We only had a Donnie's dog before we started checking daycares."

He shook his head. "I'm not hungry."

She trapped her bottom lip between her teeth. "I'll bring you something anyway. A cheese steak?"

The small smile she gave him was meant to reassure him that there was something between them that the Federal agent wouldn't learn.

His heart did a skip. "Thanks."

Jolene held his gaze for a second before she turned and followed Carter down the hall.

His hands curled into fists as he stared at the empty spot where Jolene disappeared from sight.

Why did Norris feel as if he'd lived this moment before?

Because he had.

He closed his eyes and inhaled deeply, feeling the familiar burn of heartache in his chest. He swore he'd never do this to himself again... He hadn't been enough for Ella, his ex-fiancée, and apparently he wasn't all that Jolene needed either.

He had to forget about her. Once this case was solved she'd be gone from his life and his world would be righted. Everything back in place, including the loneliness.

Sandy came up behind him and stood by his side. "You know what, Chief?"

"I have no time for games today," he said more gruffly then he'd intended. "Sorry. What?"

She jutted her chin toward the hallway. "That woman likes you. A lot. I think you should go for it."

He felt his ears grow warm. Did everyone see what he felt when he looked at Jolene? He'd thought he had kept up a good front around others. If so, maybe he was kidding himself about a lot of things. Curiosity got the better of him.

He leaned toward Sandy, keeping a watchful eye out for any of his staff. "I don't think so."

Sandy smiled up at him. "Take it from another woman. She's hot for you."

His chuckle reflected the angst churning in his gut. "If she was, why'd she leave with the Fed?"

"Maybe she wanted you to stop her. Women like to know how they stand, just like you guys do. Have you told her?"

"I thought I had."

Sandy's hazel eyes twinkled with delight. "Maybe it was the way you said it. We all hear things differently you know."

Norris scratched the whiskers lining his jaw.

Sandy walked away, leaving him standing there thinking. Maybe he and Jolene needed to talk about what happened between them last night. And about a lot more.

Thirty minutes after Jolene and Carter exited the station, the lobby was completely clear. The storm had swiftly moved inland and the sky was cloudless and bright. He'd seen sunlight dancing off the puddles on the sidewalk outside when he helped Ted move the makeshift stage and podium to the side wall. Pickett finished rolling up the carpets and began to mop the floors.

Behind him Sandy poured coffee for the emergency operator who was on loan for the next twenty-four

190

hours. Norris kept his mind on putting his house back in order and didn't allow it to wander across the street to the pizza shop. His emotions battled back and forth. He and Jolene were only acquaintances who had kissed. Once. He had no rational reason to feel betrayed by her having dinner with a fellow law enforcement officer, but he did.

As she'd stood in the hall's entry, she'd looked at him as if she waited for him to say something. *Had she wanted him to ask her not to go with Carter? Or was he wishing that was what she wanted?*

It didn't matter. She'd gone.

Ten minutes after five o'clock the six phones lines rang non-stop for thirty minutes. He had no time to think about Jolene. He rolled up his sleeves and helped his team take down the information pouring in. The fifteen so-called witnesses who called within the first thirty minutes placed Lia all over Cape James and surrounding counties. They'd also seen her with families of various sizes. Some saw her with a woman and some saw her with a man. Some reported the lone male to be Caucasian while one reported him to be an African American male who could be Sammy Davis Jr's twin. The woman was always described as white, tall with long straight, auburn hair.

Pickett quickly punched all the information into a spreadsheet and within minutes connections became clear.

***

"Here's the cheese steak you ordered." The waitress set the package down on the edge of the table and cleared Jolene's empty plate from in front of her. "How was your chef's salad?"

Jolene wiped the corners of her mouth and then placed her folded napkin in her lap. "Very good. Thank you."

The paper bag in front of her contained the sandwich. It was warm under her fingers. The delicious beefy aroma filled her nostrils and her mouth watered despite the fact she was full.

"Are you having dessert today?" the young girl asked as if they were regular customers.

"I don't think so." Jolene patted her stomach.

"None for me." Carter handed the waitress his empty platter, flashing her a genuine smile.

The girl thanked them and placed their bill on the table.

When the waitress walked away Carter's smile faded and he flattened his spine against the cushions of the booth. Jolene suspected the friendly conversation they'd shared over dinner was history and Carter was finally going to tell her the real reason he'd asked her to join him for a meal.

"You like the guy, don't you?"

The federal agent had eaten pasta in clam sauce and now had two spots of oil marking his red tie. Jolene thought to tell him his perfect image was ruined but decided to let it go.

"Who?" She knew who he referred to but kept her expression blank.

He jutted his chin toward the brown bag.

"Oh. Chief Stiles? He's okay." She pursed her lips

192

for a second and casually shrugged. "He's passionate about his job and I respect him for that."

"He might be passionate but"—Carter glanced at the other customers sitting nearby and then leaned forward—"I think he's in over his head with this case."

"I disagree. I think he's handling everything well." Under the table she refolded her napkin.

"Give me a break, Martinez. It's been over forty-eight hours since you found the girl and he hasn't dug up any solid leads."

"We've learned who she is not. The delay with the Burgesses' case put the investigation behind only slightly. He and his team continued to eliminate possibilities while waiting for the DNA results."

"I don't hold much stock in his team." Carter balled up his napkin and tossed it on the table between them. "The incident was caused by Stiles' own man."

"Norris inherited the guy," Jolene responded quickly, feeling a need to stand up for Norris.

Carter chuckled. "You're defending him."

"I'm stating facts." Carter was trying to get her to take sides and that pissed her off. They were all on the same team, damn it. She crossed her forearms in front of her on the table and leaned forward. "Look if you have something to say, say it."

"I don't want to see your career take a hit because you hitched your wagon to this local yokel."

She chuckled and smiled sweetly. "I'm touched you're concern about my career." Then she cocked her head to the side. "When did we get so close, by the way?"

"I'm simply offering professional advice."

"Again, thank you for your concern but I think my

career is on track and not in danger." She plucked the bill the from table. "Look. This was... Well, I'm not sure what this was. Informative. Unnecessary. I'm going to get back over there and help with calls. Dinner is on me. Including the tip." She slid from the booth and grabbed her coat and purse.

Carter smiled up at her. "I take it I don't need to hang around any longer?"

She held her tongue and didn't tell him to piss off. Instead she pulled a crisp fifty from her wallet. "If we need anything from the FBI we'll contact you. Stiles has your number."

Jolene handed the waitress the bill and cash on her way out the door. Cradling the twelve-inch sandwich and her rain jacket in the crook of her arm she stepped out into the sunlight. The rain seemed to wash away the grime and the world sparkled. She checked traffic before she crossed the street. The moment she entered the station she knew something was up. Excitement sizzled in the air.

The phone rang and the temporary operator answered it and put it on hold and then answered the next call and the next.

Jolene walked into the police den and saw Norris flanked by Sandy and Ted. The trio looked over Pickett's head and stared at Pickett's computer monitor.

Norris' expression was that of hunter who'd caught a scent. "What's going on?" he asked.

The phone on the next desk rang and Sandy left Norris' side to answer it.

Jolene entered the vacated space and immediately her body responded to Norris' closeness. Carter was absolutely right. She liked Norris. A lot. She stiffened her spine and fought the urge to lean toward him.

Norris' gaze met hers. "One of the local television stations made their five o'clock deadline. We immediately had a boatload of calls. Pickett's putting the information into a spreadsheet and something interesting is showing up."

"What?"

"Most of the sightings placed Lia with a white female and are concentrated in this area." He pointed to a large map of Cape James stapled to a nearby free-standing bulletin board. Blue push pins were all over it. With a red marker, Norris made a large circle in the northeast section of the town where most of the pins had been placed. "We've had how many calls?"

"Twenty-two," Pickett responded, taking the slip of paper Sandy handed him. "Twenty-three with this one."

"That one places her with a family near the lighthouse," Sandy stated, hooking her right thumb into the loop of her belt. "In the same area."

Norris looked at Jolene while he stabbed the map with a push pin. "Twelve of those calls, put her here. Eight of them are with a white woman with long auburn hair."

The team's excitement seemed to seep into her bones and Jolene's pulse picked up. "And the other four?"

"Two with families and two with a lone white male," Norris replied.

The phone on Pickett's desk rang. This time Ted took the call.

Jolene laid the sandwich she brought for Norris down on the corner of Pickett's desk and flung her jacket and purse on the hardback chair in front of it. She crossed to the board. "That's mainly a residential area. Correct?"

"Correct. There are no hotels," Sandy responded, stepping up to Jolene's side and also studying the map.

"So she probably belongs to someone local." Jolene rubbed her wrist above her charm bracelet as she thought about that. "Why haven't they reported her missing?" She traced a finger over the map, squinting at the street names and then she looked at Norris. "Wasn't Seaweed Lane the address for Greg and Cheryl Hittler?"

"It is, but we've ruled them out," Norris said flatly, looking down at her.

His icy stare told her if she'd stayed behind instead of leaving with Carter she would've known the reason earlier and there would be no need for him to explain to her now. However, she had gone. *Had that been a mistake?* She didn't think so. Her little conversation with the federal agent had convinced Carter to keep his nose out of the case unless he was asked to help.

"What did you find out about them?"

"Larry called in while you were out to dinner."

She caught the sarcasm in his tone and thought it best if she ignored it. "And?"

"He caught up with them outside their house. They'd just returned home and were getting out of their car. It seems Cheryl had won a two-night stay at an Atlantic City resort from some local radio station. They had proof of their excursion, a copy of their bar bill. Drinks hadn't been included in the package. They had to take the nights offered or lose them, so they skipped out on work."

She arched a brow. "They weren't afraid of losing

the jobs?"

"This time of year, employers are desperate for help," Ted injected, handing Pickett another note. "They'll have to plead a little but in the end they'll keep their jobs."

Jolene shook her head and then looked at Pickett. "At least it wasn't a drug run."

"True enough." Norris looked at Ted. "What did you get?"

Ted frowned. "A caller placed Lia with a family staying at the White Sands Hotel today."

"Well, we know that isn't true." Sandy stuck her pencil into her hair and scanned a notepad she held.

Jolene walked over to Pickett. "Do we have any other similarities?"

"I'm putting in everything I can, including a breakdown of physical descriptions of the people she's been sighted with. It's going to take awhile before I have it all in. We're coming up on six o'clock in fifteen minutes. The second airing of the local news."

Norris glanced at the clock and then walked over and poured a cup of coffee.

She grabbed the steak sandwich and followed him. "You better eat this while you have time. It's still warm."

"What do I owe you?" He held up the pot, asking if she wanted coffee.

She shook her head. "Nothing."

"Thanks." He replaced the pot and then took the sandwich from her. Carrying his coffee and meal he headed into his office.

He didn't ask her to follow him but she did anyway. *Was he upset she'd gone to dinner with Carter?* She guessed that in his mind, her and Carter, both federal agents, having dinner together meant a plot to overthrow his authority. He'd be right of course. Carter had meant to gain her support in taking over the case. If they were going to work together Norris had to trust her to have his back.

She dropped onto the cushioned chair in front of his desk and watched him unwrap the steak. He took a healthy bite and she silently scanned the room. There was not one personal item except for one of his shirts hanging on a hook near the door. No accolades or certificates hung on the wall behind his desk and no framed pictures of loved ones or pets anywhere. Not even a personal mug. The mug he drank from had the Cape James logo on it. She'd seen a dozen others like it in the cabinet above the coffee system.

If Norris decided to pick up and leave this job the next chief could move right in which made her wonder what his future plans were. He had no family here. Maybe this job was a stepping stone to a bigger opportunity and that was why he was guarding his ground on this case.

After devouring more than half the sub Norris looked at her. "Where's Carter?"

She leaned back in the chair and crossed her ankles. "He's probably checking out as we speak?"

"What made him change his mind?" Norris took another bite and then grabbed a second napkin from inside the bag and wiped the sauce from the corners of his mouth.

"I assured him we had everything under control."

His hand stopped in midair. His slanted eyes spoke volumes about what was speeding through his mind:

198

satisfaction, relief and by the slight curl of his lips—smugness. "*We*, huh?"

She steepled her fingers together and her bracelet slid down her arm. "I *am* part of your team, aren't I?"

Norris' smile widened. "I was hoping I could count on you. Thanks again for the meal."

Despite the words, Jolene knew the real reason he felt better. "You're welcome."

Norris looked up at the wall clock and dropped the rest of his sandwich on the tinfoil and rolled it up into a garbage ball. He grabbed the bag and dropped it in the trash bin at the side of his desk. "It's six. They're going to need help taking calls."

"I can man Pickett's phone while he keeps building the data," she offered, standing up.

"Okay."

Jolene had made it to the doorway when he stopped her.

"Hey."

She turned back to him.

"After the next round of calls, Ted and I and are going out to talk to the callers who've agreed to speak to us further."

"Do you mind if I ride along with you?"

"I was hoping you'd want to."

Jolene smiled and then let Norris handle whatever was on his desk that drew his attention.

Frank Morell, the last member of Norris' team, walked in the door with his wife Pat who supervised a suicide hotline. While Frank logged in and then immediately headed out to assist Larry at the scene of a car accident Sandy set Pat up beside her to answer calls.

For the next hour, they worked feverishly answering

the phones and collecting information. Each information note, landed on Norris' desk before being handed off to her for review and then to Pickett to pull the date and insert it. Norris had been right to hold off on issuing Lia's picture to the press. The information they'd been able to gather in the last day and half helped them weed out the crackpots who were only trying to get their names in the news.

At seven-thirty Norris came out of his office and walked over to stand behind Pickett. From there he studied the new pins in the map.

"We had forty calls," Jolene said, walking up to him. "Eight we tossed out—attention junkies."

"We'll have a lot more of those tomorrow when the morning papers hit the stands. Everyone who needs money for their next meal or fix will be looking to earn a reward."

"The way of the world," Pickett mumbled, reading the note. He then proceeded to tap on the keys.

A cell phone chimed in the room.

"Someone's phone is ringing." Sandy turned her head to locate where the muffled sound came from."

"That's mine." Jolene circled Pickett's desk. She shifted her coat off her purse and dug inside to retrieve her cell. She looked at Norris. "It's Martina."

"Use my office."

She put her finger to her left ear while she listened with her right. "Hey, sis."

"Jolene." Martina's voice shook.

CHAPTER SEVENTEEN

Jolene's heart broke while she listened to Martina. She looked up and saw that Norris watched her with concern. "Don't worry. I'll be right there."

"Is Lia okay?" Norris asked, coming up to stand in front of her.

Jolene fought the urge to step closer to him, hoping he'd wrap his strong arms around her if she did so. "She's fine. Simon was in a car accident and was taken by ambulance to the hospital. Martina has been calling my cell for over an hour."

Her teeth ground together. *Why hadn't she clipped the phone to her belt instead of leaving it in her purse?* She never kept her phone in her purse. She was an idiot.

Norris seemed to know she needed some reassurance that her brother-in-law would be okay.

She fidgeted, shifting her weight to her other foot. She hadn't depended on anyone in years. Connecting with his gaze, she wondered what it was about Norris that made her want to be comforted by him, and him only.

Norris touched her hand, in concern. "Is Martina with him?" She ducked her head and ran her tongue over her lips, choking back the emotions clawing their way up her throat. "Yes. He was lucky. A car ran a red light and hit his truck in the front quarter panel. He has a broken ankle and is going into surgery now. She tried calling me, but I didn't answer. She didn't know what to do with Lia. She had no choice. Their neighbor came over immediately and stayed with the children until my mother could get there."

Jolene skimmed her hand through her short hair. "This is not good. Lia is in the care of someone else."

Norris' warm hands gripped her by the upper shoulders. "It's okay. I'm sure Martina wouldn't leave Lia in the care of someone who wasn't responsible."

"You don't understand. I'm fine with Mrs. Evans. She is a sweet retired school teacher. But now, Lia is with my mother." She pulled out of Norris' hold and stalked around him faster than a barrel racer could round a barrel.

"I've got to go." She grabbed her purse and coat and spun around. "I'm sorry."

"It's okay. I'd drive you but…"

"I understand," she said.

Norris nodded. Concern still tightened his features.

"I'll check in with you later and let you know if we learn anything new."

"I hate how divided I feel —"

He cut her off. "I understand priorities. Go."

His words seemed to ease Jolene's angst until she maneuvered her car from the parking spot and drove toward Martina's home where she knew after years of estrangement she'd have to face her mother.

CHAPTER EIGHTEEN

Lia's face appears on the television screen.

Immediately I feel the wrath directed at me, coiling to attack. I bend over to protect myself.

"You son of a bitch. How could you?"

I squeeze my eyes closed so tightly my teeth gnash together and my cheeks become massive pillows of anger, sealing them. I fight against the wild anger building up inside of me. I won't lose control of the world again. Today was precious. I felt the sun on my face without a worry in the world. I won't go back into the nightmare I lived before.

"How could you throw Lia away as if she were trash?"

The words echoed against the walls, and though I knew no one could hear them, I feared that possibility.

"I can't continue to live this way. I'd rather die."

"Will you stop!" I scream, my hands curl into fists and I press them against my throbbing temples. "You know why."

"She was mine."

I spin around and spit in the devil's face. "She was not yours. She was never yours. You robbed Lia of her mother's love."

"I'm her mother."

"Lair." I quickly pick up the leather flogger I keep handy next to the bed. The smooth leather crosses my palm and I feel my body quake. Rebelliously, I raise the whip above my head.

Crack!

"Don't. Please stop."

I hate the sound of leather striking skin. It makes me wince. Blood laces the inside of my mouth as I proceed to drive my point home. With each whack, I feel my control flourish. I continue to act out my madness until finally, breathless, I can raise my chin and look down my nose defiantly. "I did what I had to do. I did what was right."

I turn a deaf ear to the sobs and leave the room.

CHAPTER NINETEEN

Jolene slipped through the front door and froze inside the Gomez living room. *What the fuck?* she mouthed silently. She squeezed her eyes shut, not believing what she saw. Joan Martinez, her mother, was actually in the kitchen cooking. Her mother's idea of mastering culinary skills had always been to crack an egg and scramble it so it didn't matter if the yolk broke or not before it hit the pan.

She studied the woman from whom she'd inherited her short statue. *Had Papa somehow figured out a way to create a cyborg that looked like his wife of fifty years?*

Side-stepping into the hallway, Jolene watched her mother stir then chop and then turn back to the glass-top stove and stir again. If her olfactory neurons were correct, her mother prepared a Mexican feast of shredded chicken tacos and Spanish rice. The scene was literally the *Twilight Zone*.

And the topper was this: The four older of the seven children Joan had been put in charge of were seated at the dining room table playing a board game while Sofia, Clara and Lia played with dolls in front of the television in the family room.

Un-freakin'-believable.

"Jolene. You're here. Can you lend me a hand?" Joan Martinez asked over her shoulder. "It's already going on eight o'clock."

Jolene studied her mother's cool gaze. Her father

always said her mother's eyes were the color of the Caribbean Sea surrounding Paradise Island—where they'd met. And, as peaceful as when a storm wasn't brewing there. And turning to cold gray when one was.

Over the years, Jolene recalled her mother's eyes were gray most of the time. She raised her chin and marched into the battle zone.

"These children have to be starving," Joan said. "It's not good for their digestive systems to eat so close to their bedtime. Maybe we should let them stay up later."

Jolene waved and smiled at her nieces and nephews who didn't seem to mind waiting for dinner. She dropped her coat and purse on one of the stools in front of the kitchen island then leaned against the counter and faced her nemesis. "Hello to you too, Joan."

The lines around Joan's mouth grew taut, and she forcibly whacked a head of lettuce with the butcher knife.

Joan didn't like the use of her proper name. After ten years Jolene thought her mother would realize some hurts couldn't be undone with lavish birthday and Christmas presents. They battled for years and the scars remained.

"What can I help you with?" she asked, figuring the quicker dinner was over, the sooner Joan would leave.

"The tacos and rice are almost done. I want to make some salsa. Your father loves his salsa."

"I think there is a jar in the refrigerator."

Joan waved her off before she could grab the refrigerator's door handle. "Louey prefers fresh made."

Jolene stared at her mother. *Louey?* Jolene had never heard Joan call her father by a nickname. She'd always referred to him using his proper name, Louis. *Was one of her parents dying? Was that why Joan was being...so different.* Jolene backed away. "Okay."

"After we eat I think one of us should take a plate to the hospital for Martina and check on her and Simon. Your father met her at the hospital. He didn't want her to be there alone without support, in case..."

Joan's face paled under her makeup. Then she visibly shook herself, as if dismissing the idea Simon could be seriously injured or dying.

Her nostrils drew in with her long breath. "But he's on his way here now. We weren't sure how long you'd be at work. I told him to stay with Martina and I'd be fine handling the kids, but after he learned Simon was going to be okay, he insisted on coming back to help me." She quickly wiped off the cutting board she'd used to chop the lettuce. "One of us should be with her." She studied Jolene for a second. "Nice outfit by the way. Kind of casual for work, isn't it?" Again, Joan's gaze trailed down over Jolene's dress to her shoes. "Martina told me you were at work."

As a professional woman her mother dressed appropriately for any occasion. Tonight, Joan was dressed in black capris and a robin-egg blue peasant style top that complemented her eye color. To protect the pretty top from grease and sauce splatters she wore a flowered chef's apron. Black peek-a-boo Aerosoles sandals covered her tiny feet, exposing painted toenails.

"I was. I'm helping the chief of police with a case." She nodded toward Lia. "I'm sure Martina told you what happened."

Her mother's sandy blond eyebrow touched her feathered bangs. "With the new chief, dressed like that?" She scooped the lettuce into a bowl and then wiped her hands off with a dry towel.

Jolene blinked, thinking the dress she wore was a little dressy but wasn't completely unprofessional. She shouldn't be surprised Joan focused on her attire and had totally skipped over the fact that Jolene had saved Lia's life.

She intended to show Joan her frustration by raking her fingers through her short hair, but stopped with her hand in midair. The older woman had just done the same thing.

She sighed loudly. "I didn't bring professional outfits with me since I'd intended to spend my vacation with Martina and the kids on the beach. I didn't think I'd be working."

"Aren't you people supposed to be prepared for anything and have a go bag ready? Isn't that what they're called?" Joan's stare sharpened under her penciled brow. "Or aren't desk jockeys required to be prepared?"

Jolene sensed her mother knew she didn't just sit behind a desk entering in data for the agency. She wondered if Joan and Martina ever discussed her lie. Martina had told her they spoke regularly now and on a number of occasions Martina had even encouraged Jolene to give their parents a call. In less than five minutes her mother reminded her why she didn't pick up her phone. "Usually my job requires weeks of preparation so I have time to pack."

"I see." Joan turned away and aggressively stirred the pot of rice.

The muscles of her mother's neck constricted as if she swallowed a ton of emotion.

Jolene drew back her shoulders. To think her mother worried about her was outlandish. She never had. Their father had been the nurturing parent until he'd become an unfit drunk. By the time the loveless marriage hacked away the man's soul, Martina and she were teenagers and more than capable of taking care of themselves and making their own decisions.

"So, you didn't bring work clothes," Joan said flatly, starting their conversation at square one again.

"No." Watching her mother closely, an odd feeling settled in Jolene's chest and she rubbed her hand over the discomfort she felt below her heart.

"And you didn't have time to shop?"

"Not really. I had an early meeting with a federal agent and the chief of police this morning." Jolene didn't know why she felt the need to explain her actions to a woman who never cared what she did, but she couldn't seem to stop talking. "And then the chief and I worked the case all afternoon. I couldn't very well show up at the police station in short shorts and a tank top."

Her mother examined a tomato she'd plucked from the metal basket sitting on the draining board. "You're too old for short shorts."

In her head, Jolene heard the click of the lock securing her defenses, guarding her heart and sanity. "I'm twenty-nine, mother."

"You're closer to thirty than twenty-nine."

Whatever was the response on the tip of her tongue, but to keep peace for Martina and Simon and the children, Jolene refrained from speaking her mind. Which was the right call, because Lia had finally caught a glimpse of her and came running to her side.

"Hey, little one." She lifted Lia into her arms.

209

Lia wrapped her legs around Jolene's waist and her arms around Jolene's neck. "Mama."

She knew it was wrong for the girl to call her Mama. She should've corrected her and suggested the use of another nickname. Like auntie. But after what Lia had been through, Jolene felt she needed a safe bond. Hopefully they'd find her mother soon and the attachment Lia felt for her would dissolve easily.

But for the moment, Jolene couldn't help herself. Laughing, she snuggled the child, breathing in her innocent scent mixed with sunscreen. "I bet you and Clara played outside all day again. Did you have fun?"

"And Sofia." Nodding enthusiastically, Lia's soft locks tickled Jolene's forearms.

"Awesome. Fresh air and sunshine is good for you." She jostled Lia onto her right hip and tapped the tip of Lia's button nose. The girl giggled.

"As long as they wear sunscreen and don't get too much sun," Joan interjected and then checked the food on the stove. "And are made to drink plenty of cold water."

Jolene caught sight of her refection in the slider doors. She looked small. She felt small. She hadn't felt this way in years. She hated the feeling.

She noted the way her mother stood, tall, erect with her chin up, looking down at the frying pan.

"I put sunscreen on her this morning before I left. And I'm sure Martina did again later."

"Yes, I'm sure she did," Joan replied softly. Her tongue crossed her lips before she tapped the spatula on the edge of the pan and placed it on the caddy. With squared shoulders Joan faced Jolene. "Martina turned out to be a great mom and you will be too, one day."

Wearing a small, but genuine smile, Joan's expression grew tender while looking at Lia. Then she turned her caring eyes to Jolene. "I hope."

What the hell? Unconsciously Jolene shifted her weight from one foot to the other, wondering why Joan was pretending to be someone she'd never been. Her mother hadn't wanted children herself. She'd made that fact clear a thousand times and in a thousand ways while Martina and Jolene were growing up. *Why would she want to saddle her daughters with children? Did she realize the mistakes she'd made?*

Jolene looked at the children surrounding the table to make sure they weren't listening in on their conversation. They were too involved with their game to care what went on fifteen feet away from them.

She turned and stared into Lia's cherub face and simultaneously a tug pulled at her womb and her heart. "I'm going to help make dinner. I'm starved. Are you?"

"Yes," Lia said loudly in a most definite manner.

Jolene let her joy show. "Good. Why don't you go feed your baby and then put her down for a nap before it's time to eat?" She gave Lia a squeeze and then lowered her to the floor. "Tell Clara and Sofia to do the same."

Lia ran past the table of game players and hopped down the step to the family room.

When they were alone in the kitchen area again, Jolene turned to Joan. "What's going on?"

"What do you mean?" Joan grabbed a dishcloth.

"This." Jolene fought to keep her voice even. "You never enjoyed cooking. And you were never a kid person."

Joan silently wiped off the granite countertop.

Jolene slapped the stone top, drawing her mother's attention.

Joan exhaled and leaned into the counter between them. In a hushed tone she said, "I wasn't the best of mothers, Jolene. But in my defense, I was building a career. Your father was supposed to take care of you and Martina, but he broke his—"

Joan's hands clenched the dishcloth so hard water spilled on the counter. Her lips drew into a thin line and her gray eyes shimmered with tears. "The past is the past. We forgave each other our mistakes. All of us but you, it seems."

"To forgive anything I need to understand what you're talking about? What were you going to say? Dad broke what?"

Joan's lips rolled together into a tight seal. Then she quickly glanced at the kids, snapped the stove burners off and ordered Jolene outside. Without waiting for Jolene's response, Joan marched to the slider.

Once they were outside and their privacy assured she turned to Jolene. "I know you're confused about your childhood."

Jolene folded her arms across her chest and leaned against the slider's frame. Confused was not a word she'd use to describe how she felt about her childhood. She was very interested to know why her mother thought she was. "I'm not confused. You were never around."

"That was because your father and I had an agreement. I earned the higher wage. His job as a boat mechanic was done at night or on the weekends when the boats were at dock. We decided together that I would open my own practice. Everything was fine, or so I thought, until it wasn't." Joan bit her lip, obviously fighting back emotions.

Jolene crossed her arms thinking about all the hours Joan hadn't been at home and was presumably at work. "Was there someone else?'

"What?" Joan's earrings swung against her cheek with the motion of her head. "No. Something happened. Then your father became depressed and started drinking."

"What happened?"

"I'm embarrassed to tell you." Joan picked up a forgotten toy from the cement patio.

It was as Jolene had thought. Her father became an alcoholic because of her mother. Jolene ground her molars together and waited for her confession. "What happened?" she asked.

Joan placed the small truck in a nearby toy bin. She inhaled and faced Jolene.

"Without me knowing, he'd started to gamble. At first his losses were small. Nothing I'd really missed out of our household budget, but then the amount grew. He lost tens of thousands of dollars before I found out. I never thought he would steal from you and Martina."

Jolene's heart cracked. "Our college funds." Her mother had always been wise concerning finances. She insisted Jolene and Martina save at least a third of whatever they earned at their part time jobs.

She remembered Martina's and her sister's surprise when it came time for them to go to college and their parents had to re-mortgage their home to help pay the bills. "He lost our college funds?"

The knuckles of her hands became as white as her complexion. "Yes. He was in debit beyond his ears and

213

in a last attempt to get the bookies off his back he forged my name and withdrew the money from your accounts. Of course by that time he was an alcoholic and wasn't thinking straight."

Jolene staggered back and sat on the patio glider. Behind closed eyes, memories, like pieces of a puzzle, fell into place. All these years she blamed her mother for so many things. Not having the time to attend school events. Not having money to buy new items young girls thought they had to have because they'd die a slow death if they didn't get them. Not loving them the way a mother should. Always, always working, at her law firm. Never at home.

A memory of her mother wanting to hold her when she was fourteen popped into Jolene's mind. They'd had an argument. *Over what?* Jolene couldn't recall. She'd pushed her mother away and ran to her father. She recalled her mother's hurt expression. She'd thought her father walked on water. He hadn't. All those years her mother had been trying to keep their family from falling apart. And worse, how sad for her mother to carry the burden of the secret that was unfair to her as well as her daughters.

Jolene pressed a hand to her mouth as bile tickled the back of her throat. Her entire collection of childhood memories now seemed a lie.

She heard her mom approach her and then a soft but shaky hand smoothed over her head.

Jolene jumped up and backed away. "Why didn't you tell us?" Tears moistened her cheeks and she swiped them away. She sensed her mother wanted to move closer, to comfort her.

"You loved your father so much. You've always

idolized him. I couldn't take that away from you. Or him. He needed your admiration to help him get through his addiction treatment. It took a year before he could look into my eyes and accept that I stilled love him."

Tears trailed down her mother's face.

Jolene choked on the thickness clogging her throat. "All these years you let me think the worst of you. *Why?*"

"Because I loved your father, and you and Martina."

Jolene stiffened her spine. "Does Martina know about this?"

Her mother nodded.

"How long?"

"For some time now."

Growing anger tightened Jolene's shoulders. "And she didn't tell me?"

"I asked her not to. I wanted to tell you myself. I tried to talk to you many times when you were home but you always shut me out. I couldn't talk to you over the phone, you'd hang up on me before I could explain." Her mother sighed and took a step toward her.

Jolene backed up.

"When I learned you were coming to visit I decided I was not going to let you walk away from me again. I didn't want you to be angry with me on your thirtieth birthday. You're old enough now to understand how life happens. How people make mistakes. How they right the mistakes and ask for forgiveness. Your father did both. I forgave him. He received Martina's forgiveness. He wants yours too. We both do." Joan's hands wrung together. "You've been so angry and whether you believe me or not, your anger has affected your life. It's time to let the past go and build a life which doesn't revolve totally around danger and pain."

Her mother wanted her forgiveness but Jolene couldn't erase all the hurt and rationalizing she'd harbored over the years, like dust that clings to an old book. She needed to digest what Joan had told her and work it out in her head and in her heart.

From inside the house Jolene heard her father's booming voice and the children's squeals and she quickly backed toward the gate to the yard. "I don't think I can see Dad right now. I need time to think." She bit down on her lip, checking the emotions which made it hard for her to breathe, to think straight.

Joan's pleading smile faded. "I understand."

Watching the slider door for her father to appear, Jolene said, "I'm going for a drive."

Joan nodded. "Take the time you need. I'll tell him you were called back to the station."

Jolene started toward her escape exit and then halted, snapping her fingers. "Oh, my keys." She turned, looking toward the house. "They're in my purse. It's inside."

"Wait by the front door," her mother replied then headed inside.

Two minutes passed before the door opened with her purse strap laced over its handle. Jolene stood in the shadow of a nearby butterfly bush, looking at it. This was the first time she could recall she and her mother were on the same side. Her stomach felt like a cobra coiled inside it, waiting for the best moment to strike.

Jolene rushed to the door, grabbed her purse, and then walked quickly away. As she climbed into her vehicle her mind raced back over the years. How could she consider herself a good investigator if she hadn't seen what was going on within her own family for decades? She was once a child, yes, but she'd been a U.S. Marshal for nearly five years. She should've known something, had some kind of hint.

She turned over the engine and signaled out into the street. She needed a drink.

With relief, she drove away from her past. And in her rearview mirror she saw lightening light up the sky.

CHAPTER TWENTY

A few minutes before ten Norris pulled his Jeep in front of the small cove shack he'd rented at a premium price for its solitude. The roar of waves beyond the swath of light from the deck called for him to lay his head down. He pushed himself out of his Jeep and grunted. This was the first time he'd been home in two days and he needed to shower and shave, and then snag a few hours of sleep so he could think straight.

He reached the rear of his vehicle when his yard was flooded with the glare from headlights. The ocean sounds had concealed the sound of an engine, and he hadn't noticed the approaching vehicle that cut through the sea grass along the winding narrow trail he considered his driveway.

Who'd have reason to follow him? It wasn't one of his team. He'd checked in before leaving the station. Could it be the drunk he'd arrested for causing a full-fledged fight at the downtown bar last week? That guy was stupid enough to seek revenge.

Or could it be the woman who seemed to break the speed limit every time he was on duty. The one who offered him her services so he wouldn't write her a ticket?

Or had he come too close to learning the truth about who set Lia adrift on the ocean?

His hand found his gun and he thought to draw his weapon and take aim but the vehicle continued toward him at an even pace. An uneasiness tightened his gut. His leg muscles became taut, giant springs enabling him

218

to leap away if he needed to.

The dark shadow drew closer.

His breath caught in his lungs, waiting for the moment the truck would speed forward. And he released his breath only when the vehicle rolled to a stop a few feet away from where he stood his ground. Norris' heart jump-started and he put his hand up to shield his eyes from the glare. He squinted, searched for any familiar detail to tell him who'd followed him home. He heard the driver's door creak before the headlights cut off. He blinked. No interior lights had come on to reveal who the driver was.

"What's this place?"

Jolene. He exhaled and snapped his holster. "I thought you went home for the night?"

"That had been the plan." Jolene slammed her SUV's door. "You live here?"

"Yeah. Did you try to call me?"

"No." She scanned the area, not once connecting with his gaze. "This place is definitely secluded."

Something was on her mind. *Had Carter contacted her with a possible DNA match? Or had something happened to Simon?* "How's your brother-in-law?"

Jolene wobbled into the soft glow cascading from the mercury light near the shack's rear corner. She steadied herself by holding on to the hood of the vehicle and rounded the front of her car.

Norris wondered if she was distressed over her brother-in-law's accident or if she'd been drinking.

She lowered herself onto the SUV's bumper, looking even more drained than he felt.

"Simon was damn lucky. He has a broken ankle, a cracked rib and bruises and cuts from the air bag. His injuries could've been much worse." She kicked off her shoes and then tapped the sand from their soles. "Martina called me while I followed you into this path. He's out of surgery and is resting."

"You followed me? From where? The station?" He had to be tired. He never noticed the tail.

She chuckled softly and shook her head while placing her shoes on the bumper next to her.

"What?" he asked.

"Nothing." She waved her hand. "Yeah, I followed you from the station. Now we're even."

Her small smile faded.

For a second, he wondered what she found funny and then his mind turned to the night he'd followed her to the beach. Their time together had ended with a kiss that had him wanting a hell of a lot more from her. He let his gaze wander over her curves. His cock twitched as he recalled the feel of her supple body against his.

When she inhaled deeply he couldn't help but notice the plump tan skin pushing against the scoop of her dress. Then she sighed heavily and with that sound of her distress, the desire to cup her firm breasts in his palms disappeared. Something troubled her.

He stretched his arms, shaking off the memory of her body as he changed his stance.

"Something important must've happened for you to follow me down a dark trail instead of calling me? Carter?"

"No. Not Carter. Nothing to do with Lia's case."

"What then?"

With her head down, she shuffled her feet, digging her painted toenails into the sand. "I needed to talk to someone."

220

He waited, listening to the crash of the waves, giving her time to sort through her feelings and come up with the words to express them. When a minute turned into two long minutes his concern made him ask, "About…?"

"Maybe I should go?" She pushed off the bumper and stood straighter.

He reached out and snagged her wrist above her bracelet so she wouldn't turn away. Her soft skin heated the rough pad of his index finger and underneath it her pulse quickened. He couldn't deny he wanted this woman.

"Don't go. Stay."

With his free hand he lifted her face to look at him. His heart flip-flopped when he stared down into her soulful eyes. They were filled with such raw emotion he wanted to pull her into his arms and stop whatever caused her pain. *Was her problem with job or family?* "You don't need to tell me what's going on. Just stay."

Her gaze wavered. "Do you have anything strong to drink?"

He smiled. "I have beer."

She scrunched up her nose.

"Vodka? There's an unopened bottle in the freezer. I might have orange juice."

The corner of her lips pulled up slightly. "Forget the juice."

She was sassy. He loved sassy. He let go of her and stepped back to give her space.

She slipped on her shoes and then followed him along the wooden planks that served as his sidewalk.

The old screen door screeched when he opened it. Using his backside, he held it ajar for her.

"Do you want to come in or would you rather we sit on the deck?" he asked over his shoulder while he unlocked the padlock that secured his home.

"The deck. I'd like to listen to the ocean," she answered. "I can't hear it from Martina's place and I find it relaxing."

"Okay. I'll get our drinks and meet you there in a few minutes." He reached inside and flipped the switch so the tiny lights along the deck railing came to life. Norris kept an eye on Jolene until she disappeared around the corner.

He stepped inside and scanned the two-room shack. One room was his kitchen, living room, bedroom combo. The far wall had two French doors overlooking the deck and ocean. The second room was a tiny bathroom, installed in the cabin when indoor plumbing became the thing.

Quickly he entered the bathroom, ripped off his shirt and washed his face and ran the washcloth over his chest and under his arms. He toweled off and pulled a clean T-shirt from the shelf in his closet and yanked the moss-green shirt over his head. He ran his comb through his hair before entering the kitchen where he quickly poured three fingers of vodka into a tumbler. Then he grabbed a beer for himself.

Taking a deep breath to calm the eagerness making his nerves zing, Norris headed out to the deck via the French doors near his La-Z-Boy recliner.

He found Jolene by the railing. The ocean breeze pinned her dress against her shapely legs and hips. His cock hardened at the sight of her heart-shaped ass. Good God he wanted her.

She turned and looked at him. Normally, he wasn't

222

attracted to women with such short hair, but Jolene's jagged cut fit her. It accented her high cheek bones and showcased her almond-shaped eyes and adorable ears.

"Here you are." Norris handed her the tumbler.

"Thanks." Jolene took a sip of the liquid and let the heat it produced in her throat escape through clenched teeth. She turned and once again leaned against the railing and looked out into the darkness. "Did you ever feel as if your life has been an illusion? That you don't know what's real and what's not?"

He opened his beer and tossed the lid into a nearby recycling bucket. "What do you mean?"

In the dim light, he saw her neck muscles work.

She took tiny sips of her drink, letting its heat escape through her full lips and then she stared off into the darkness. "Have you ever believed in something so much you missed all the signs telling you that you were utterly wrong about it?"

Norris swept his tongue across his suddenly dry lips. *Did he ever*. The deep pain he'd felt when he discovered his life was a lie still plagued him. His heart had been mutilated. He didn't intend to ever fall into the dark hole again.

Jolene stood next to him silent, not really asking for anything more than someone to be near.

Her hands trembled slightly.

He looked down at the Lynx tattoo on his foreman. It reminded him of the strength he'd nurtured. What happened between his ex-girlfriend and himself wasn't something he'd shared with anyone, but Jolene's deep-seated sadness made him want to open up to her.

He leaned his forearms on the railing and let his beer dangle from his hand. He didn't look at her but kept his gaze focused toward where the dark sky met the sand dunes. "Yeah, I did."

"Makes you wonder if you're as good a cop as you thought, right?" Her nostrils pulled in when she inhaled deeply.

"Everyone second-guesses themselves at some time or another."

She nodded . "True. True."

"You're damn good," he said, hoping to dispel whatever worried her.

She smiled at him. "So are you."

For a few minutes they drank in silence, listening to the ocean's repeated melody.

Jolene emptied her glass and turned toward him. "Do you want to go for a swim?"

Her delighted tone caused him to arch a brow. Apparently, she wasn't ready to tell him what was bothering her. "Are you serious?"

"Yes. Yes, I am." She padded across the deck and set her glass down on the table positioned between two Adirondack rockers in the deck's private corner. "I need to do something physical. Join me, or not," she said, walking by him. "Grab me a towel. I didn't bring my beach stuff."

Then she disappeared around the corner.

No beach stuff meant no swimsuit.

Holy shit.

Feeling all of his blood heading south, Norris swallowed. He had to remain in control of his desires. For some reason, Jolene was very vulnerable now. He didn't want to take advantage of her or hurt her.

***

What she said was crazy but she needed to do something wild and impetuous. Her heart was pounding so loudly the sound of the waves crashing against the shore were only a backdrop to its throbbing. There was no doubt she'd become an adrenaline junkie over the years and Norris was her fix of choice tonight. She wasn't going to think about tomorrow and what hooking up with him would mean. She needed to get her mind off a boatload of shit and she knew he was the man who could do that for her.

She'd slipped out of her dress and waded up to her hips in the surprisingly warm water before Norris reached the narrow beach with the towels.

"Don't you know you shouldn't swim alone?" he called to her as he flung out the blanket. He picked up her dress and lay it and the towels on the edge of the blanket.

"I'm not swimming yet. Join me. The water is beautiful." Then she turned and dove into a wave. The water was silk against her skin. Only when her lungs felt like they'd burst, did she push off from the sandy bottom and come up for air. When she swiped the water from her eyes and looked to shore Norris had disappeared.

"What the hell?" She took a step forward, scanning the path over the dune only to jump back when Norris surged out of the water a few feet in front of her. "Son of a bitch. You scared me."

"Good. We're even." He flung his hair back and droplets arched into the air. "I thought you got caught up in a riptide."

In the moonlight reflected on the water she admired

his broad shoulders and the coarse hair covering his chest. Jolene's heartbeat raced. "So, you dove in to save me?"

"You look good in red," he said, ignoring her question.

Looking into his hungry gaze, her nipples puckered under her lace bra.

A swell pushed her from behind like an invisible hand and she moved toward him.

Norris' strong arms caught her and he lifted her up against him so tightly her breath swooshed from her lungs.

She smoothed her palms along his wet biceps, longing to feel every ripple of his hard muscles.

A wave jostled them and she realized Norris was naked.

Immediately, her skin grew feverish, despite the cool water. She looked at him devilishly through wet lashes. "No suit?"

"Forgot it." His gaze dropped to her mouth for a second before lowering further to where her lace covered breasts pressed against his chest. With an intake of air, his gaze rose and connected with hers. "Do you want to swim to the old pier over there?"

"I sort of like it right here." She pulled herself against him.

"*Hmmm.*"

Despite his erection nudging her leg, his expression turned pensive. His hold on her relaxed and Jolene worried she'd made a fool of herself.

"I want you, Jolene, but if you don't want me to make love to you tell me now and I'll walk out of this ocean."

His fingers caressed her back.

Certainly not. She had never wanted a man more. With one hand, Jolene broke the thin strap of her panties, slid them off and tossed them over her head and into the Atlantic. Then she pulled herself against Norris again and greedily captured his mouth. She opened her lips to him and he pushed his tongue, laced with beer and salt water, inside of her.

His warm hands drifted down over her backside and cupped her ass cheeks. He kneaded her flesh and in turn rubbed his erection against her stomach.

His fingers sought her entrance and stole her breath with their teasing.

She broke free of his demanding lips and gasped. Heaven wasn't only above them.

Jolene laughed and tilted her face up to the stars. Norris took the opportunity to graze her exposed neck and tickle her cheeks with his whiskers. Electric charges followed the trail of kisses he placed on her shoulder and then lower to the swell of her breasts.

Wanting to pleasure him too, she laced an arm around his neck and pushed back. Then she dragged her free hand down his solid abdominal muscles and closed her fingers around his thick shaft.

His deep-throated moan made her core tighten with desire. She wrapped her legs around his hips and felt some relief with his shaft nestled against her clit. "I need you in me now, Chief."

"Rubbers are on the beach in my jeans, Agent Martinez," he mumbled between clenched teeth as he turned them toward the shore.

She dug her nails into his shoulder.

"*Oww.*" He winced, nearly dropping her into the

water. "What the fuck?"

Nose to nose, she stared into his heart. "Pill. And recently had annual exam. You?" She pecked his lips and drew her tongue across them.

A wave jostled them and Norris quickly found his footing. "Right after... I've haven't been with anyone since."

She suspected as much.

Jolene pressed her smile to his lips and arched up and guided him inside her.

His neck, his shoulders, his arms rippled under her hands while he slowly took ownership of her body.

Jolene rolled her hips, allowing him to bury his throbbing member completely within her warm walls. She watched his beautiful eyes close to half mast.

She wasn't as patient as Norris and began to rock against him wanting their heat to build to an inferno.

Her sigh broke his restraint and he matched her thrusts and drove deeper into her until she shuddered. Norris' arm tightened around her waist and after several intense thrusts the universe disappeared above them.

Jolene was still floating, clinging to his shoulders when he whispered in her ear, "Welcome home."

She laughed. "Do not tell me you greet all new arrivals this way."

"Hell no. Only the really special ones."

She smoothed his damp hair back. "And exactly how many have been special?"

"One." He held her head between his large hands and kissed her deeply.

CHAPTER TWENTY-ONE

Outside, the birds burst into song. Through the French doors Jolene saw shards of yellow and pink shoot up into the early morning sky above the ocean.

She sighed. The world could wait to greet her a little longer. She was right where she wanted to be, in Norris' bed, with her leg draped over his hairy ones.

Her body felt deliciously mellow as if she'd gone to a five-star spa. Last night, Norris had taken her in the sea, in the shower after the sea and in this bed after that. She felt totally rested and relaxed even though she'd had little sleep. Since waking she told Norris about her life with her parents and that churned up years of pent-up anger and self-doubt.

He hit home when he noted she could've gone anywhere for a vacation, but had come home. Maybe on some level she had wanted to face her past. The past couldn't be changed. She had to forgive those who'd kept secrets from her because ultimately they'd had her best interests at heart. And then she had to move on with her life.

Jolene thought about her parents. She was part of the reason this feud, for a lack of a better word, had lasted so long between her and her mother. She had rebelled against her mother as a teenager and had carried the grudge into her adult years, refusing to bend and listen to her mother when she'd tried to talk to Jolene. It was true: Mom had reached out many times over the last ten years but Jolene wouldn't have any of it. Even Martina had pleaded with her to talk to their mother. Now she felt terrible for causing her parents so much pain.

Her poor listening skills… Another reason she would not make a good parent.

Norris fidgeted, smacked his lips, muttered something unintelligible and then relaxed into the mattress.

Jolene adjusted the sheet over his waist. He'd been right when he reminded her if life hadn't happened the way it had, she wouldn't be in his arms last night. He was so damn levelheaded, and optimistic and handsome. *Why hadn't some other woman snagged him up?*

Jolene snuggled into the crook of his muscular arm and began to play with his chest hair, pulling one course curl straight and watching it spring back into a tight coil.

"Are you having fun?"

Jolene gathered from Norris' rough, sexy voice the little bit of sleep they'd had last night wasn't enough for him. She should've let him sleep instead of rousing him for a third romp around two a.m., but he looked too damn sexy with his hair a mess and his broad chest exposed. It was all his fault she was horny.

"I am." She shifted and smiled up at him, loving the desire in his drowsy eyes.

"Good. I want you to have a great time, so you'll come back tonight." He pushed her bangs back and pressed his full lips to her forehead.

"I think you pretty well sealed that deal several times last night." His beard tickled her nose and she giggled. She combed her fingers through its fullness.

230

She grew wet between her legs remembering how the coarse hair felt, tantalizing her breasts and stomach and the inside of her thighs. She wanted him again but instead she rested her head against his chest and listened to his calming heartbeat.

They lay silent for a few minutes while she continued to play with his chest and he brushed his fingers lightly over her upper arm. She loved the way he touched her, as if she were fragile and might break. It made her feel girly and she didn't feel girly very often.

"What time is it?" His rock-hard abdomen muscles bunched under her palm when he pushed up on an elbow and stared across the room at the microwave's digital clock. "Four thirty."

"Say you don't need to get up for work yet," she pleaded.

He looked down at her. "Woman if you want sex again I can tell you it's not going to happen. I've had exactly fours sleep in the last two days. And I haven't made love three times in one night, ever. I'm spent."

She tugged his beard playfully. There wasn't much he didn't know about her past after her rundown, except for Stefan. She told Norris she'd been in love once and the man had died. However, she left out the part that Stefan was part of a Russian mafia ring she'd been sent to destroy. She also didn't tell him she'd been the one to fire the kill shot that took Stefan's life. "I thought you were a Special Force Army veteran and were used to days with lots of action and no sleep."

He chuckled, twining his fingers with hers. "You got the Army veteran right, but special forces, no.

I was a grunt. Did what I was told for six years before getting out and going into the Norfolk Police Academy."

Norris lifted her hand and brushed his lips across her fingers, sending shivers running through her.

She loved the tiny lines that formed at the edges of his eyes when he laughed. She fought the urge to reach over and touch them. She didn't want to sidetrack their conversation. There was so much she didn't know about Norris and she wanted to know everything. "You're from Western Pennsylvania, right? How did you end up in Norfolk?"

His full lips pressed flat for two seconds. "You want the truth?"

"Of course."

"A woman."

She felt her heart wince with jealousy. "Ah."

"Ella and I met while I was on leave for a long weekend. One of my Army pals was from Norfolk and invited me to join him and his family for a Fourth of July barbeque. She was the friend of his sister. Afterwards, Ella and I stayed in touch. We saw each other whenever we could. A year later, I was out and I thought why not give the relationship a real go so I applied at the Norfolk Police Academy and the rest is history."

"Not all of it. What brought you here to Cape James?" She felt him stiffen next to her and noted his jaw clench. Whatever it was had hurt him badly. She suspected it had to do with Ella, since she no longer seemed to be in the picture. "If you don't want to tell me, it's okay."

He sighed and repositioned his arm under her. "I

caught Ella screwing another man. I beat the hell out of him and almost landed my ass in jail."

His gruff words rushed out of him as if he thought them instead of intending to voice them. The vibrant forest-green color of his eyes deepened the way the earth darkens when a cloud moves in front of the sun. She knew then; he'd loved Ella once.

In that instant, she both hated the woman for hurting this good man and adored Ella for screwing up so she could be here lying in his strong arms.

Jolene stroked her hand over his heart, longing to sooth away his pain.

"We were in engaged to be married in three months," he said.

"*Ouch.*" Jolene flinched with empathy. "Did you know the guy?"

Norris inhaled deeply, held it as if he counted off from ten, and then blew his warm breath out slowly. "He was my partner."

"*Oh fuck.*"

"Exactly my reaction too. Fortunately, Carson didn't press charges. I guess he felt like an ass." Norris swiped his hand over his face before he glanced down at her. "You know how they say guys fall for women who are like their mother. In my case, it was true. Ella was my mom's twin through and through. She traded up for someone she thought could provide her with the better life she felt she deserved."

"Ah. Right. Your mother is on her fourth husband," Jolene said. "I'm sorry."

He shrugged. "I'm over it."

"Are you?"

"Sure." He looked down at her. "Why did you

question that?" The aching memories still etched his face. She rolled her lips together and shrugged.

He shifted higher on his pillow. "Really? After last night, you think I'm not over her?"

"I think you want to be."

Norris slid his arm out from under her and climbed out of bed. He grabbed a pair of sweat pants off the floor where he had peeled them off the night before.

She'd upset him. She hadn't meant to. She was only being honest about what she saw in his eyes. Whether he wanted to admit it or not, he still had feelings for Ella. And just like the advice he'd given her earlier, he would have to accept the past and let it go.

Jolene propped herself up on the pillows and admired his body.

His gaze went immediately to her breasts and she felt a rush of wet heat between her legs again. She tugged the sheets up and covered herself. "How many women have you dated since moving here?"

"A few."

She skimmed her feet along the sheets where his body heat lingered and brought her knees to her chest. She wrapped her arms around them. "How many is a few?"

"Okay, if you must know…" He yanked the drawstring of his sweat pants tight around his narrow hips. "I hadn't gotten around to asking anyone out."

"Not one?"

"You have a problem with that?" He crossed to the old wooden trunk standing at the end of the bed and opened the lid. From inside, he grabbed a T-shirt and let the lid drop with a thud. "I haven't had time to meet anyone."

Inside, she smiled. She was the first woman he'd chosen to be with.

Then her smile faded. Did he think there was a possibility of a happy ever after between them? She longed for an HEA for herself, one day, but now… Impossible. "Yet here you are with me. Why?"

His head popped out from inside his shirt. "What do you mean, why? You're hot. We have a lot in common. I like you. I assumed you liked me."

He was right. She did like him. In fact, more than she should. He looked so damn adorable with his hair messy. "You're a great guy but I'm not going to be staying here in Cape James. I have a life and career back in Pennsylvania."

"I know."

"I don't come home often," she said quietly, watching his reaction.

He remained silent. His expression unreadable.

"You're good about this…?" She waggled her finger between them. "*Us* being temporary."

"Sounds like a line I should be saying." He stared down at her.

He was protecting himself. He wanted her to believe he'd used her for sex but her instincts told her Norris longed for more in a relationship, more than she could give. "Then we're on the same page."

His icy stare slashed at her soul.

"Same book too." With long strides he walked by her and headed to the bathroom. "I'll be right back."

Jolene sat and waited for the door to close behind him before she flopped back on the mattress. She bumped her head on the railed headboard and immediately covered her mouth to conceal her whimper. She'd screwed up royally. *Why hadn't she just told him the whole truth instead of using her job as an excuse?* She wasn't the woman he needed. He didn't have to say the words for her to know he was the type of guy who wanted a lifetime with one woman and a family. She never allowed herself that dream. However, she had to admit while he kissed her, held her, made love to her, she had pictures of herself in his embrace years from now.

"Fuck. Fuck. Fuck." Clutching the sheet, she stared up at the white bead-board ceiling. Yes, she had known the second his gaze flickered to the side he was lying about the number of women he'd dated since the breakup. Why hadn't she simply accepted his answer *of a few* as the truth instead of probing and pissing him off.

For some reason, Jolene's heart sank to her stomach. Admitting what he had to her, wouldn't have been easy for any man. Guys seemed to have an unwritten code: They didn't share their feelings under any circumstances. For Norris to reveal the source of his pain must mean he trusted her. And what did she do then? She reminded him she was out of here in a few days, taking his secret with her.

She listened to the toilet flush and then the water in the shower turned on. Norris needed to wash away her scent.

"Nice going, Jolene. You're an idiot," she mumbled, running her fingers through her short hair. She pulled the sheets to her nose, closed her eyes and drew in the smell of their love making. He might want to forget last night but she never would.

She shot up and stared ahead. She was falling

236

for him. Had she wanted him to confess he was falling for her too? Was that why she asked?

What the hell was she thinking letting herself get involved with a man who lived more than three-hundred miles away from her home base?

Someone she could easily love.

***

Norris stood in the shower with his fists planted against the tile wall and water rushing over his bowed head. Jolene was right about Ella. He wasn't over his ex. Until he'd met Jolene he had thought about Ella every day since he walked out of their apartment after finding her and Carson together. She totally captivated him. Now Jolene was the woman who preoccupied his thoughts, so much so he had to remind himself to concentrate on his job. With her by his side every day, it made the task hard.

He had wanted her from the first moment he'd seen her. She was the first woman he'd felt anything for since Ella.

He'd believed once he slept with her the attraction would diminish, but if his hard-on was any indication how over Jolene he was, he hadn't had nearly enough of her yet. It wasn't only his body that wanted more of her. She was funny and smart and he loved being in her company.

If last night wasn't enough to prove how much he was over Ella, what more could he do?

He clenched his jaw thinking about the woman who had ripped his heart from his chest and stomped on it. He didn't care what Ella did any longer.

He needed Jolene to believe him. He'd been totally open with her because he wanted her to know. *Didn't that show Jolene she meant something to him?*

Apparently not because her response was to tell him she was leaving and that this thing between them was only temporary.

He looked through the clear shower curtain and noted the bathroom door remained closed. Jolene wasn't going to come to him.

He had a decision to make. And his gut told him, he'd better do it quickly.

CHAPTER TWENTY-TWO

I watch him through a blurry haze. How can he sleep so peacefully, knowing Lia probably cried for her mama every day, especially at bedtime?

Every part of me aches to hold my baby. The pain is almost unbearable.

The bastard would pay for shipping my sweet, sweet little girl away. As if she was nothing more than a flawed item to be returned.

The welts on my thighs sting against the sheets and I wince. I need to find the strength to gain control before he kills me. I can't bare to think Lia will never feel my kisses again. She will forget me. Like my father did.

I curl my fingers into tight fists, intending to lash out at him and beat him into submission, but I can't. He is in control now and I can only voice my pain silently, to myself.

Lia was mine, damn it! I found her you bastard. Not you. I cared for her and loved her.

I swear on my mother's life somehow I will get Lia back. Somehow. I will make you pay for all the years you made me suffer. I will teach you a lesson. I promise.

CHAPTER TWENTY-THREE

Jolene studied her bracelet's every charm while she waited for Norris to come out of the bathroom. Among the many she collected over the years, she found the dragonfly. It had been from Stefan, her first real love. He saw her as carefree and filled with aspirations. The angel that was clasped next to it she had bought in Stefan's memory.

Jolene sighed. Even if she removed the bracelet she would carry her past, like Norris did. Between them, they had too much baggage to make a stab at any kind of relationship.

The bathroom door popped open and Norris stepped out, followed by a cloud of steam. He wore a towel draped around his narrow hips and his thick wet hair was slicked back.

Jolene stood from the couch.

Norris frowned. "Where are you going?"

"I think I should go." Jolene bent over and picked up her shoes and turned away from the sight of Norris' bare torso. Her intention was to walk out the door before things became more complicated between them but he quickly crossed the room, snagged her by the wrist and yanked her back against his chest. Within a second, she found herself trapped in his strong arms again.

From behind, he pressed his strong thighs against hers. Her dress grew damp from the towel. She looked over her shoulder and met the hot flames dancing in

Norris' hooded eyes. Over the past week, they'd played a philandering game of cat and mouse. She sensed the game was about to morph into something more and both of them would walk away changed forever.

"Are you sure you want to get involved with me?" she asked, feeling the strong beat of his heart hammer against her shoulder blade.

"Yes."

She had watched his full lips part with the whispered word. It was all he had to say in his deep, sexy tone to send her blood free falling through her veins. A week ago, having sex with him would've just been sex, but now, this time, the act would mean something. They had shared too much. Loving him would make saying goodbye nearly impossible.

His hand tightened on her wrist and her heart tripped over itself.

The Lynx tensed when his other hand rose to trace a finger along her jawline, under her chin and then circled up and over her lips. He made no move to kiss her. He made love to her lips with his finger, tracing them, playing with her V lightly, and gently parting them, and then his finger stilled.

Her breath caught in her lungs waiting for the moment he would relax his grip on her and back away. She didn't want him to change his mind. She had never wanted a man more than she wanted Norris at this moment. And he wanted her. She felt his hard need nestled against her backside.

Then it occurred to her that he was waiting for her to make the next move. He was allowing her to make the decision which would cement their relationship.

Sometime over the last week this man had learned a

lot about her, enough to capture her soul. She dropped her shoes to the floor. Parting her lips, she drew his finger inside her mouth.

Jolene felt his chest expand and knew her move had been the right choice.

Slowly she lapped at the rough pad, enjoying the salty flavor. With each nip and suck, she felt his need for her grow.

She released him and he immediately trailed kisses to her neck. His teeth grazed her life's artery and nipped at her neck's cord, sending electric charges to her center.

His arm held her in place and he ground himself against her.

She whimpered with pleasure and liquid warmth saturated her panties.

He pulled his finger from her mouth and wet both her lips before lowering his hand and slipping his hand inside her dress and cupping her lace covered breast. He circled her nipple with the damp finger. The roughness of the lace was slightly painful against her nub, yet the sting excited her. Her breast grew hard in his hand while the other ached for attention.

He pulled his hand free of her dress and stepped back.

Cool air rushed into the small space between them.

Jolene whipped around and laced her hands over his neck, pressing her wanting body against his and kissed him hard.

"I'm going to kiss every part of you." He lifted her up. Her breasts squashed against his broad chest and with her toes barely touching the floor, he carried her to the bed.

Dawn sliced through the room and across the bed and provided a romantic ambiance to the room. Over his shoulder, she noted how sparsely furnished and tidy his space was. She wondered if he spent any time there at all. He certainly hadn't since she met him a week earlier.

As he released her, he grabbed the hem of her dress and peeled it from her body. Then he reached for the towel.

She slapped his hands out of the way and while holding his gaze loosened the towel and flung it to the floor. With her palm flat against his hard abs she slid her hand along his hot skin and until her fingertips reached the mass of course curls surrounding his manhood. Then she twisted her wrist and oh so slowly laced her fingers around his shaft.

Norris seemly wobbled and Jolene took control of the situation much like he had initially.

He kneaded her ass cheeks through her panties and she slowly increased the speed at which she pumped her hand up and down, up and then down, letting her pinky brush across its base. She couldn't believe it possible, because Norris was well hung and standing quite erect when she gripped him, but his erection grew larger and harder in her fist. The feel of his heat radiated up her arm and into her blood escalating the urge to have him inside her.

Norris' chest rose and fell.

She arched her back, wanting to press her mound against his shaft, but her hand was in the way, so she pressed against it. Little charges of electricity shot through her womb. She grew hotter and wetter. Fighting her own climax, her knees quaked.

She pressed against his hungry hands and sought relief from the sensation causing her vision to cloud over as if she moved toward a higher level of awareness. She circled his head and drew the hot sticky precum over his thick shaft.

"Woman, you're…going to make me…cum." His growl was more than primal this time. It came from deep inside his being.

He leaned into her at an angle that wouldn't obstruct her movements.

Jolene bit down on her lip.

He was nearly at the ledge of ecstasy and as much as she longed to go down on him and take him over the edge, she wanted to feel the breadth of him stretch her throbbing muscles and push inside her.

She pleasured him with her hand for a few seconds longer and then at the right moment she released him and pushed him away. "Condom. Now."

Coming back from the edge of bliss, he blinked. It took a second to register the words she'd spoken. He nodded and reached for the nightstand.

Inside the drawer, she saw alongside the box of condoms a TV remote, a flashlight, a box of chocolate Junior mints and a switchblade. Norris was a man prepared for anything.

Holding the foiled wrapper between his teeth, he slammed the drawer closed. His Jeep keys fell to the floor with a jangle. Cursing at the delay, he scooped them up and tossed them into the drawer with his wallet before he ripped open the foil package and slipped the condom over his erection.

Matching his urgency, Jolene peeled off her bra and panties and tossed them on top of Norris' clothing on the chair.

Norris turned; his erection jutted toward her. His gaze drifted over her body. "You are so damn beautiful."

All the hours in the gym and the pain of overworked muscles were worth it, she thought, stepping toward him.

Norris gripped her by her waist and lifted her up and gently placed her on his bed. The sheets felt cool against her skin.

Then he walked near the foot of the bed and stood there admiring her. He reached out and, lifting her foot, kissed the inside of her ankle.

Jolene gasped and involuntarily lifted her bottom off the bed at the sensation of his lips on the sensitive skin. He was taking control again and she was more than willing to let him. So long as he gave her what she needed.

Slowly he placed butterfly kisses up her calf. She gripped the sheets, stealing herself against the pleasure.

When he stopped at her knee, she pleaded, "Don't stop."

"I have no intention of stopping." He laid her foot down where her legs were spread wider apart. Then he did the same to the other foot and leg.

Her nerves sang as she waited for him to climb on top of her, but instead he only reached forward and flicked her clitoris. She cried out with pleasure. "More."

"Patience. You must learn patience," he answered without any urgency in his voice and for a second Jolene wished she had brought him to his knees before giving up control. He could've gotten her off with his tongue until his cock was ready for the next round. She had no doubt there would be more lovemaking in her immediate future.

"Fuck patience. I'll work on my patience later. I want you inside me, now," she growled.

His sly grin told her she wasn't going to get what she wanted until he was ready. "Soon enough."

Without pulling his gaze from hers, he rounded the bed and lowered his face to her nipple. He blew across the hard nub and she shuddered. Then before the sensation dispelled, he captured her nipple with his mouth. He made a meal of one and then the other while his hand drifted over her flat stomach.

Jolene arched up, wanting more of his mouth, tongue and fingers, and he obliged. He played her body like it was a cherished instrument, tweaking, stroking, nibbling until she thought she'd go out of her mind. When he sucked on her clit, she felt herself waver on the edge of bliss. When he pushed his fingers inside her the white wave crashed over her thoughts without warning. She shuddered against his hand and mouth and felt any power she possessed seep from body through her toes.

Before she fully recovered, he climbed between her legs and pushed inside her.

"Oh my! What the hell took you so long," she cried out. She trailed her hands over the strong muscles of his back and then dug her nails into his tight buttocks, prompting him to probe deeper inside her. Jolene rode Norris until he cried out and shuddered to release.

Before their euphoria had subsided, Norris' phone buzzed on the nightstand. Breathless he answered it: "Stiles."

"Chief." Jolene heard a bit of eagerness in Pickett's

voice. "You okay?"

"Yeah. You woke me." He looked down at her and smiled.

"Sorry, but I didn't think you'd want me to wait until you came in," Pickett answered.

Frowning, Norris pushed off Jolene and sat on the edge of the bed. He scooped up the towel and placed it over his lap. "What's up?"

"I think you better come into the station right away."

Pickett sounded both excited and apprehensive.

"Are we really going to play a game?"

"It's Mackey. He says he's seen the girl, Lia."

Jolene's nails inched up his spine and then down again, causing him to shiver. Her soft hand cupped his ass and it took all his willpower not to throw the phone out into the sand dunes. All he wanted to do was hold her for the entire day with nothing on his mind but how he'd pleasure her next. However, he was the chief of police with a huge case. He had to follow up on every lead until they got a break. "Is he drunk?"

"Yes and no."

Norris clenched his jaw. "What the hell do you mean? Come on. It's a yes or no question."

"He walked in here on his own. Straight as an arrow, but he'd had a few… You can smell it on his breath." Pickett spoke in a rush, apparently sensing Norris was losing his patience. "He had tonight's paper in his hand. He told me he had information about the girl."

"He's probably looking for the reward money so he can buy more booze," Norris said. He admired Jolene's breasts when she stretched. He chuckled quietly when

247

she winked and nestled under the sheet. With her short hair ruffled and her lips plump from kissing him, she was a sex goddess.

"He says not, Chief. He doesn't want a cent."

Norris' attention jumped back to Pickett. "What does he want?"

"Justice for someone in this world."

CHAPTER TWENTY-FOUR

Jolene parked her SUV on the street instead of pulling into the driveway. She didn't want to wake anyone in the Gomez household. At this time of year, by six a.m. the sun already erased any coolness the night had provided. Carrying her heels, Jolene quickly tiptoed across the warm blacktop and scurried into the backyard. If she was lucky, she could be in her pajamas before her parents rose, thus avoiding any questions about where she'd been all night. She couldn't lie and say she went for an early morning run since she was wearing the same clothing she had on yesterday.

"Where have you been?" Martina gave Jolene the condemning walk-of-shame stare before she shoved the filled tray into the coffee pot and hit the on button.

"*Shhh.*" Stepping into the air conditioning and softly closing the slider door behind her, Jolene felt like the rebel she'd been at sixteen. "You're home?"

"I got home about ten minutes ago," Martina answered in a hushed tone.

Jolene listened for any sounds of stirring before responding. "Are Mom and Dad still here?"

"They're sleeping in my bed." Martina opened the cabinet next to the sink. "They'll be up soon. Dad has a doctor's appointment in Norfolk at eleven. His hip has been bothering him. Mom's driving him over. Last night I told Mom and Dad I'd be back to take over this morning. They were going to reschedule Dad's appointment but I insisted they didn't."

Guilt slivered into Jolene's consciousness. She was so out of the loop when it came to what had been happening in her family. "I should've stayed to help them."

Martina waved her off. "Please. They're pros at handling my gang. They babysit whenever I need them."

Feeling like an outsider to the family circle, sadness made Jolene frown. It would take time, but somehow she would make her way back inside the close-knit family.

Her sister looked exhausted and the guilt stabbing Jolene's gut intensified. While her sister was experiencing probably one of the most stressful nights of her life, she'd been having the best sex of her life with a handsome lawman.

"Well, I can help out today and you can get some sleep." She crossed over and dropped her purse on the counter top.

"What about Lia's case?"

"I can take a few hours. If anything breaks Stiles will call me. How's Simon?" she asked quickly, pushing the chief out of her mind.

"He's good. Better than they expected." Martina pulled two mugs from the cabinet, set them next to the coffee pot and then faced Jolene and leaned against the counter. "Doing fine actually."

Jolene chuckled quietly. "He pissed you off, didn't he?"

Martina's lips curled upward for a second before her lower teeth trapped her upper lip. Her dark lashes shimmered with unshed tears. "Yeah. And then he made me laugh."

Martina had thought she might lose Simon. Seeing her sister's problem, Jolene rounded the bar and wrapped her arms around her. Martina had always been there for her, even when Stefan had been killed. Her sister hadn't known about Stefan, but she hadn't been able to hide her grief when she'd come home for a few days after she...

Jolene had never told Martina anything about Stefan, other than his name and that she had loved him. Her sister hadn't pried her for information. She had only offered Jolene comfort. Now it was her turn to console Martina.

"He's okay. He's a tough guy. And before long, he'll be one-hundred percent again."

"I know," Martina mumbled against her shoulder.

"I'm sorry I didn't make it to the hospital," Jolene whispered.

Martina's breath was warm against her ear. "It's okay. I'm okay."

"Sure you are." Jolene rubbed her back. "And so is Simon. I'm sure he'll be home soon enough, bugging the hell out of you."

Martina laughed and then pulled back. "I know he will and then I'll threaten to pack his bags and send him off to his mother."

Jolene schooled her face to look anxious. "You wouldn't? Rosa is a great cook. He might not come home again."

Martina shrugged. "Rosa is not me."

Jolene smoothed Martina's hair back from her face. "This is true."

The coffee dripped into the pot and the rich aroma called to them.

Jolene stepped back from Martina's embrace.

"So, do you want to tell me about last night? Mom told me you two talked," Martina said while she filled the mugs. "And then you left."

"We did." Jolene slid onto a stool and accepted the warm mug Martina handed her. "And yes, I had to get away and think. Don't ask me why. I just did." She set the mug down and rubbed her hands together.

"I understand," Martina replied. "I did the same. Blew my mind that I never suspected any of what she told me."

"I know." Jolene pressed the heart charm her mother had given her when she'd graduated high school into the pad of her thumb. The heart held both of their birth stones. How she had wanted to believe her mother loved her then, but she came to believe she hadn't. Now she knew she hadn't seen the truth.

"And I was older than you." Cool air spilled from the refrigerator while Martina glanced over her shoulder at her sister.

"You still are," Jolene answered and dropped her hands to the bar.

Martina laughed and handed her the French Vanilla creamer they both adored.

"I checked in with Mom around eleven." Jolene poured her cream and then handed it back to Martina. "She told me everything was good. Lia gave her no problems and the kids were all tucked in."

"She told me you called. I called her right after you had. I didn't want Dad to run back to the hospital to keep me company. I knew Simon would be okay by then."

"I should've been there."

252

"I was fine. And you have a job to do." Martina placed the creamer back in the refrigerator and slid onto the stool next to her. She took a sip and then peered over her mug. "So how is the chief?"

"How should I know?" Jolene sipped her coffee, ignoring her sister's smirk.

Martina bumped her elbow against hers.

"Come on, sis. Anyone with eyes can see the attraction between the two of you. And I know you like I know myself. You didn't drive around all night and you didn't go to a hotel. You were with him last night. How was he?"

Jolene nearly choked on her sip of coffee. "I have no idea what you mean? I was—"

"Your dress is wrinkled. And you have whisker burns along your neck."

Without thought, Jolene covered her neck.

Martina chuckled. "Your dress lay on the floor all night, didn't it?

Jolene face grew warm. "You think you know me?"

"I know I know you."

Martina's cup didn't hide her grin.

Jolene opened her mouth to respond when her cell phone in her purse chirped the first notes of *Born To Be Wild*. It was the ring tune sound she'd assigned to Norris. Why she had no idea. Wild was not a word she'd use to describe him. Maybe she had because she longed to get wild with him again. The thought of him inside her made a warmth flow outward from her stomach.

Martina set her mug down. "What the heck is that noise?"

"My cell." Jolene dug her phone out of her purse

and quickly muted the ringer. She walked into the family room, feeling her heart beating against her sternum at lightning speed. She tingled all over in anticipation of hearing Norris' deep voice against her ear.

She also sensed Martina's gaze on her back.

"U.S. Marshall Martinez." Jolene spoke briskly into her phone, pretending the call was from her headquarters instead of the man who had rocked her world last night.

"I take it you're not alone," Norris said.

He didn't need to be in the room for her to respond to him. Just the sound of his voice made her knees quake. She had it bad for Norris.

Behind her, flowing water splashed against metal.

Jolene glanced over her shoulder and saw Martina had vacated her seat to give Jolene some privacy by rinsing off the kitchen sponge and wiping off the already sparkling stove top.

"Affirmative. Did you get a solid lead?"

"Not sure. Our town drunk, who is not so drunk at the moment, swears on his mother's grave he's not only seen Lia, but has spoken to her?"

"Really? Where?"

"Outside the rear entrance to a local bakery. The bakery in a strip mall on Hudson Avenue." Norris cleared his throat. "I'm going to drive over there and check with the management of each store in the mall. If the car was parked out back, it's probably owned by an employee. Did you want to ride along?"

She glanced at Martina. She'd really would like to be there if the lead broke in the case, but Martina looked so tired...and she'd promise to stay. Never had she been divided been family and duty, but the choice was clear. "I promised Martina I'd stay and watch over the kids while she gets some rest. Maybe I can find more out from Lia. She might remember something about the bakery. But if anything breaks, call me and I'll be right there."

"Family first. Good. I'll check in with your later."

The connection between them was severed before she could respond. She imagined the excitement on Norris' face while he headed out of the station. He loved the hunt as much as she did.

"So. Who was that?" Martina asked over her shoulder when Jolene laid her phone on the counter.

"Stiles. He has a lead. He's going to check it out."

Martina turned and arched her brow. "Without you?"

"It's his case. I am authorized to assist him, when and if he needs me. Right now, he's not sure how reliable the source is for this lead. If something comes of it, he'll call me." Jolene sipped her coffee and grimaced. It was cold. She placed her mug in the microwave and then looked at Martina who now scrubbed the hundreds of tiny handprints from the refrigerator door. Jolene knew well the effects of stress.

Martina was a ball of energy at the moment, but soon she'd crash. "Why don't you go lie down in the guest room? I'll make breakfast for everyone. Then I'll take the kids to the park and out to lunch so the house is quiet for you."

"What happens if you need to go?"

"Then I would bring the kids home to you before meeting him." She took the sponge from Martina and shoved her out of the kitchen. "Go. Sleep well."

Getting breakfast ready for nine people was a challenge but Jolene handled the job fairly well she thought and within two hours everyone was fed and dressed, teeth were brushed and they were all out the door, leaving Martina sleeping soundly. Thankfully, Jolene's parents had filled their travel mugs with coffee and left immediately for her dad's appointment. She wasn't ready to speak to them.

CHAPTER TWENTY-FIVE

The sun warms my face and the salt air laces my tongue and fills my lungs while I cruise through town past quaint shops and busy cafes. This two-hundred-year-old seaside settlement is my home, even if I wasn't born to it. Just the same, I love it and it loves me in return. But I think I must go away for a while until this hype about the girl quiets down. I need to go somewhere peaceful where I can think and not worry every moment that I will be jailed for what I did.

I didn't mean to harm the girl. I meant to give her back to her family, but would anyone of sound mind believe me? Hell, I wouldn't believe me.

It shouldn't take long for Lia's story to become old news. A few months perhaps. The media hounds will sniff blood somewhere else in a few days. I simply can't take the chance my supposedly better half would do something to cause the police to look in our direction.

"Stop!"

The shrill voice cuts off my next thought and without hesitation I slam on the brakes, sliding, tires squealing, coming to a halt mere inches from one of the old sycamores lining the street. My lungs, like bellows, suck back my exhale.

"There," she wails. "It's Lia. It's my little girl."

I feel the veins in my neck strain. My head throbs as if it's been hit with a sledge hammer. My hands become steel grips around the metal they grasp and I fight back against the anger welling up inside me. I must remain calm and in control. I can't let her ruin my life, again.

A seaward gust swirls through the row of buildings, cooling my brow and a bead of sweat rolls down my back.

I see the curiosity in the eyes of those passing by. They wonder what is wrong with me. I tell her to shut up. She grows silent but continues to fume.

Ahead, parked near the traffic light, I see a police car.

I need to leave before they wonder why I've stopped, but I can't. She is holding me in place.

I close my eyes against the sting in my temples. I know she is watching Lia. I feel her longing to run to the girl and embrace her. I know her pain is great but she needs to let the girl go back to her own mother.

What I did was the right thing to do.

I repeat the words: "What I did was the right thing to do."

CHAPTER TWENTY-SIX

Above Jolene the clouds swirled in the blue sky, reminding her of pinwheels in a feisty wind. She threw back her head and laughed freely while the swing she sat on spun and then slowed to a halt and then twirled her even faster in the opposite direction. How foolish she must look to the other women who sat on the nearby benches chatting while keeping one eye trained on their children.

If she ever became a mother she wouldn't behave like them. Sharing gossip had never held an interest for her. She intended to be as she was now, acting like a damn fool and enjoying every moment of making memories with her kids.

Jolene dropped her feet to the ground. Over the past week, while tending Lia, more and more she considered herself in a mother's role. Before she'd come home to visit this time, she'd brushed away the notion like swiping a fly off her arm, but now freeing herself from the idea wasn't easy. The longing she'd kept buried for so long grew stronger each moment she was with her family, and with Norris. He was definitely the kind of man she'd imagined for a life partner when she'd allowed herself to indulge in the dream of having her own family to come home to.

"Don't stop, Aunt Jolene," Diego her oldest nephew whined. "The swing will take you back again. Daddy said it's called send-triple force."

A woman sitting on a nearby bench smiled at her

259

and then drew in a deep breath and rested her hand on the arm of the older woman sitting next to her. The younger woman appeared to be of the sandwich generation, caring for a grandchild while the child's mother worked and caring for her own mother too.

"You mean centrifugal force." Bringing her attention back to her nephew, she pronounced the word again slowly so he'd hear each syllable. Then she glanced over his head and did a head count of the other children. When he pronounced the word correctly, she smiled and mussed her nephew's hair. "And good for you for listening and learning."

"My dad is pretty smart."

She noted the pride in his eyes before Diego's gaze dropped to his scuffed sneakers where he jabbed the rubber mulch with his shoe tip.

Jolene could see the nine-year-old was worried about his father. For a while she'd been able to take Diego's mind off his father's accident, but the mere mention of his daddy had brought last night's event to the forefront of the child's mind. He was too young to have the weight of such worry on his shoulders. She grabbed him into a bear hug. "Yes, he is. Now, you better help me stand."

She faked acute dizziness which lightened the boy's mood and caused Diego to laugh.

In the distance she heard the musical chime of the mobile ice cream vendor. It grew louder as the cart drew closer to the north side of the small park. She stopped and Diego looked up at her. "I think everyone looks really hot, don't you?" Jolene glanced toward the mock pirate ship where the rest of the Gomez gang and Lia played.

"Aye," Diego answered as if addressing his ship's captain.

Staying in the seafaring mood, she responded, "Man and wench needs more than water to quench the thirst don't you think?"

Jolene saw the spark of recognition and delight take hold in his eyes before he turned his head and searched for the ice cream truck.

She reached into her shorts pocket and pulled out a twenty-dollar bill. "Do you think you could fetch us some ice? Cherry for all of us," she said with the best seafaring voice she could muster.

"Aye, Captain. I'd be your man." He snatched the money from her fingertips and raced off across the park, beating out other children who'd heard Mr. Icicle's call.

Jolene grabbed her bag off the nearby bench and retrieved a container of hand wipes and headed toward the other children.

Ten minutes later, she sat crossed legged on the grass surrounded by the children enjoying a fruity flavor that took her back to her childhood. Their chatter and the joy on their little faces made her heart ache in a strange way. The yearning moved downward to her belly. Even the muscles in her arms craved to hold a little one, a part of her and someone else.

Jolene turned her head and blinked away the moisture clouding her vision. She had managed to walk the group by herself for several blocks without incident. So far there had been no cuts or bruises to the children while they'd scampered around the playground. Nor had any fights broken out between them. She had managed to keep them safe and entertained. Maybe one day she could be a mother.

261

Her cell phone on her belt buzzed. She looked at the screen and saw Norris was calling her. Thinking he might have news, she checked Lia's position and scrambled to her feet. "Norris, give me one second." She spoke into the phone and then looked down at Diego. "I need to take this call. You're in charge. Everyone stays seated until I return." She looked directly at each child before backing away.

She dropped her cherry ice cream into a nearby garbage can and then put thirty-feet between herself and the children before she again acknowledged Norris. "I'm back."

"Where are you?"

Norris sounded exceptionally gruff and she wondered what had changed since she left his bed five hours ago.

"I'm at the playground near Martina's house. She needed to sleep so I brought the kids here."

"Is Lia with you?"

The nape of her neck prickled. She swiped the hand, still chilled from the icy treat, over her hairline. "Yes. Why? Did you learn something?"

"The owner of the bakery in this strip mall remembered Lia. A woman brought her in last week to pick out a theme for her birthday cake. I've met Tessa the owner a few times. She's a sharp lady. I think she can help us."

Out of nowhere, jealousy pricked at Jolene's heart and immediately she wondered about the circumstances under which Norris had met the bakery's owner. She locked her jaw, knowing she was being idiotic. Norris had met hundreds of townsfolk over the past nine months since he'd become Cape James' Chief of Police.

She had no claim on Norris and he had none on her. They each had a past.

She pushed away the feeling and focused on what Norris was saying.

"The woman had been in a few other times, but always by herself. Tessa said the woman told her she was Lia's mother and they would be celebrating Lia's birthday on June 12th."

Jolene's stomach rolled. "The day we found her."

"Right. The cake she ordered was never picked up."

His simple statement added to the sorrow she already felt for Lia. "Are you thinking something happened to the mother?"

"No one has reported anyone missing, yet."

That was true. And in the hours since the media picked up on Lia's story and her picture was released to the public, many sightings of her being accompanied by both a woman and a man had been reported, but none in connection with a missing woman. "Did the woman leave personal information with the bakery?"

"No."

Jolene rubbed an itch under her bangs and then swatted away a gnat. "Not even a phone number?"

"No. She paid cash in advance."

"That's odd."

"I haven't ever ordered a cake but I've ordered flowers and…"

His voice died and Jolene wondered if he thought of his ex-fiancé.

Norris cleared his throat. "It could be our mystery woman didn't want anyone to know where she stayed."

"Did she at least give a name?"

"Martha. No last name."

"A first name is at least something," Jolene replied.

"I think we need to look at home rentals again," Norris spoke in a wistful manner. "If she was hiding from someone—"

"They could've found her," Jolene cut him off.

"Yeah. She has to be somewhere she wouldn't be missed or discovered for a few days."

Jolene heard a car door open and close and knew Norris had climbed into his Jeep.

"Tessa is going to meet with our sketch artist later this afternoon," Norris continued. "Since she was up close and personal with the woman for a short time, her sketch should be reasonably precise. With a picture of both of them, maybe we'll get closer to learning who they are."

"Right."

An engine starting broke into the silence hanging between them.

"What are you thinking?" Norris finally asked.

"I'm wondering why Martha parked in the back of the building... It's not the safest place to leave a child, even if she was locked inside the car." Jolene saw the Gomez gang had finished with their treats and were beginning to get restless. Her parents should be back from Norfolk soon. Then she could catch up with Norris. "That's where your witness said she parked, right?"

"Yeah. She did. Maybe Martha is an employee of one of the other stores."

"Wouldn't Tessa at least have seen Martha at some point though?"

"Depends when Martha might've worked. Tessa is in the bakery from four a.m. to noon. They might never have crossed paths."

"It's possible, I suppose," Jolene agreed.

"Once we get Martha's sketch from Tessa we'll make the rounds again. We'll question the store owners about their policy on employees entering the store from the back door and also check who has access to their store's back entrance keys."

So far there had been a lot of footwork and probing done in this case, Jolene mused, but finally Norris had found a solid lead. "So where are you headed now?"

"Back to the office. I need to catch up on a few things. Then once Tessa arrives, I'll talk to her some more and see if she remembers anything else about the woman."

"I'll join you there."

"I thought you were watching the gang?"

"Until my parents come back from my dad's doctor appointment. They should be back very soon. The plan is they'll stay with the kids until Martina comes back from the hospital from visiting Simon."

"Then you're free later? Tonight?"

She wanted to say yes, but she knew if she spent another night with Norris it would be much harder to say goodbye to him later. She couldn't deny she was beginning to have strong feelings for him. She had to keep things on a professional level going forward. "I can help you with the case if you need me."

"The case?"

She heard the questions in his voice. She didn't want to hurt him, but she knew if they continued on the way they had been, stealing heated glances, touching each other in passing and sharing each other's pasts and thoughts, when it came time for her to leave she would hurt him much more. "Can I call you when I get home? The kids are getting anxious."

"Sure." The phone went silent. He disconnected the call without saying goodbye. She'd already disappointed him.

"Aunt Jolene can we go play on the pirate ship some more?" Angel, her second oldest nephew, asked.

"Sure. We can stay for another half-hour."

Angel hooted and most of the children raced toward the playground once again. Sofia and Lia however headed toward the sandbox where a few other children played.

Jolene took a seat on a bench between the two spaces. While she watched over the children, her mind remained on Norris. There was so much she wanted to say to him and yet she knew she couldn't. It was best if she concentrated on the case and forgot about the amazing time she'd had last night.

Suddenly the old woman across the way screamed. She shot off the bench, shouting at the younger woman, accusing her of abuse. The younger woman tried to calm her but the older woman cried out louder, claiming the younger woman was a stranger to her. She slapped away at the hands trying to restrain her.

Jolene checked on the child who was with them. Sadness made the child wrap her arms around her belly. She had obviously seen this scene play out before.

The old woman broke loose of the woman's grasp and ran toward the street. Jolene darted in front of her. She held out her hand but didn't touch the woman. "Madam, do you need help?"

Wide cloudy blue eyes, the woman studied Jolene oddly for a few seconds. Then they rounded and brightened with recognition. "Yes. Yes. Thank God you found me, Anna," she said, throwing herself into Jolene's arms. "Where have you been? That woman you left me with hates me. She loves the brat more than she does me."

"*Shhhh.*" While she tried to calm her, Jolene felt the curvature of the woman's spine under her hand. "It's all right. I'm here now."

The younger woman came into her view. The apologetic, stressful expression she wore melted Jolene's heart. Would she or Martina be in similar shoes in years to come with their parents? If her parents' mental capacity began to fail, she didn't want Martina to shoulder the whole responsibility. She wanted to be there for them too.

Jolene signaled the woman with a sly dip of her head that she understood the situation. With a raised index finger she asked for a few moments and continued to talk to the older woman as if she'd known her all of her life. When the older woman calmed down Jolene waved to the other woman to join them.

Miraculously, the older woman lovingly recognized the younger woman this time and after a minute of chatting, the younger woman led her mother back to the bench. Over her shoulder, she mouthed a silent *thank you* to Jolene.

Jolene glanced at the sand box and realized the girls weren't there. Her heart kicked up a notch. She looked toward the pirate ship and saw Sophia running up the gangplank. Ahead of her was another child. It wasn't Lia. Above the sail's railing she saw the top of a head with hair the color of Lia's and she relaxed.

She called to the gang it was time to go. Slowly, one

by one, they appeared on the deck. All of the Gomez gang—minus Lia.

"Is Lia down below?" She bent over at the waist and peered through the window into the lower portion of the ship. She saw no movement inside.

"I didn't see her," Diego responded.

Jolene spun toward Sofia. "Sofia, where's Lia?"

"Her daddy came for her." Sofia skipped down the gangplank. "He talks funny."

"Her daddy?"

"Ah, ya."

Jolene stooped and looked directly into her niece's eyes. "She knew him? She went with him?"

"Yes." Sofia's ponytail bobbed.

Jolene's chest tightened around her heart. She stood and scanned the park. And then the area bordering it.

Touching the pocket where she'd placed her cell phone, she hesitated for a split second, knowing she had to call Norris and let him know she'd lost Lia, and likely to the person who tried to kill her.

***

We were blocks away from the park when I heard the sirens wail. I tightened my grip on Lia and lengthened my steps. We'd put another half block between us and the woman who had made my baby part of her family. Then I realized Lia had to run to keep up with me. The oversized, matching sunglasses I'd brought to conceal our features slid down her nose and teetered there for a step and then fell to the sidewalk.

Quickly, I stooped down next to Lia, picked up the glasses, wiped them off with my T-shirt and plopped

268

them on her nose. She giggled back at me and I can see how happy she is that I found her.

A police car sped by, reminding me we need to keep moving. I'd hoped for more time and to be a little closer to the town's edge before the woman noticed Lia was gone.

I brushed my thumb over Lia's soft cheek and then rose to my full stature, feeling confident. No one had or would give me and Lia a second glace. We were simply a mother and daughter out for walk on a beautiful day, wearing matching teal-colored T-shirts and similar ball caps covering our hair.

Ahead, flashing lights catch my attention. It's the chief of police's Jeep heading our way. Behind my glasses, I close my eyes. I hear the sound of my heart clearer when I do. The steady beat, even though its pace has quickened, is reassurance I'm alive and in control.

Lia and I watch the chief speed by and then we resumed our walk. According to the mayor, who Mark had breakfast with this morning, the chief of police still had no clue who Lia was or where she lived. It seemed the relatively new chief of police was chasing his tail. Or the tail of the beautiful U.S. Marshal who had first sighted Lia floating in the ocean. I wonder if the woman with Lia today was the U.S. Marshal. She was certainly pretty in a pixie type of way.

There was no time to ponder trivial things. Once we reach the house, however, I will need to act fast and gather our belongings and leave before Mark breaks out. It took everything in me to overtake him earlier. I don't know if I have the strength to do it again.

We need to disappear again if Lia is to remain safe.

CHAPTER TWENTY-SEVEN

Norris saw anguish on Jolene's face when she glanced his way. He knew the pain causing her to pace back and forth between the entrance to the park and the toddler swing set. Her arms were dead-locked around her mid-section and her fingers worked over the charms on her bracelet.

He knew her well enough already to know that when she played with her bracelet, she worried about something She blamed herself for Lia's disappearance.

Child snatching happens in the blink of an eye. The witnesses' descriptions of the moments before Lia disappeared had to make Jolene realize she wasn't to blame. If she hadn't intervened and stopped the elderly woman from leaving the park, the old woman could've run out into traffic.

But how had the man found out where Lia was being kept? They'd had no idea Lia's father—if he was indeed her father—had been watching Lia and perhaps the Gomez home, waiting for the opportunity to snag her.

Norris tapped his pencil against the pad in his hand. *How had he found Lia? Why would he want her back? He'd tried to kill her. Did he intend to accomplish what he'd set out to do? If so, why would he want the child dead? Had she witnessed something she wasn't meant to?* The list of questions rattled off in his brain.

"If that's all, Chief, I want to take my granddaughter and mother home," the woman who

270

stood in front of him said, bringing him back to their conversation.

"Sorry. Yes. I have your information. Here's my card. If you think of anything else which might help us locate the girl, please give me a call. Maybe you saw someone before your mother darted away."

The woman accepted his card and quickly pocketed it in the bag slung over her shoulder. "I will. Thank the Marshal again for helping me. I'm sorry my mother's actions caused—"

Norris lay a hand on her forearm. "The only one to blame for this situation is the person who kidnapped the little girl."

Relief softened the woman's face before she turned and took the hands of both her charges and rushed them from the park.

Norris turned around, slid his pad and pencil into his breast pocket and watched Jolene again for a few seconds. She didn't look as if that truth would ease her pain so easily. If she was going to be any good to him and help him nail the bastard, she'd need to let the anger and guilt go and concentrate on the facts.

There were three paths leading into to the park. Both Pickett and Frank who responded to the location immediately took up posts at two entrances while Jolene covered the third, sealing off the park. It wasn't a tight seal however. The grounds were lined with fencing on two sides where the traffic was heavier, and the other two sides were bordered by shrubbery. Not impossible to push through.

All of the occupants in the vicinity had been interviewed immediately and then dismissed, including the Gomez gang. Jolene had called Martina who arrived at the playground a minute after him. Now the entire area, including the sandbox Lia had been playing in, had been photographed. They found no useable footprints near the sandbox. It appeared the man never stepped close enough to lift Lia from the box. Apparently, she'd known him. He'd called Lia and she simply went to him. But why would she do that if he'd tried to kill her before?

Jogging toward Jolene, he was intercepted by Pickett and Frank. "Did you learn anything?"

Pickett shook his head. "No. Everyone I interviewed said they were focused on the old woman and Jolene. They said the old lady fought Jolene like a tom cat, but Jolene hung on."

Norris looked at Frank.

"Same story here, Chief. All eyes were on them."

"How about the little girl who was playing in the sandbox with Lia?" Norris asked, knowing she was probably their best witness.

"Her mother let me talk to her," Jolene spoke behind him.

Turning, he looked down at her and immediately sympathy softened his heart. He'd seen her tired before, and stressed, but now she appeared beaten. Her tan skin appeared grayish and her bottom lip was blood red from her teeth's assault. She was literally sick over losing Lia to the bastard.

He longed to draw her into an embrace, tuck her head under his chin and comfort her with the beat of his heart, but for the sake of their professional reputations he wouldn't. It was best if she remained focused on the job and not something personal.

"What did she say?"

272

She notched her chin a little higher. "That he was a giant. His shadow covered both of them."

"That's pretty perceptive for a child. How old is she?"

"Six. Her mother says she is a student in a summer art course. She notices details that way."

"Smart kid," Pickett mumbled.

Norris looked back to Jolene after scanning the "scene gawkers" who stood outside the park's perimeter. He'd hoped to spy someone who had deception curling his lips so they could end this nightmare quickly. It was a foolish wish. Whoever had Lia was long gone. *But where?* "Anything else besides a shadow?"

"He had mousey brown hair, long, pulled back into a ponytail and he was clean shaven," Jolene answered.

Pickett's normally lazy gaze flashed disbelief. "She said that?"

"Her exact words were, 'He had hair like my brother's mouse and he didn't have a hairy face like my dad.' Her dad's whiskers tickle her. I took it to mean he was clean shaven."

"Clean shaven… Right." Pickett scratched on his pad and then in good humor added, "Did she say his eyes were chocolate drops or the color of the sky."

The deputy quieted his chuckle when he glanced Norris' way.

"She couldn't say. He wore sunglasses."

"Tattoos or scars?"

Jolene stuffed her hands into her pockets. "No, but he wears a ring. Gold with a black stone."

Jolene continued to scan the area, hoping to spot the guy. Norris had no doubt if she did see a man fitting the six-year-old's description she'd chase him down and hogtie him. He couldn't deny he might look the other way for a moment if it was their man. Anyone who treated a child the way Lia had been treated deserved an ass-kicking session. But, he highly doubted the guy and Lia were still within a mile of the park.

"Jeans?" Pickett rapid fired questions and Jolene shot back information.

"No. Shorts. Brown, similar to the lady's hat over there."

They all looked in the direction Jolene pointed and saw a woman wearing a wide-brimmed straw hat.

"Okay. Tan. How about his shirt?"

"White with some buttons." Jolene unconsciously touched her breast bone with a long, painted nail.

The tip of Pickett's right sandy brow peeked above his sunglasses dark frame. "Maybe a golf shirt?"

"That's my thought," Jolene said.

Pickett's smile made Norris want to pull Jolene close and let his deputies know she was his.

Frank whistled softly. "That kid was a gold mine."

Norris could see his deputies were dancing in place, anxious to comb the town for the guy.

"You were right to get permission to talk to her right away, Jolene," Pickett said. "Often times, parents don't want their children involved in any way for fear of retaliation from the perp. Her description is going to help us find this guy. How about his shoes?"

"Sneakers. White. They had letters on the side."

"Nike?"

"No. She said the first letter was an L."

Norris cleared his throat. "An L?"

"Lake. They're cycling sneakers," Pickett said.

274

Jolene looked at Pickett. "Do you know the brand?"

"I have a pair."

"Where did you buy them?" Norris asked.

"At Cycle Haven."

"Cycle Haven?" Norris clenched his jaw.

"What's wrong?" Jolene asked.

"Cycle Haven happens to be in the same mall as Tessa's bakery."

"Did she see him leave the park?" Pickett continued on with his questioning not noticing Norris had gone silent.

"No," Jolene said, not taking her eyes from him. "The older woman's screaming frightened her and she ran to her mother."

Norris slid his cell phone from his pocket.

"What are you thinking?" Jolene asked.

"It's nearly two," Norris said. "Tessa should be at the station with our sketch artist. I need to look at the sketch."

"Do you know who took Lia?" Jolene felt hope thread around her heart.

"I might..."

CHAPTER TWENTY-EIGHT

Thank goodness an available cab had stopped at the intersection just as Lia and I reached it. I knew time was of the essence the moment I saw the chief of police heading toward the park. I don't think anyone in the park recognized me, but I can't be sure. If someone at the park had known who I was and we walked all the way home, we would've been greeted by the chief and his deputies. That hadn't happened. Not yet. But something prickled the nerves under my skin and in my head I heard this tiny voice urging me to get out now before it was too late.

I stuff my favorite dress, sweater and some personal items into my overnight bag and zipper it closed. From Lia's room, I hear her giggle. She is so happy to be home. Thank goodness he hadn't had time to remove her belongings.

The whip he uses to keep his power over me still lies on the bedroom chair. I quickly check the lock to the secret room where he's trapped. It's intact and I only hear silence beyond it.

Quickly, I race down the hall to Lia's room and see her little suitcase overflowing with stuffed animals and dolls.

"Honey, there's not enough time to take everything." My heart swells with love as I look down at the child. I dump the contents of the suitcase onto the bed and quickly proceed to fill it with a couple of changes of clothing and shoes for Lia. It might be a day

276

or two until we find a new home and I can shop for us both. "Pick one. We need to leave now."

"But I want all my friends. I missed them."

I kneel down beside her and smooth her soft hair away from her face. I missed her so much—but now isn't the time to cuddle. "I know. They missed you too. I'll tell you what. I'll send for them and they'll join us in a few days." I lie which I hate to do to my daughter, but we really have to leave before the police stop us. Once we are settled I'll buy her dozens of new friends.

After a two-second deliberation, Lia said, "Okay. I want Boo-boo bunny and my fairy princess though."

I smiled. Lia was so much like me. Decisive. Loyal. And as beautiful as mother. "Fine. You can bring them both."

I hustle her down the hall, through the kitchen and out into the garage.

A few minutes later we're northward bound in his foreign compact car. In less than a half hour, we'll be out of Chief Stiles' reach, and if luck is on our side we'll be in Canada before nightfall.

The stream of sea air cruising through the open window tousles my long hair. I will look a mess until I can take the time to brush it out but I didn't care. All I care about is that Lia is safe.

I chew my lip. I really should stop and see mother before I leave the country. She would be so happy to see I won the battle with him, but I really can't chance being caught. The police would take Lia away from me forever. I'm the only mother Lia remembers.

I would die without her.

Time will provide opportunities to see mama later.

CHAPTER TWENTY-NINE

Norris' instinct had been right.

Bright sunlight filtered through a high window. It was a window meant to provide air, light and a means of escape in case of fire, but not a view. The empty room decorated in princess pink and purple and filled with soft cuddly creatures and toys pulled at Jolene's heart strings while the padlock on the door made the bile in her stomach turn to hot acid.

Dresser drawers were open and contents askew. Clothing frantically pushed to the one side kept whomever had opened them from closing the drawers altogether. Opposite the brass bed, upon a child-sized table, Jolene saw the remains of milk in a tiny china teacup and a half-eaten chocolate chip cookie almost as wide as the saucer on which it lay. The milk appeared to be fresh, not curdled which meant Lia had been there recently.

What kind of monsters were these people? Paradise wasn't paradise if one was imprisoned in it.

They had caught a lucky break with the bakery owner. When the image of the woman who had bought Lia's birthday cake came across Norris' cell phone, the owner's face illuminated with eagerness. Jolene saw the piece of the puzzle they'd been searching for fall into place in his eager expression. He hadn't met the woman with long auburn curls but he'd met someone who favored her. Definitely a relative of hers. Mark Branka.

They had wasted no time racing to the beachside

home—the house she'd thought of as a dream home.

Even the sea which lay a mere one-hundred yards away seemed stilled as they'd entered the quiet home through the open garage door. Norris had sent Pickett and Frank around the perimeter. They had no warrant, yet. But after discovering a trail of blood droplets leading inside the house through the kitchen the point became moot. The bloody tee cloth they found lying in the highly polished sink sent images of Lia's death whirling through her mind.

She'd been thankful when Norris said he'd follow the trail of blood into the west wing of the house while she took the right wing. She didn't know if she could handle the sight of a child mutilated.

She turned her head slightly at the low-key squawk of Norris' two-way hand radio. His muffled reply had her holding her breath until silence owned the next ten seconds. Norris hadn't cried out for medical help which in her mind meant Lia wasn't there. Surely he wouldn't be able to control his outrage so well. She wouldn't.

Jolene focused on the details of the room and picked up the white unicorn lying on the floor at her feet. She knew it was foolish to think Lia might've left a clue behind about the fact they'd taken her. She was only a child after all, but just the same, she hoped and searched for the smallest of hints. "Where did they take you?" she whispered, trying to put herself into the darkness that was Mark's and his relative's minds.

Disappointed there was nothing there to help them find Lia, Jolene headed back to the main living area.

"Clear. There is no one here," Jolene said holstering her gun and entered the living room. Her heart pounded in her chest even though disappointment weighed on it.

Norris let go of the mike he'd clipped to his shoulder earlier and slid his weapon into the sheath at his back. "It's Branka's silver compact that's missing from the garage," Norris responded, joining her by the plush cushioned sofa. "I've already issued a BOLO on it and every cop within one-hundred miles will be watching for the vehicle. They won't get too far."

"If they intend to drive to safety." She bit down on her bottom lip, causing a pain she could control. She didn't need a splitting headache right now. "What if they decided to escape by sea? Or—"

Norris cut her off. "Branka doesn't own a boat."

The shear determination on his face told her he knew what she'd been about to suggest and would do anything in his power to prevent Lia from dying out on the Atlantic, but the angst welling up inside her couldn't let her dismiss the idea so easily. "They're desperate. They could steal one."

He took her hands in his. "If they do pirate one, we'll hear about it. Launching and sailing a boat is not an easy task especially when you're a novice sailor. I don't think they'd try it. But I'll have Sandy notify the Coast Guard to be on the lookout for any small crafts beyond the boat lane."

"What about the blood?"

"Someone broke the mirror in the master bath."

"They argued."

"Possibly."

Norris' cell phone chirped and he looked at the screen.

"What is it?" Hope pitched her voice.

His mouth tightened and he shook his head. "Nothing to do with this case."

She blew out her frustration. "So, we wait, again."

"It's the hardest part of this job," he said softly.

He inched toward her and his hands reached out as if he meant to wrap his arms around her, but Pickett chose that moment to enter the house through the garage. Norris quickly stepped back from her.

"Chief, we didn't find anything to make us believe anyone might've escaped by way of the beach. There are no recent footprints in the path leading over the dune."

Norris cleared his throat and turned to face his deputy. "Okay. Tell Frank to head back into town and run his routes. You secure this property until we get the state forensic team in here. I want every room photographed and prints lifted. We need to learn the identity of the woman with Branka."

"Yes, sir."

Jolene looked at the artwork hanging on the walls. They were prints, bird's-eye views of ocean landscapes. On the mantel sat a small golden airplane. She picked it up carefully by the edge and turned to face Norris. "Does Mark have a pilot's license?"

"I don't know." He scrutinized the trophy in her hand.

Norris' radio crackled. "Chief."

He keyed the mike on his shoulder. "Go ahead, Sandy."

"Fire Chief Turner sighted the Branka car on Flat Handle Road. He knows the car. He rode in it a few times with Branka."

Norris' gaze snapped up to meet hers. "The airport."

"I guess that answers my question," Jolene said, rushing toward the open garage door.

Norris was right behind her, ordering Sandy to get in touch with the small airport's management and connect them to him right away. "Warn them not to engage with Branka. He could be armed."

Norris shouted to Pickett to lock up the house and meet them at the airport ASAP. Jolene jumped into Norris' Jeep and before she'd closed her door properly he was already backing up and spinning the vehicle around.

"We're fifteen minutes away." Norris turned on the lights mounted to the top of his vehicle.

"Isn't there security at the airport?"

"Ben. He retired from the force ten years ago. It's a small airport. Mostly pilots who give air tours and do fly-by advertising. Celebrities and some rich folk use it when they visit the area. Most of them house their planes in a hanger. All the others are tied down. The staff who are usually on duty during the day are the check-in secretary, a mechanic and Ben. The place is locked down at night. My officers cruise the area several times a night."

Jolene clung to the door handle when Norris took a hard left onto a side road that served as the main entrance to a bayside campground.

"Short cut," he said, tossing her a smile.

Through the two-way radio, Sandy announced Mark was not at the airport yet. The fire chief had turned around and was following him at a safe distance and reported they were within two miles of the small airport.

Norris spoke into his mike while maneuvering around a motorhome on the narrow highway: "Sandy, find out from the airport's secretary where Mark's plane is housed."

"10-4, Chief."

"If he does keep his plane in the hanger, we'll need to be careful approaching it." He glanced at the digital clock on the dashboard and immediately the tension lining his face intensified.

"He'll need to do a check of his plane before he takes off."

Norris glanced at her. His eyes softened. He recognized that she tried to alleviate his worry that they would arrive too late.

"I have my pilot's license," Jolene said. Her shoulder bumped against the door panel when Norris turned right off the two-lane highway and onto what appeared to be a dune path that put them heading north again.

"If you were trying to get away with little time to spare, would you do a full check?" he asked.

"I would, especially if I didn't want to harm the girl," Jolene said.

The stop sign ahead seemed to appear out of nowhere and they jolted to a halt.

"What if he doesn't care if he harms Lia?" Norris asked. "Once he's up in the air, he could dump her into the ocean and we might never find her again. No body. No trial."

She pointed ahead to Flat Handle Road and then gripped her seat. "Move."

Norris jammed his right foot down on the accelerator. Smoothly he wove around traffic and eight minutes later they sped through the open gate leading into the airport. They skidded to a halt and a gray-haired male security officer rushed to the driver's door.

"Did you see Mark Branka, Ben?"

"I didn't see him. I saw his little compact however. There was a woman driving it. She drove by me as if she knew where she was going. She parked near the hanger's rear door. Then she and a little girl got out and went inside."

"Could they be waiting for Mark?" Jolene asked.

"I don't know. Either way, she has Lia," Norris pointed out.

"Anyone else in the hanger?" Jolene asked.

"Nah. Lucus called in sick today. It's only me and Lois working the place."

Norris nodded. "Pickett is on the way. Close off the entrance. Have him keep an eye out for Mark."

"Will do, Chief."

Jolene grabbed his arm. "The hanger door is opening."

Norris leaned forward clutching the steering wheel. "It's the woman Tessa saw."

From this distance, the woman's facial features were not clear, but her long auburn hair led Jolene to believe Norris was right.

The woman gave the door a last shove and then rushed back into the hanger. A moment later a small plane rolled out onto the tarmac and quickly picked up speed while heading toward the runway. Norris jumped out of the Jeep.

"What are you doing?" Jolene rushed around the front of the Jeep.

"I'm going to stop her from taking off." Norris drew his gun and took aim.

"Not with that," Jolene slapped his hand down. "Lia is in the plane."

"I'll shoot the tires out."

"She's four-hundred yards away. If you miss, you could hit the fuel tanks and the whole plane could go up in flames. Listen to me. I know what I'm talking about."

Norris frowned. "Okay. How do you propose we stop them?"

"Get back in the Jeep." She headed for the passenger door.

"And do what? Drive in front of them?" He threw his arms in the air. "They'll either fly above us or crash into us which could get us all killed."

"That is a Cessna 172 Skyhawk. It's a prop plane which carries its fuel in the wings. All we need to do is bump the tail section enough to damage the controls. Without the tail flap and rudder the pilot won't get lift off or be able to control the direction of the plane. She'll have no choice but to stop."

Taking her advice, Norris jammed the Jeep into gear and gunned it toward the runway where the plane had begun to taxi.

They swerved onto the runway behind the vintage silver plane.

Jolene held her breath. It seemed an hour had passed before Norris nudged the Jeep's push-bar against the tail of the plane, bending the horizontal stabilizer. The plane swerved and then hopped into the air like a bird with a broken wing. The pilot tried two more times to get the plane airborne before she veered off the runway. Yet, she remained on the gas, apparently thinking she could make a run for freedom across the field next to the runway.

The plane hit a ditch and dove nose first into the

ground.

"Lia," Jolene cried, already holding on to the door's handle.

A second later, they saw the pilot's door open and the woman jumped from the plane and raced across the meadow.

Jolene reached out toward the dashboard, bracing herself for a sudden stop.

The Jeep skidded to a halt fifty yards from the plane.

"You check on Lia." Norris unclipped his seat belt, furious and determined. Then he jumped from the vehicle. "I'll get the bitch."

Her lips tight, she answered with a nod.

What would she find when she reached the plane? Ben had seen Lia walk with the woman into the hanger over ten minutes ago. *Would she still be alive?* A dead person wouldn't fight back and would be easier to throw out of a plane.

Jolene's pulse thundered against her temples like a bass drum accentuating each dreadful thought while she raced, arms and legs pumping, toward the aircraft. She hesitated, holding the handle of the door for a second and pleaded to God before she yanked it open.

Lia was buckled into the rear seat and clutched a stuffed bunny.

Jolene released the air packed into her lungs that had pressed against her heart.

Lia looked a little frightened but unharmed.

"You're okay, sweetie. I'm here."

Immediately a smile lifted the child's lips into a bow and she let up on the choke hold she had on her stuffed animal.

"Mama , Auntie Jolene. We go bye, bye."

Mama. As Jolene climbed inside to unbuckle Lia she peered through the open pilot's door and saw Norris tackle the woman full force. She winced imagining the pain he'd caused the bitch.

Good.

Norris rose and yanked the woman to her feet and Jolene saw she no longer had a full auburn mane. Her hair was slicked back and mousey-brown.

CHAPTER THIRTY

Jolene stood outside the interrogation room watching Mark Branka through the two-way mirror. He seemed anxious, repeatedly bouncing in his seat as if he was about to jump and race for the door. However, when he caught his refection in the mirror his wild search for an escape halted and his gaze altered into hard, cold ice.

He couldn't possibly see through the two-way glass and know she studied him, so was his reaction one of self-loathing? Did he regret his actions, what he did to Lia? To her mother?

In the few hours since Branka's capture, everyone who knew him seemed baffled by his arrest including the entire police force. Norris had described Branka as an up-standing citizen who was the benefactor of many community charitable endowments, including a new addition to the local library. And the mayor, who was with Norris at the moment and stunned by the turn in the case, described Branka as a man's man, living a jet-set life style, zooming off at a moment's notice to many exotic locations accompanied by numerous beautiful women. The mayor admitted he hadn't spent much time with Branka since Branka's return to the little sea-side town a month ago. However, it wasn't until this past week Mark called him and they'd golfed together. On another evening, the mayor, his wife along with several other couples had dinner at Branka's beach-side house, which was after Lia had been rescued—perhaps after he'd killed the girl's mother.

When questioned whether Lia's rescue had been discussed at the gathering, the mayor had stated "yes, of course." The story had been the evening's breaking headline news, but he didn't recall if Branka had added anything to the conversation. The mayor stated Mark had reacted like the rest of them, shocked.

The man was a good actor. He wasn't normal. In fact, being in a room with Branka made Jolene's hand itch to hold her gun, finger on the trigger.

Norris came up behind her. She gripped the butt of her Glock. "Are you ready for this?"

Norris' hand encased her left one, giving it a little squeeze. She shook out the tension from her right hand while she looked up at him. "Do you think he killed Lia's mother?"

"I don't know. People around here who know him never saw him with a woman who had a child."

"Everyone has secrets."

"That's true." Norris studied her for a second as if trying to uncover her secret before he continued, "Well, Branka certainly had someone living with him. The forensic techs are still combing his house. They've found women's clothing, makeup, perfumes, jewelry and they've pulled several sets of fingerprints from different areas in the house, and hair from clothing and the master bathroom shower drains. It'll be a few hours until the prints are processed."

"And they'll only give us an answer if the persons they belong to have been printed before."

"Right," Norris responded sounding a little less hopeful than he had a moment ago. "The best chance we have of unraveling who Lia belongs to and where her mother might be is through Branka."

Jolene looked back at the man they'd arrested. "Why did he take the time to dress in women's clothing?"

"Disguise." The chief's wide shoulder lifted and fell against her own. "I guess we'll find out. Ready?"

Norris opened the door to the tiny interrogation room and allowed Jolene to enter first. Inside the stuffy space, their perp sat at the stainless-steel table centered in the room. His head and shoulders were now bowed low like a heavy weight was yoked to him. Slowly, his head lifted and he stared up at them with red-rimmed eyes. Sorrow filled their dark depths. Mascara trailed down from his dark, moist lashes onto his rose-colored cheeks, making him look like a drag queen who'd walked a city block in a downpour.

Jolene had no pity for him. Anyone who did what he'd done to Lia deserved none.

When he saw them Mark asked, "Where's Lia? Where's my little girl?"

"Safe," Norris answered.

The closing of the door behind them echoed in the room.

Norris acknowledged the cadaver-pale man who sat next to Mark Banka.

Banka had shrieked for an attorney the moment his rights had been read to him. His corporate attorneys appointed a young local lawyer for the time being, until they sorted out the facts and hired a criminal attorney. Apparently the allegations against Mark had them in a state of shock.

With an inexperienced attorney at his side, Norris and Jolene were going to push the rules as far as they could to learn the truth about Mark and about the identity of Lia's mother.

"Where are you keeping her? I need to see her," Mark pleaded, clutching the table's edge.

"That's not possible at the moment. You have my word, she's safe."

Mark slid his gaze to her and his upper lip curled. "*You* have her. Don't you? She's not your daughter. She's mine."

Jolene remained silent, thinking if Lia had been hers, the girl would never be mistreated.

Norris pulled Jolene's chair back from the table and they took their seats.

Staring at the man sitting across from her, furry stirred in Jolene's gut. Her sharp inhale of the stale air was hidden by the scrape of her chair as she scooted it forward. She had to remain calm and collected and not let her personal feelings surface during this interview. Over the last week she had become very fond of Lia. They needed to nail this bastard, so he'd never harm her again.

Keeping calm, Jolene looked directly at him. "Mr. Branka—"

"Miss Branka," the man snapped, cutting her off. "My name is Miss Martha Branka."

Anger, frustration and even sadness suddenly inundated his glare. His chin lifted higher and he reached up with his handcuffed hands to his shoulder and apparently reached for the auburn hair that was no longer there. "I am not Mark."

Branka's head lowered again, pressing his chin to his chest while his attorney whispered in his ear. Branka gave the impression he was becoming submissive but the way his glare remained dark and glued on her, Jolene's muscles remained taut.

Jolene glanced at Norris whose narrowed eyes were fixed on Branka. His Adam's apple slid below his collar before he relaxed back in his chair. He flipped open the file sitting on the table in front of him and without exhibiting another sign of surprise he spoke in a calm tone, "You're Martha Branka?"

Branka's gaze shifted to Norris. Immediately, his tongue peeked out and swept over his lips.

By the slight sway of his body, Jolene knew without looking under the table the man had crossed his legs at the ankles before he demurely placed his hands on the table and smiled. He acted like a woman interested in the man sitting before her. *What was Branka's game?*

"Yes. That's my name," Mark responded sweetly.

"Sister to Mark Branka?" Norris asked again to make it clear the man understood what he asked.

"Yes."

Jolene saw Mark's attorney shift uncomfortably in his seat, edging away from his client.

Norris leaned forward and took a second to read from the file. The silence comprising the five seconds weighed on all of them.

Without lifting his bowed head, the chief studied the accused. "Your mother is Dinah Branka and your father was Matthew Branka?"

"Yes. I'm their daughter. Mark's my twin brother."

Norris cleared his throat and then tapped the paper in front of him. "Our records indicate Martha Branka was stillborn and is buried in Saint Paul's cemetery in New London."

Branka's penciled-in eye brow drew upward. "Your

292

records are incorrect. As you can see, I'm sitting right in front of you. Flesh. Blood. Bone."

This ludicrous game Branka played wasted time, Jolene thought. "You really expe—"

Probably sensing she was about to pounce on the man for his ridiculous claim to be his dead sister, Norris stopped her from standing by slipping a hand under the table and pressed down on her thigh. Her hot glare met the chief's cool one and immediately she was reminded she'd get more from Branka with sugar than threats to tear his throat out. She sat back and clamped her lips tight and watched Mark's body language carefully.

"If you're Martha. Where's Mark?" Norris asked quietly.

Branka leaned back on the chair. The handcuffs scraped against the table top when he dropped his hands to his lap. His smile turned devilishly wicked. "He's locked away in hell."

There. Jolene swallowed hard before she realized she had. Now Mark's eyes didn't only look cold, they shimmered with malice. Norris must've seen the depth of darkness in them before and that was why he'd stopped her from calling the man crazy a few seconds earlier.

She'd seen hatred, greed, lust and every degree of desire to inflect pain in the eyes of men who didn't deserve to ever walk free, but never had she seen the madness that was in this man's eyes. *Was Mark Branka truly insane or was he a great actor?*

Jolene placed her arms on the table, leaning forward. "And exactly where is he locked away?"

Branka's impish glare cut her way. "Close but not close enough for anyone to hear you when you scream out for help. It's the place he's kept me for years."

Norris asked, "Is Mark here in this room?"

"I guess you could say he is."

"Can Mark hear us?" Jolene asked calmly.

Mark moved his head slowly to the side and back, once as if listening for something. "No."

"Why not?" she continued, appearing to be very interested.

"Because I won't let him."

The amused smile on Mark's lips caused a shiver to crawl up her spine.

"Can he hear you?" Norris took the lead again, drawing Mark's attention.

"If I speak to him."

"Can I speak to him?"

"No."

Norris arched a brow. "Why not?"

Mark's mouth pinched into a hard line. "Because I won't go back there."

The air in the room seemed to sizzle. So much so, they could almost hear the snap, the pop, the zap that might cause a person's heart to stop momentarily. Even Mark's attorney felt it. He rose cautiously from his seat and backed away from his client until the wall stopped his retreat. The young man looked as if he might piss in his pants. Jolene couldn't blame him one bit.

Mark remained so still even his chest didn't rise with a breath.

Unflinching, Norris held the man's flat stare. "Okay. I understand."

Jolene tapped Norris' arm. "Can I speak to you a moment, Chief? Outside."

They rose. Mark's attorney left a wide berth around

294

the table and followed them until Norris stopped him at the door. "Stay with your client."

Jolene recognized the lawyer's move as a reach for freedom... Norris shut the door in his face.

Norris rounded on her and swept a hand through his thick hair. His calm temperament evaporated. "Do you think he's acting?"

His perplexed expression revealed he'd never faced a psychopath with multiple personality disorder before—if Mark Branka were indeed crazy. She still wasn't convinced the man wasn't just jerking them around.

Jolene had to give Norris credit for remaining composed while he'd spoken to Branka. The first time she'd run into someone who was certifiably loony she'd nearly blown her cover to get the hell away from the girl.

She pushed away the memories and focused on the present.

"I don't know." She barely shook her head while wrapping her arms over her chest. "He's pretty damn convincing."

"How do we find out?"

Thinking on the answer to that, Jolene crossed to the two-way mirror while Norris continued to guard the door.

Inside the room, Mark's attorney remained by the door keeping a watchful eye on his client.

Mark had his handcuffed wrists laced behind his head. He pressed his forearms against his temples as if he were in tremendous pain. With eyes squeezed shut, his lips moved quickly. She'd bet silently too, because his lawyer didn't appear to hear him.

"Lia is the key." She turned to Norris. "He took her. He dumped her in a little raft on the ocean. Then he snatched her again. He has to have reasons why he did it at all. Whether he's insane or not, we need to find out where Lia came from. And where her mother is. We need to press him. Hard. If he truly thinks he's Martha then we'll need to get an expert in here ASAP, and if he is toying with us, we might get him to slip up."

"Okay." Norris crossed over to her and also watched Mark through the glass. "He saw you in the park with Lia. He seemed threatened by you, like you were trying to replace him as Lia's mother. You're the trigger that will set him off."

"You might be right."

"You okay with this?"

Jolene knew her uneasiness showed so took a deep breath to help her pull it together for Lia's sake. "Yeah. I'm fine."

Norris touched her shoulder and squeezed. "I'll be right beside you."

"Let's do this."

Mark's attorney remained by the door after they reentered and took their seats.

Norris looked at the young attorney and pointed at the empty chair next to Branka.

Once the man slid onto his chair, Jolene said calmly, "Lia is a wonderful kid. I'm sure her mother misses her."

"I'm her mother."

"If you're her mother, why would you try to kill her?"

Metal clashed against metal when Branka slapped the table. His teeth gnashed together, but somehow, he muttered, "I never did such a thing."

Jolene latched onto his wild stare. "It was a miracle I spied her on the ocean. You know the Atlantic. She was just a speck in the water. She almost floated out to sea."

Branka jumped forward in his chair, his fingers scraping the tabletop before curling into fists. "Mark did that to her. I love Lia with all my heart."

"Mark, huh?" She chuckled under her breath, hoping to infuriate him enough that he'd trip up. He didn't take the bait.

"Yes. Mark," Branka answered in the same bereaved tone.

"You really expect me to believe you're not Mark, playing us?" she pressed. "You look like a man dressed in women's clothing. Why?"

"Am not a man. I am a woman. I'm Lia's mother."

It was Jolene's turn to slap the table. "No. You're not. Where is Lia's mother?"

Branka's red lips sealed.

Jolene sighed. "Okay. You want me to believe you're Martha."

"I am Martha."

"And you've been caring for Lia?"

He bowed his head. "Yes."

She tilted her head slightly, wanting to see Branka's eyes. "You love her?"

"Yes."

"Then how could you let Mark dump Lia into the ocean? You said he was the one who did it, right?"

A tear rolled down Branka's cheek. "He locked me away. I couldn't stop him."

"Like you've trapped him now?"

"Yes." Branka swept the tears away with the back of his hands.

Jolene licked her lips. Branka seemed frail, but she knew how cunning he had to be to pull off what he had done. She didn't want to piss him off and shut him down if he was deranged and truly thought he was Martha. She wanted the truth. "How do you lock him away and control him?"

Martha looked toward the tiled ceiling and inhaled. "I can't explain it."

"So why did he try to kill Lia?" Norris asked quietly.

Mark looked at the chief.

"We want to understand." Norris' expression was a picture of sincerity and sympathy.

"He didn't mean to harm her. He only wanted someone to find her…"

"Why?" Jolene asked.

"Because he said Lia wasn't mine."

Jolene let a second pass before she spoke. "But you just told us she was."

"She is now."

"What do you mean, now?"

The sound of four people breathing kept silence at bay in the small enclosed area while Branka chewed on his bottom lip.

Jolene lay her hands on the table, palms down and spoke softly, "We know Lia isn't your daughter. Where did you find her, Martha?"

Tears spilled down Mark's cheeks. "Her mother didn't want her. Lia was crying. The woman ignored her. She was too busy shopping."

Norris leaned forward and keeping his voice even

and calm asked, "Where was she shopping, Martha?"

"Obor Market."

Out of the corner of his eye, Norris glanced at her. He questioned if she recognized the market Branka mentioned. She shook her head.

"I've never heard of the place. What city or town is it in?"

Mark raised his eyes to meet the chief's and then shifted them to her. "Bucharest, Romania."

Norris exhaled. He dropped back on his chair and looked at her, dipping his head. They had their answer to where they would find Lia's family.

CHAPTER THIRTY-ONE

Sitting in the Dulles airport, listening to the boarding calls for departing International flights, Jolene smoothed back the girl's soft curls. Lia had been identified as Belinda Ferenc. She'd been abducted by Martha, aka Mark, from her mother Aleksandra Ferenc, then age seventeen, while Aleksandra was working her family's stand in the Obor marketplace. Mark, or Martha at the time of abduction, had brought Belinda into the United States via his private jet, first landing in Canada and then in a small airport in North Dakota.

It took only a week to locate Aleksandra who traveled the countryside with her family selling their wares. The American Consulate working with the Romania government, located her in Kosice Region. Belinda's father was listed as unknown. Apparently, an English tourist from the United Kingdom.

From the reports Jolene read, Belinda's family lived day to day. They had little material wealth but they had family and love. Aleksandra contacted the authorities who were in charge of her daughter's case every opportunity she had.

Through a translator, Jolene had spoken with her and the woman seemed truly joyous that her baby had been found and that Belinda was coming home to her.

For now, Mark Branka was being evaluated for mental competency before a trial commenced. He sat safely behind bars.

For him, this nightmare started months prior to

Jolene finding Lia drifting in the boat lane, when his father died. Feeling he needed to tell his mother of his father's passing, he'd gone to see her. She'd been admitted into a psychiatric hospital twenty-years prior for claiming Mark had died in childbirth and his twin Martha had lived. The woman had made Mark, as a child, act and dress as Martha whenever Mark's father was away from home.

Through therapy Mark had suppressed the second identity his mother's abuse had inflicted on him, but the moment Mark faced her again, Martha had gained control. It had taken him months to fight his way back from the dark hole—and that was when he discovered Lia.

During his interrogation he stated he'd no recall of how she was kidnapped or brought to his seaside home. Apparently, she'd been living at his house for a while and he felt no one would believe him that he hadn't known about her or that he hadn't brought her there himself.

Later that night, while he slept, he heard Martha call the girl's name. He knew he had to leave the child somewhere so he took her to the beach the next morning, before Martha had an opportunity to resurface. He'd hoped someone would find the girl and return her to her family. He hadn't meant to harm her.

Thinking about his interview caused Jolene to shiver. She swiped her hands over her arms and tugged on her light sweater, the one she wore whenever she flew.

The speakers overhead crackled. "International flight R-743 to Paris will begin boarding at Gate B-7 in three minutes."

301

With a sigh and mumbling under her breath, Jolene stood up from the hard-plastic chair and stretched her back before picking up her and Lia's carry-on bags.

The counter attendant's voice rose over the terminal's din while she repeated the announcement for the final call of the first leg of their trip. A trip she'd volunteered for—not wanting to hand Lia off to yet another stranger. A trip arranged by FBI Special Agent Carter.

From Paris they would fly into Henri Coanda International Airport in Bucharest where they would meet with Lia's family at the American Embassy.

Disappointment that Norris had not shown up to say goodbye added to the weight the carry-ons exerted on her shoulder while she searched the faces of the hundreds of people who raced through the D.C. terminal. She hadn't really expected to see him—they were beyond the security check after all—but she'd harbored hope she'd see his smile one last time.

He'd promised her he would say goodbye to the little girl before she was returned to her mother. Also, the last three days since Branka's capture had been a whirlwind and they had a lot of unspoken words hanging between them. They'd had no time to talk about their feelings for each other or if there would be a future for them. She'd no clue when, or if, they would speak again, since she was to fly to her home base in Pennsylvania when she returned. She didn't expect to return to Cape James any time soon. She had a career of her own. One she loved.

Maybe it was best he hadn't come… Maybe what they had was over, rather than being a stepping stone to something more. Now, she didn't lie awake at night thinking about Stefan, but after being with Norris, she couldn't imagine a more perfect partner for her. Norris had awakened feelings in her she'd buried and thought she'd never, ever feel again.

Sorrow weighed down her heart. She'd thought she'd done the same for him but now she was unsure.

Maybe Norris decided saying another goodbye was fruitless. She already had her next assignment.

Still.

Pushing her disenchantment with the handsome chief to the side, Jolene pasted on a smile and looked down at Lia who clutched Boo-boo bunny in the crook of her arm. Then Jolene pointed toward the ceiling-to-floor window behind her. "Are you ready to take a ride in that big airplane?"

Lia looked warily over her shoulder at the large plane and shook her head no.

"It'll be okay. I'm sitting beside you and you can hold my hand the whole time if you want to. I also brought my iPad so we can watch *Cinderella* and *Frozen* together. You like Elsa and Anna, right? We'll have fun?"

Lia's chestnut locks shimmered against her tan skin when she nodded her approval.

"Good, girl." Jolene took Lia's tiny hand in hers and they moved in line behind a group of college students who chatted idly about the adventures they were going to have in Paris.

Oh, to be so excited over something again... Jolene thought. Norris' face popped to mind and she smiled.

She looked down at her charm bracelet and winced. The Lynx charm Norris gave her the night before she departed Cape James sparkled against her skin. With her free hand she touched her lips and recalled the tender kiss he'd given her and the way he'd stood in the middle of the street watching her drive away.

She would miss him. Hell, she already did. If he were here she'd tell him without hesitation that somehow over the past ten days, she'd fallen in love with him.

"I almost missed you."

She whirled around to face the familiar baritone voice behind her and immediately felt fireworks detonate in her heart. "Norris. How?"

She looked past him for any airport security who might be chasing him down for breaching their lines. Seeing none, she focused on him and noted a backpack hung from his shoulder and his cell phone's screen flashed an airline ticket.

"Nor," Lia exclaimed before Jolene could say more. Still holding onto Jolene, Lia grabbed Norris' hand too. "Look what Auntie Jolene gave me? My own bracelet. It's just like hers."

"Hey, kid." He smiled down at Lia. "That's beautiful. You two could be twins. Are you ready for another adventure with Jolene and me?"

The little girl nodded happily.

"What do you mean with *us*?" Jolene pointed between them. Her heart skipped. "Are you coming with us?"

Norris let his backpack drop to the floor and wrapped his arm around her waist. "You didn't think I was going to let you go so easily did you?"

He lifted her hand to his lips.

Her heart pounded in her chest. Its rhythm vibrated throughout her body.

The soft kiss against the inside of her wrist, just above her bracelet, lingered while his gaze latched onto hers. He'd gotten the message before she spoke. "I-I hoped you wouldn't."

"That's good to know." Lowering his head, his warm breath tickled her ear. "Because I don't intend to let you go."

She leaned back, searching the depths of his eyes. "I think I've fallen in love with you," she whispered, hoping he felt the same way about her and would profess his love.

Instead, Norris arched his eyebrow quizzically and *humphed*. "You think, or you know you have?"

Her knees weakened and she allowed herself to be drawn against his hard body. "I know."

"Good, because I'm planning to be in your life until I take my last breath. I love you, Agent Martinez."

Norris sealed his promise with a kiss that told Jolene his heart belonged to her, forever.

EPILOGUE

April was such a pretty month. Wildflowers sprouted to life everywhere, and both the sky and sea sparkled as if renewed.

Jolene smoothed out the last wrinkle on the patio tablecloth that covered the serving table, soon to be laden with food. She stood and placed her hands on her back, covering her kidneys as she stretched for a moment. Taking a deep breath, she enjoyed the sun reflecting off the cool waves and sandy beach in front of her and Norris' home.

He'd bought the land from his landlord soon after they returned from Romania and replaced the old cabin with a modest seaside house which had real door locks and all the modern necessities. The path leading to it, while still secluded, had been widened and the ruts eliminated. That had been nearly three years ago.

She thought of Lia often, wondering what the pudgy-cheeked little girl would look like now, at almost five years of age. *Was she happy?*

Jolene knew the girl likely wouldn't remember her if they'd ever met but Lia would always be in Jolene's heart. Finding Lia, had changed her life in so many ways.

Crossing the patio, she thought how much she loved this haven. It was the first place she and Norris had made love. It was the place where she realized she loved him. It was where they'd said their vows, promising to love one another for eternity.

306

Giggles filled the air and Jolene smiled at the vision before her. Norris tossed their daughter, August into the air. The ruffles on the rear of her flowered swimsuit fluttered while her chubby legs and arms flayed in the air. They looked so happy and she hated to interrupt their fun, but her family and Norris' father would be arriving soon to enjoy an Easter feast and she needed Norris' help to finish setting up the tables.

"Hey, hon," Jolene called to Norris who once again cradled his daughter. "If you don't put her back down and help me, we'll never be ready for our guests."

"She wants me to play with her," Norris said, still holding August and walking over to Jolene. "What's a dad to do? You know she rules the house." He bent down and kissed Jolene lightly on the lips.

They'd been married for two years and he still drove her crazy with desire for him. She laced her arm around his neck and pulled him down for another kiss, a long deep kiss.

With August settled on his hip, Norris pulled Jolene closer and captured her mouth again, pushing his tongue into her mouth and tasting her.

"Should we leave and come back?" Jolene's mother asked behind them.

Norris pressed his forehead to hers and stared into her eyes that promised he'd finish this thing between them later. "No. We're good."

Jolene turned, ignoring her father's smirk and zeroed in on her mother's grin. "What are you all smiles about? It's not the first time you caught Norris mauling me."

"No, and I bet it won't be the last time either," Joan said. "But that is not why I'm smiling. Martina has a surprise for you."

"What?"

They heard the shrieks of the Gomez tribe as they exited their extended mini-van. A few seconds later, Clara rounded the corner and sprinted to the patio. She was followed by a strange, dark-haired girl who appeared to be her age.

"Auntie, Jolene. Uncle Norris. Look who's back," Clara said.

Jolene's hand drifted from Norris' waist to rest over her heart and she stepped forward. Her heart stalled in her chest. "Lia," she whispered. She knelt and stared into the girl's dark eyes, fighting the overwhelming urge to touch Lia. She didn't want to frighten her.

"I know you don't remember me and my husband, Norris. I'm Jolene, Clara's aunt. We knew you when you were little. You weren't much older than our daughter August is now." She pointed to Norris and August standing behind her. "We've thought about you every day since we last saw you."

The girl continued to stare at her, playing with the drawstring on her shorts and poking the toe of her flip-flop into the crack between two patio blocks. "I am happy to meet you."

Of course, Lia had a European accent.

Jolene's chest tightened around her pounding heart as the craving to embrace Lia grew.

Lia's gaze dropped to Jolene's charm bracelet. "I like your bracelet. I have one too."

Lia held up her wrist.

Joy spiraled through Jolene when she recognized the gift she'd given Lia years ago. "I know, I gave it to you."

Lia's face brightened as if she'd met Santa Claus.

"You speak English very well," Jolene said. Jolene looked up to see Aleksandra standing beside Martina.

"Yes, pumpkin," Aleksandra said in broken English. "Hello, Ms. Jolene. It's nice to see you again."

"It's nice to see you again too." Jolene came to her feet and looked at her sister. "How did you manage to do this?"

"You know that church project I've been working on?" Martina grinned. "We're sponsoring Aleksandra and Belinda. They want to become U.S. citizens."

"Lia, come see the cupcakes Aunt Jolene made," Clara said and tugged the girl away. "They look like bunny rabbits."

Jolene stood and reached out for Aleksandra's hand. "That's wonderful. Really wonderful."

Carrying more totes filled with food and drinks, Simon, Norris' father Harlan, Jolene's father Louis, and Pickett entered the patio area. Pickett had been invited by Norris because the guy had no family in the area.

"Let's get this celebration started," Simon said, holding up a twelve-pack of beer in one hand and two bottles of wine in the other.

After the feast was consumed the men settled into the living room to catch up on the baseball games, except for Pickett. He walked along the beach with Aleksandra, chatting while they kept an eye on the children playing tag with the waves rolling to shore. Martina and Joan sat side by side on beach chairs playing with August.

Jolene stood on a sand dune, surveying the scene. She sighed with satisfaction.

Norris walked up behind her and wound his arm

around her waist, pulling her against his hard body. "What are you thinking?"

"It's amazing."

He rested his head against hers. "What is?"

"How one person's actions can change so many lives."

Over the past few years, she'd let her spiked hair grow to her shoulders and Norris now pushed it to the side and kissed her neck. "I think it's pretty astounding that goodness found a way to grow from such a bad seed."

Without breaking his hold on her, she turned and leaned against his muscular chest.

"You know, you're right. If Mark's mother hadn't done what she did to him, you and I wouldn't have met, and August…" Jolene's heart hitched. She glanced over her shoulder at their daughter.

With a finger on her chin, Norris turned her face back to him. His hungry lips found hers and the past slipped away. In his eyes, she saw her future and it was all good.

THE END

From the Author

Thank you for reading Loved By Darkness. I hope you enjoyed it as much as I did plotting and writing it. My family and I would really appreciate if you'd leave a review. Let other readers know what you thought of the story. Also, if you'd like to be the first to know what is happening and receive free reads, join my newsletter at www.autumnjordon.com

Now, a bit about me. I'm an award-winning novelist, recognized by the Romance Writers Of America as a Golden Heart Finalist and a Golden Leaf winner for His witness To Evil, and by the Kindle Book Reviewers as a 2013 Best Indie Romance Author Finalist for Seized By Darkness. Awards are nice but it's the reviews of my readers that mean so much more.

I love to travel, making new friends along the way. Often, it is on my trips that I dream of adventures for my characters and schemes to put them into danger of losing their hearts to their one true love— just like I did with my own hero.

To learn more about me. Join my newsletter. It's call AJ Revealed for a reason.

Thanks again for your support.

Autumn Jordon

Made in the USA
Middletown, DE
21 August 2019